Highland Mist

Donna Grant

An Ellora's Cave Publication

www.ellorascave.com

Highland Mist

ISBN 9781419966903
ALL RIGHTS RESERVED.
Highland Mist Copyright © 2009 Donna Grant
Edited by Mary Moran.
Cover art by Dar Albert.

Electronic book publication October 2009
Trade paperback publication 2012

With the exception of quotes used in reviews, this book may not be reproduced or used in whole or in part by any means existing without written permission from the publisher, Ellora's Cave Publishing, Inc.® 1056 Home Avenue, Akron OH 44310-3502.

Warning: The unauthorized reproduction or distribution of this copyrighted work is illegal. Criminal copyright infringement, including infringement without monetary gain, is investigated by the FBI and is punishable by up to 5 years in federal prison and a fine of $250,000. (http://www.fbi.gov/ipr/)

This book is a work of fiction and any resemblance to persons, living or dead, or places, events or locales is purely coincidental. The characters are productions of the author's imagination and used fictitiously.

The publisher and author(s) acknowledge the trademark status and trademark ownership of all trademarks, service marks and word marks mentioned in this book.

The publisher does not have any control over and does not assume any responsibility for author or third-party Web sites or their content.

*In a time of conquering
There will be three
Who will end the MacNeil line.
Three born of the
Imbolc, Beltaine and Lughnasad Feasts
Who will destroy all at the
Samhain, the Feast of the Dead.*

Prologue
Sinclair Castle, Highlands of Scotland
February 3, 1607

Being a man was never easy. Being a Druid as well as laird was even harder, yet Duncan Sinclair had managed to do both, as well being husband and father. The latter two gave him the most joy though.

He turned his head away from the hearth to his wife laying in bed, holding their newly born daughter, the last of the three spoken of in the prophecy, a prophecy that could alter the course of the future.

Duncan rose from his chair before the fire and walked to the bed. He rested his hand on the babe's head.

"Don't think about it now," Catriona said softly, so as not to wake the babe.

"It's all I can think about. The fate of the world rests on their shoulders, Cat."

Catriona chuckled, her green eyes crinkling at the corners. "You worry overmuch, husband. We have our third daughter after years of thinking I would have no more children. We are Druids. We will raise them as they should be and help them to learn and harness their powers."

Duncan groaned. "Powers. The Fae must know what they are doing to give our children those kinds of powers."

The babe stirred and gave a small cry. "She has strong lungs, just like her father," Catriona said as she rocked the infant.

"What should we name her? Moira and Fiona will want to know first thing in the morning."

"How about—"

Duncan held up his hand to quiet his wife. "I thought I heard something."

No sooner were the words out of his mouth than the door to the chamber crashed open.

"*You*," Duncan hissed. He ran to his sword at the end of the bed and quickly palmed it.

Alistair MacNeil sauntered into the chamber with six men at his back. "So it's true. The brat was born on Imbolc just as the prophecy foretold."

"You will die for daring to come into my home," Duncan ground out. He raised his sword and lunged at MacNeil.

MacNeil quickly stepped away. "A fool I am not, Sinclair. I'm no match for you."

Out the corner of his eye, Duncan saw Catriona leave the bed and huddle in the corner with their daughter in her arms. He would not let harm come to them.

"You and your men are nothing," he said to MacNeil.

Laughter followed his words. "Do you really believe I only brought six men with me? I came to kill your daughters, Sinclair. I brought my entire army."

Duncan took a step toward MacNeil only to have a soldier step in his path.

Duncan easily blocked a downward swing from the man's sword. MacNeil smiled as he watched Sinclair fight. It was turning out just as he planned. And it was time to add a little something.

"By the way, Sinclair, did you know there is a traitor in your midst? It's a pity you'll never know who it is." He chuckled when Sinclair growled low in his throat. It was just the reaction he wanted.

"Don't worry," MacNeil continued. "Your family will soon be joining you in Hell with all the other pagans."

At his nod, his men rushed to surround Sinclair, who merely raised a blond brow and beckoned them to charge. MacNeil grudgingly gave Sinclair credit. The man fought valiantly even against such odds.

To his surprise, Sinclair cut down two of his men in the space of a heartbeat and wounded another, further proof, in MacNeil's mind, that the man wasn't mortal but was in league with some demon, or the devil himself, to have such strength.

The last soldier would soon be defeated, and he couldn't take the chance of fighting against Sinclair's superior skills. MacNeil saw his chance when Sinclair pivoted after blocking a blow. In one smooth movement, he stuck his sword into Sinclair's back and twisted the blade.

An ear-piercing scream rent the air as Sinclair's sword clattered to the floor and his body crumpled, unseeing eyes staring at his wife.

"Murderer," Catriona screamed.

MacNeil turned and stared at the woman standing before him, her raven hair streaming around her while her green eyes blazed with fury. It was a pity she was a pagan for she could have given him good, strong sons.

He sheathed his sword and walked toward her, stopping inches away, his fingers brushing the dagger hidden up his sleeve. The infant's cries at being left in the corner echoed inside the chamber.

"I'm only ridding Scotland of your kind, Catriona," he said before he slit her throat.

Her green eyes widened in astonishment before they closed and she fell beside her husband. He stared at the couple, their blood pooling and mixing together.

"Get the infant," he commanded his remaining soldier.

MacNeil left the chamber and smiled at how easily they had taken the castle. The fighting had all but stopped, and the sounds of his men celebrating their victory could now be heard.

There was only one task left.

His men crowded outside the nursery chamber and parted as he neared. Inside, he spotted the two young girls lying in the middle of the floor, their lifeless bodies covered in blood.

"Were they the only children?" he asked.

"Aye, laird."

MacNeil sighed with relief. It was done. No more prophecy hanging over his head like an axe ready to fall. Or so he thought, until he heard the infant wail, reminding him there was one more life to take.

Yet a thought took root. With her sisters dead, was she a threat? He could raise her as his own and use her Druid skills and supposed powers to his advantage. Without the threat of the prophecy he would be free to pillage at will, but how much more powerful would he be with the power of the Druids by his side? No clan in Scotland would stand a chance against him.

"Come. Our work here is done," he said.

"And the babe?" one of his soldiers asked.

"Bring her."

Chapter One
Highlands of Scotland
April 1625

☙

Conall MacInnes no more wanted to enter the gates of MacNeil castle than he wanted to gnaw off his own hand, but for the sake of his clan he was doing just that.

"It's a good time to ask them about Iona," Angus said as they rode through the gates.

Conall looked at his friend. "Aye. I'd thought of that."

The mere mention of his sister brought a spasm of pain. It had been nearly a year since her disappearance and no trace had ever been found. No thanks to the Druids he kept hidden. He pushed aside his thoughts and concentrated on the task at hand.

Angus grunted as they dismounted, his giant form standing taller than any man, Conall included. "I don't know if forty of our men are enough to bring into this pit of Hell."

"It's a peace talk. I couldn't very well bring an army," Conall stated, though he wished he had brought more. He looked up and spotted Alisdair MacNeil's lanky form walk toward them.

MacNeil kept his gray hair shorn to his neck. His light brown beard was full and graying slightly, but he still carried himself like a young warrior. His command over his clan showed when men bowed their heads and women refused to meet his eyes as he passed.

Not exactly what Conall would call a good leader if everyone feared him, but then again, MacNeil was known in the Highlands as a butcher who didn't know the meaning of mercy.

"I was afraid you wouldn't take my offering seriously. Many say you're too young and foolish to come," MacNeil said once he had reached them. His hazel eyes roamed over Conall's men as if sizing them up for battle.

It was on the tip of Conall's tongue to say he didn't take the offer seriously. "Lairds will do much to keep their clan safe and happy."

"Even to one such as me?"

Conall could literally feel Angus readying himself for a fight. "Aye, MacNeil, even to one such as you."

"But I have to wonder," he said, and paced in front of Conall. "Why? All the others have refused and challenged me on the battlefield."

"I've battled many a clan, but I want peace for mine. And if the price for such is to have a truce with you, then so be it."

"You aren't afraid of me?"

Conall saw the surprise on MacNeil's gaunt face. "Nay, I'm not."

"My soldiers outnumber your clan, but still you say such words."

"Loyalty is what counts. It wouldn't matter if you had ten thousand soldiers if none are loyal to you."

MacNeil nodded thoughtfully and clapped him on the shoulder. "Come and drink with me. We've the finest ale around. And while we drink we can talk of peace."

Conall followed slowly. His gut told him something wasn't right. He took in the state of MacNeil's bailey. It was filthy, no children ran around playing or women talking in groups. The people wouldn't meet his eyes, but the soldiers dared him to make a wrong move.

Brutality hummed from them. Conall knew it would be a miracle if they left here unscathed, for the laird may want a truce, but the soldiers did not. The quiet stillness of the bailey unsettled Conall. He was used to the chatter and sounds of everyday life at his home, not the silence of a graveyard.

He saw his men glance around warily. None were fools. The MacNeils had proven themselves time and again as the enemy, why should today be any different? It most likely wasn't, but he had to think of his vow to his mother to bring Iona home. In order to bring her home he had to put aside his personal feelings.

"We're here for peace between our clans," Conall reminded his men and himself. "Regardless of what the soldiers try, ignore them unless I tell you otherwise."

They entered the bleak hall to find it full of soldiers and a few women serving mead, but the MacNeil himself was nowhere to be seen. Conall's guard immediately went up as he surveyed the filthy state of the castle and its inhabitants.

Old rushes full of bones and urine coated the floor. The women's clothing was tattered and torn, barely hanging on to their bodies. Unlike the soldiers, whose clothing was dirty but not shabby. Candle wax hadn't been cleaned from the floor or the rushlights. All in all it was a disgusting place to step foot in, and he was immensely grateful that his mother had run such a clean castle.

His eyes ran back around the hall, this time looking more thoroughly at the men. Most were in groups, giving him and his men a wary eye, but a few stood alone. Conall was a man to take advantages when they came his way. Now was one of those times.

He grabbed a goblet of ale and made his way toward a lad who lounged against the wall. As he approached, he noticed the lad's youth and hid his smile at how easily he would gain information.

The lad looked up and immediately greeted him. "Laird MacInnes."

"You know me?" Conall asked, and watched him closely.

"Aye," he answered, and visibly swallowed. "A clan knows everything of their neighbors."

"So you know of my sister Iona and her disappearance?"

"Nay," the young lad answered quickly—a little too quickly—and lowered his head.

He's lying.

His unwanted power recoiled at the lie issued from the lad. Conall wanted to bellow his fury. He tamped it down and prodded further, softening his voice. "Surely you have. As you said, you know everything of my clan."

The lad raised his troubled eyes and bit his lip. "I remember it being said she'd disappeared."

"But you know nothing else?"

"Nay. I must get to the stables to…ah…they need me," he finished lamely, and ran off.

Conall seethed with unbridled rage. There would be no truce talk now that he knew the MacNeils had something to do with Iona's disappearance. Now they would talk of revenge and battle.

Although he hated to admit it, his powers came in handy in times like these. He took several deep breaths before he was calm enough to return to his men to tell them of his findings. Just as he turned, a flash of light grabbed his attention.

Swords. Drawn swords at that.

This wasn't a peace talk. It was a trap. He whistled and threw down his goblet. In seconds his men's swords were drawn. A blur of MacNeil plaid surrounded him. He raised his sword and looked his enemy in the eye, promising each a long and painful death.

The sounds of metal against metal clashed around him as his men fought. Out the corner of his eye he spotted Angus as he threw a brute of a man over his shoulder before plunging his sword in the soldier. In a glance he noted that all his men were surrounded and fighting valiantly.

With a diving roll, he ducked a deadly swing of a sword and came up ready to see his sword stained with blood. His blood cried for revenge, demanded revenge. Revenge for Iona. Maybe once his family was avenged then the helplessness that filled him would leave.

The five soldiers who surrounded him didn't make a move. Conall studied each until he found just the man he sought. The soldier had a wary look in his eye. He nearly laughed when he winked at the soldier and saw his face turn red. The soldier raced at him, sword swinging wildly. With a swift downward arc of his own blade, Conall ended the man's life.

The other four rushed him at once. He blocked a killing blow that left his arm feeling as though it were on fire, but he ignored the biting pain. In quick succession he sent two more soldiers to their deaths and turned to face the last two.

One of them backed away, and Conall turned his full attention on the remaining man. The soldier ran at him. Conall easily sidestepped and brought his claymore down to slice the back of the soldier's knee. The man crumpled, screaming in pain, his sword and the battle forgotten.

Conall then found himself facedown on the floor, a heavy weight on his back, pinning him down. He spotted an arm and quickly rolled the weight off. One glance told him the soldier was dead. He sat up and found Angus standing above him.

"I cannot believe me eyes. What are you doing on the ground when there's a fight, man?" Angus asked with a twinkle in his eye.

Conall rolled his eyes and gained his feet as more MacNeil soldiers charged. His sword was drenched in blood when he saw a man who wore no plaid but a leather jerkin and breeches stumble over a dead body while fighting a MacNeil. The soldier raised his arms, about to end the stranger's life. Conall wasn't about to let the man die, not when he was fighting MacNeils.

With a downward slice, Conall killed the soldier he had been fighting and leapt over several more before he thrust his sword between the stranger and the MacNeil soldier.

The soldier's sword clanged into his. He smiled at the surprise on the soldier's face before he twisted his arms up and around. The soldier's sword flew from his hand and, finding himself suddenly bereft of a weapon, he turned and scurried away. Conall laughed and turned to the stranger.

"You saved my life," the stranger said, his black eyes guarded.

"I'm Conall MacInnes. And you are?" he prompted.

"Gregor."

Conall ignored the fact Gregor hadn't offered his surname and held out his arm to help him to his feet. "Good luck to you. I needs find the MacNeil."

"I know who can tell you."

He looked at Gregor. "Who?"

"Her," Gregor said, and pointed to the top of the stairs.

Instead of wondering how Gregor knew of the lass, he simply stared. For the first time in his life he was speechless. Standing atop the stairs was a lass so beautiful she put sunsets to shame. Waves of dark hair flowed over her shoulders nearly to her waist. She was a tiny thing, but there was no denying she was a woman by her lush curves and ample breasts. Though the blue gown that clung to her nice shape was in better repair than the servants, it was still worn and faded.

He licked his lips as his eyes raked over her delectable body once more before he raised his gaze. Lips perfectly formed, full but not too wide, parted slightly as she raised her stubborn little chin. Her angelic oval face held no expression, but her big almond-shaped eyes were riveted on him.

"Who is she?" he asked Gregor.

"MacNeil's daughter."

*****

Glenna stared down at the battle, her mind frozen by the sight of the black-headed giant in the bold green and blue MacInnes plaid, swinging his claymore with one arm as if it weighed no more than a feather. The muscles flexing in his arms and bare back bespoke hours of training, and his quickness for a man of his size was almost uncanny.

His wide, brawny shoulders shoved men aside as though they were nothing more than weeds needing thrown out. Because he didn't wear a shirt beneath his kilt she was able to see the hard planes of his stomach and the tapering of his waist. Long, muscular legs supported him as he pivoted and steeled himself for a blow.

But it was his face she longed to see more closely.

When his eyes met hers, she knew he would forever change her life. This man had her soul in the palm of his hands without even knowing it. He had to be the man Iona had spoken of.

Some unknown force kept her rooted where she stood and her eyes on the MacInnes laird. Even when he ran up the stairs to her she waited instead of dashing away, waited instead of killing him as her father bid.

He reached her and his silver orbs burned into her, his square jaw hard and unyielding, and hair as black as pitch tied at his nape. "You're the MacNeil's daughter?"

His deep, husky voice poured over her like water. "Aye."

"Where is he?"

"I don't know." It wasn't a lie. She didn't know. MacNeil had fled after ordering her to kill the intruders. She hadn't even had time to ask him exactly how she, a mere woman, was supposed to kill trained warriors.

It wasn't the first time she had been ashamed of her father and she doubted it would be her last. After all, a laird should stay with his soldiers, not flee.

Two other men joined the MacInnes laird, one without a plaid and another with a bushy red beard. Red beard asked, "Is she lying, Conall?"

Conall. A good, strong name that suited this Highland warrior, as did his gray eyes, high cheekbones and chiseled features.

"She's speaking true, Angus," he answered without taking his eyes from her.

Of course she spoke the truth. The urge to roll her eyes at the idea of her lying was strong, but she dared not show them any emotion. She had learned that the hard way from MacNeil.

"What's your name, lass?"

The laird took a step toward her. The mere size of him would intimidate the bravest man, and she was far from brave. She swallowed, her mouth now dry, and tried to keep her expression blank. "Glenna."

"Well, Glenna, be a good lass and point me in the direction of your coward father."

She knew this was her one and only chance to escape from her father successfully. So she tamped down her growing fear, and hurriedly said, "There's only one way to get him. Take me."

Those striking silver eyes narrowed on her and he took a step closer. "Why? Why would you willingly give yourself to the enemy to be used as bait?"

To be free she yearned to scream. Instead, she said, "You want revenge. He wants me. It's the only solution."

After several heartbeats of watching him look her over, he held out his hand. "You've sealed your fate, lass."

Oh aye, she thought, and looked at Conall. It was the brief message she had been given by her only friend Iona that there would be a man to claim her who made it easy to hand herself over to him.

A man who would free her.

Those had been Iona's words, and it had been those few words that had kept Glenna going through each day. Surprisingly, it hadn't taken as long as Glenna had expected. Less than two months, actually, and she had been prepared to wait years.

She followed Conall and walked among her dead kinsmen. Hatred for the MacInnes' men should have seeped into her heart, but instead there was nothing. An empty, numb void resided in her chest thanks to her father and the clan that had shown her their loathing. With Conall in the lead and Angus and the unknown stranger behind her, she was hidden from view. Conall kept a hand clasped around her arm as if he feared she would run.

If he only knew how desperately I yearn to be free of this he wouldn't bother, she thought.

While they waited she counted the MacInnes' men and all forty still stood, though most had wounds that would need tending. A low whistle sounded from Conall, signaling his men it was time to leave.

One by one they crept from the hall. She looked around the near-empty bailey and heard the call go up for more MacNeil soldiers. Panic seized her heart, and she wondered if she would be free from her prison.

That one glance was all she was given as Conall roughly hauled her up behind him at the same time he nudged his horse. Before she knew it, she was out the MacNeil gates for only the second time in her life.

"I'm free," she whispered into the wind, and grabbed hold of a rock-solid abdomen as the horse raced from the castle.

The men splintered into different groups to confuse the MacNeil soldiers. Soon they stopped and hid behind trees, waiting for the rest of the MacInnes' men to catch up. Conall dismounted and reached to help her down. His gaze held her immobile as he slowly lowered her to the ground. Big, strong hands engulfed her and made her feel even smaller than she actually was. She hated being so short, but it had been her lot in life, and being next to this giant made her feel as small as a flea.

Of all the things she should be thinking about, this wasn't one of them. She began to turn away and spotted the blood on his arm. "You're hurt," she said, embarrassed that it came out so breathless.

He looked down at his arm and shrugged. "Don't fash yourself. It's but a small wound." He dug in his sporran and tugged out a piece of cloth.

"You should tend to it now."

He wrapped the cloth around the cut on his lower arm. "I'll have it tended to when we reach my home."

She helped him tie off the bandage and stepped back. "You've touched me more in this short time than anyone in my entire life," she said as she rubbed his horse's neck.

"People touch each other every day," Angus said, and moved closer to them.

Glenna didn't say more. All her life she had been treated differently, and she needed them to think she was as normal as they were. She was saved from having to explain by the arrival of the stranger.

"Ah Gregor," Conall called. "Come meet my friend and clansmen Angus MacDuff."

Glenna got her first good look at Gregor. His blond hair flowed freely to his shoulders except for two small braids that hung next to his face, and his stance was that of a man who feared nothing. But his black eyes guarded much. She watched him saunter to Conall and noted they were similar in shape and both clearly over six feet in height.

Angus and Gregor clasped hands and Conall told of how he had come upon Gregor.

"What were you doing there anyway?" Angus asked. "The MacNeils aren't known for their kindness."

All three men looked toward her before Gregor answered, "I was there on a personal matter. I owe you my life, Conall."

He had stated the last as if it pained him, and Glenna realized he was a man who didn't like to be beholden to anyone. And though he smiled easily enough, it didn't reach his eyes. He interested her, mostly because he had been at her home and she hadn't even known. Just what else had the MacNeil hidden?

"You're welcome in my clan anytime," Conall said, and clasped Gregor on the back. "Any man who fights the MacNeils is an ally."

Her mind raced at what she had heard from Gregor. What had he been doing at the castle? She had never seen him before, yet he acted as though he knew the MacNeil.

It wasn't long before the rest of the MacInnes' men surrounded them. They quickly saw to their injuries while studying her. Her chest began to ache and clench tightly as if a great weight rested there while the back of her neck began to throb painfully.

She looked up and spotted the looks of hatred and malice directed at her. Surely the soldiers couldn't be the cause, but she knew in her heart they were. She had felt this pain in her own home, but it hadn't been nearly this terrible.

Her limbs grew heavy to where she could barely lift them without great effort. Her breath locked within her lungs. The more she fought, the more excruciating it became.

Pain infused her body as she struggled to keep it from showing on her face. The looks ate away at her resistance until she had to lean against the horse or crumple under their weight. Fear nestled itself comfortably in her stomach and threatened to bring about the old demons.

"What are you going to do with her, laird?" one man asked.

She strained to tamp down the fear so she could hear his answer. Had she been a fool to take Iona's words to heart? How could any captive trust their captor as easily and surely as she trusted hers?

"She's my prisoner. I plan to trade her for my sister Iona."

Glenna gasped and tried to stay on her feet as Conall's words sunk in and the blackness threatened to take hold.

Iona? Saints help me.

Chapter Two

The first thing Glenna saw when she opened her eyes was an intense silver gaze boring into her. Conall's strong jaw, a nose that had been broken at least once and black brows that arched ever so slightly, loomed above her.

"We thought we'd lost ye, lass," Angus said as he came to kneel beside Conall.

Conall frowned. "You should have told me you needed to rest."

"It wasn't that," she said.

"Then what?"

Her gaze traveled to the men who still stared with open hostility. "They hate me because I'm a MacNeil." She couldn't believe she had fainted, but the embarrassment over that quickly left as the pain began anew.

"That's true enough," Angus said. "Can't say as I blame them, lass. It was a trap the MacNeil set."

Years of hearing servants whisper words of MacNeil cruelty when they had thought she wasn't listening came to mind. Just what had he done? Would her shame at being a MacNeil never end?

"Glenna?" Once again Conall forced her attention to him.

"I'm sorry for what the MacNeil has done. It's unforgivable. I've heard whispers before but nothing solid until today. I had no idea..."

He shrugged his massive shoulders. "Maybe. Maybe not. Regardless, you're now my prisoner," he said, and brought her to her feet. "Are you well enough to ride? We've wasted enough time."

The pain abated as the men focused their attention on their mounts instead of her. Her relief was short-lived though once Conall set her in front of him, and the contact of his hard muscled chest against her back was as foreign as the soil she was on. But she felt safe. Safe for the first time in her life.

Iona.

Tears misted her eyes so that the beautiful budding green landscape around her blurred. Iona, her one and only friend. Glenna would give up her life to know where Iona was, and if she was safe. She had begged MacNeil to tell her something, anything of Iona, but he had refused.

MacNeil had said Iona had come to MacNeil Castle to teach her, but Glenna had been unsure just what Iona had been sent to teach until talk of magic had begun. Then Glenna had known MacNeil was using Iona.

Unbidden, a memory of bruises on Iona's arms came to mind. She had questioned Iona about them but had never gotten an answer. None of the questions about where Iona had come from were answered either.

Glenna had thought Iona had run away from her home, but seeing Conall, she had to wonder if that was the case. From what she had seen so far he was nothing like MacNeil.

MacNeil said Iona had left, but had she really? Or had she run from MacNeil Castle? Glenna wouldn't blame her if she had. Many times she had wanted to escape MacNeil's bonds, and many times she had been caught before she had even reached the gatehouse.

"You're quiet. I would've thought you would question me until my ears ached at what I was going to do with you," Conall's deep voice reached her as they passed beneath a huge fir tree.

"I know what you're going to do with me. Instead, I'm looking at what I've been denied." It was true she feared what was before her, but Iona's words comforted her. Not to mention, knowing she was with Iona's brother helped ease some of those fears.

"Denied? What are you talking about, lass?" His voice rumbled in his chest at his question.

She gazed greedily at the many trees and flowers they passed. "MacNeil has kept me within his walls all my life."

"And the touching?"

She turned her head over her shoulder and looked at her capturer, his wide, full mouth only inches from her. "The only person to touch me was MacNeil and even then only occasionally."

"Why?" he questioned, his eyes narrowed.

"Why does the sun set in the west?" She shrugged. "I was never given an answer, though I asked many times."

"How old are you?"

She snorted. "Old enough to have been married with children."

"And why aren't you?"

"He's refused the few brave souls who have asked for my hand."

"What reason did he give?"

"MacNeil never gives a reason."

"No child should be raised like that," he said, and drew her against his chest. It was probably a reflex on his part, but Glenna couldn't help but like this close contact with him. He was pleasant to look upon and had treated her with more kindness than she had seen from her own clan.

The women ignored her, the soldiers mocked her, and the children ran screaming from her. She closed her eyes and willed those memories to fade. She couldn't stop shaking, yet from the cold or from being near Conall she didn't know. Touching and being touched was not something she was accustomed to, yet these men thought nothing of it. And here was a man who had saved her. Yet he didn't know it.

"Are you cold, lass? You're trembling."

"A wee bit."

Conall wrapped his plaid around her and settled her more comfortably against him. He didn't know what to make of her, but he knew he would come close by the time he arrived home.

He breathed in the clean scent of her and wrinkled his nose as a tendril of her dark hair tickled his cheek. With a small adjustment of his head he was able to have a view of her face.

She had a high forehead, dark brows that accented her almond-shaped eyes. Her big, dark eyes hastily took in everything while her luscious mouth parted as she gazed at the sights. He looked at the trees and sky and didn't see anything unusual, but he might have a different perspective if he had been locked within stone walls.

Her lips were full, ripe…kissable. Now what the hell could have made him think that?

She hadn't lied about her childhood. His ability to know when someone was indeed untruthful came in handy in situations like this. He let his thoughts wander over her and what he had learned.

Much later he called a halt to their steady progress. "We need to rest the horses if we're to return before nightfall."

The men dismounted to water their horses. He slid from his horse then turned and reached to help Glenna dismount. "I won't bite, lass," he said, adding a smile when she hesitated.

She allowed him to assist her, though she was suddenly more cautious. He wasn't surprised to find his hands spanned her tiny waist. Her head barely came to his chest, but he sensed a power in her that she had yet to find.

And God help everyone when she did find it.

He watched her slight figure as she made her way to a rock and leaned against it. He grabbed his horse's reins and led the animal to the small stream.

His gaze drifted over his men and the easy way they talked, laughed and touched.

Those simple pleasures he had taken for granted and wondered what life would be like without those small things. But his mind refused to dwell on that when he had bigger concerns.

Like the MacNeil.

The war Conall had wanted to prevent was no longer avoidable...it was inevitable. Especially now that he knew MacNeils were responsible for his sister's vanishing.

Glenna had offered herself, and in doing so would not only bring MacNeil and allow Conall to exact his revenge, she would also provide him with a means for Iona's safe return. Only then, after fulfilling his vows to his mother and father, would he be free to pursue the vow he made to himself — to see every MacNeil who had a hand in taking Iona die by his blade.

He ran his hand down his face and sighed deeply. His eyes opened to find Gregor beside him, a hint of worry in his dark eyes.

"I'd watch your men around Glenna. Their hatred is having an effect on her that I've never seen."

Conall swiveled his head until he spotted her. She walked near him and studied the surroundings. Her slim hands reached out and stroked the trees, their leaves and anything else she could grasp, her touch reverent as if it would shatter at her contact.

Yet he saw by the tightness of her mouth, her pale complexion and the fine sheen of sweat that Gregor had stated the truth. She glanced up and gave him a weak smile.

He motioned her to the water. "Come drink."

"Och, but it's cold," she said when her fingers dipped into the icy water.

"Aye. This stream is fed from the snow atop the mountains. It will get a wee bit warmer during the summer."

She leaned down and brought the water to her lips. Her eyes closed. Water beaded and dripped from her mouth. It ran down her chin to her neck and disappeared to hidden places Conall itched to touch and see.

His body hardened instantly. His hand yearned to follow the path of the water and see if her skin was as soft as it looked. He cursed and blamed it on the fact he hadn't been with a woman recently, and he would be sure to remedy that as soon as he could.

"Mount up," he called when she had drunk her fill.

He settled her on his horse, her petite body molding to his as if they were one. His hand dropped to her trim waist and rested on her flared hips. By the way she sat with her back straight and body tense he knew she was in some discomfort, but all he could think of was looking over her shoulder at the swell of her breasts. He said a brief prayer that she didn't feel the bulge of his desire pressing into her back and again wrapped his plaid about her before taking the reins.

They traveled hard and fast, and when most women would have complained, she said not a word.

He had just slowed his horse to a walk when she turned her head, and asked, "Do you hear that?"

He listened but heard nothing other than the sounds of the Highlands. "What is it you hear?"

"Music. Beautiful music," she whispered, looking toward the sky.

"There's no music, lass." *And now I need to add your sanity to my growing list of worries.*

She didn't say more about the music, and for that Conall was relieved. Could she be addled? Is that why none of the MacNeils would touch her? Nay. That couldn't be the reason. There had to be something else, something she wasn't telling him. They rode in silence, and it unnerved him to be so comfortable with her. She was the enemy after all, even though she was innocent.

After a while, he glanced at the sun and was surprised they had come so far. It amazed him even more that she wasn't like most women he knew who would have been screaming like shrews to be taken from their homes by a complete stranger, regardless that she had practically asked him to take her.

But Glenna was nothing like the women he was used to. In some ways she reminded him of his mother who had been strong-willed and headstrong.

When they could go no farther without resting the horses, he halted and dismounted. He turned and held out his arms. She slid easily into his arms, but when his hands left her, she crumpled.

Conall caught her before she hit the ground. "I've got you," he said, and carried her to a boulder. "Rest. I'll bring you water."

While he retrieved his waterskin, he noted the many hostile glances his men gave her. A dull ache in the back of his neck began to pound, signaling that there might be trouble. Trouble he didn't want or need.

Then again, his people deserved revenge for the many deeds of violence given to them by MacNeil. Even Conall's own father had sought that revenge only to die by a MacNeil's sword on the battlefield.

Still, he wouldn't allow his clan to harm Glenna. Revenge would be taken, but against the MacNeil, not an innocent lass who was his daughter by a quirk of fate. He returned to find her asleep, her dark hair flying around her as the afternoon breeze quickened. With a finger, he reached up and smoothed a lock of hair from her thick, black eyelashes.

Her eyes flew open at his touch. Fear lurked in her beautiful brown depths as well as determination and spirit. Spirit the MacNeil hadn't been able to kill though Conall would bet his sword MacNeil had tried. He handed her the water and turned to give her a moment of privacy.

Glenna took the water and trembled from Conall's gentle touch. The cool water touched her lips and her body demanded more. She hadn't realized how thirsty she had been and she drank greedily.

She kept her head bent but watched Conall and his soldiers. Her chest began to tighten as breathing became difficult.

Not again. Please not again.

The pain lessened when Conall called for them to mount. She wanted to cry in relief until she tried to stand. Then she wanted to cry from the pain searing its way through her legs and lower back. She had never been allowed on a horse before and hadn't been prepared for this.

All those years of yearning to ride, but now she would be glad to never see a horse again after today.

Gradually, and more slowly than she would have liked, she walked to Conall and noticed he had put on a shirt. It took every effort she had to walk upright and not show them how much she hurt. She reached Conall to find him sitting astride his horse instead of waiting to help her mount.

He held out his hand, and said, "We've a tough trek ahead. I need you on back."

Nay. I want on front. I don't have the strength to hold on. But the argument died on her lips when she saw the determined glint of his eyes. She had seen that same look in MacNeil's eyes and knew better than to argue, though the urge was strong, stronger than it had been in many years.

"All right."

He easily swung her behind him, and she found his thick, muscled neck and black hair within heartbeats of her touch. A brisk spring breeze swept around her, and she hastily wrapped her arms around him for warmth.

His stomach muscles jumped at her touch. She heard his sharp intake of breath when she laid her head on his back. She wasn't given long to rejoice in her effect on him as his horse leapt into a gallop. She was forced to hold on for dear life while her body screamed silently in pain.

When they began their descent over a rock-covered mountainside, she squeezed her eyes shut. With every breath she knew it was her last, and her hold became a death grip. The sound of rocks sliding loose and falling increased her fear tenfold.

"I cannot breathe, lass."

"I'm sorry," she mumbled into his back, her eyes still shut.

"These horses are the surest-footed creatures around."

"Uh-huh," she murmured.

He chuckled. "You won't plummet to your death while riding with me."

But his words did little to ease her fear.

* * * * *

Conall moved Glenna in front of him once they cleared the pass. A shiver shook her and he pulled his plaid around her. The heat from her body seeped into his saffron shirt, scalding him. He hardened instantly and cursed his luck.

In the next heartbeat she leaned her head against his chest. His body once again responded to her. He knew he had gone far too long without a woman when the simple touch of a maiden set him on fire.

He was more than a little surprised when she fell asleep in his arms. Her upturned face looked so innocent and trusting, that he wondered if his course of action had been the right one, but then he hadn't had much of a choice. Glenna had been right. The only way to get MacNeil and find Iona was to take her. He still didn't like the thought of kidnapping her, but there wasn't another way.

As much as he hated to admit it, he was attracted to her. She was a MacNeil. An enemy. But she stirred his loins like no other. Her simple touch, hesitant and featherlight, brought out his protective instinct that hereto now had only been given to his family. It disturbed him to no end that she could stir such strong feelings within him.

It had been awhile since he had held a woman this close. Ever since his sister vanished he had foregone any kind of physical pleasure and concentrated on being the laird his father had wanted him to be.

His mother's dying wish that he bring Iona home had been his driving force. He had given his mother his word and nothing would stop him. Nothing. Honor was all he had left and nothing would be able to change that.

"The music grows louder," she mumbled, and snuggled closer.

He froze. Music?

How could he have been so dimwitted? He knew what she heard. The Druids. They were calling to her, one of their own.

By St. George's baldhead, his life had become infinitely more complicated if that was possible. His life was based on honor yet now that would be sorely tested.

For more generations than he knew, his clan had kept the Druids hidden.

Now he would have to break a vow. The one he had made the day he had become laird to protect all Druids, or the vow to his mother to find Iona.

Chapter Three

Glenna awoke to the smell of horse, pine and...man. She jerked straight and would have fallen to the earth if Conall hadn't caught her.

His powerful silver gaze questioned her wits, and she couldn't blame him. "I forgot where I was," she said quickly as the plaid fell from her shoulders.

He didn't speak as he tucked the plaid around her and pulled her against his chest. "We've still a wee bit of riding ahead. Rest while you can."

But she didn't hear him. The music had grown so loud she could scarce hear anything else. It pulled at her soul, urging her toward some unknown force, and she instinctively knew she would find her answers if she just followed the music.

Her heart squeezed tight. Soon. Soon she would know who she really was, just as Iona had promised. Her heart was lighter than it had ever been, but her body ached too badly to rejoice. It became difficult to hold her head up, so she rested her cheek against Conall's strong, muscular chest.

With each step the horse took, pain exploded through her body. Her belly grumbled with hunger and she prayed he didn't hear it.

"We'll be stopping for food soon," he said into her ear.

Would her embarrassment never end? She listened to the hauntingly beautiful music as she gazed at the wild surroundings of fir, yew and pine trees and the occasional clump of heather. The trees were budding and flowers sprouted from the earth as the sun's rays warmed the cold ground.

Strikingly beautiful is how she would describe the Highland landscape, and the mountains that rose around them only added to the majesty of the scene. Anger for all she had missed these past years welled up and nearly consumed her in its intensity.

For years she had tried to understand MacNeil's need to keep her at the castle, but the more he refused to answer her, the more resentful she had grown. He had never been a very caring father, so it had been easy to stay away from him. And she had escaped him. Finally. Thanks to Iona's foretelling of Conall.

"Tell me about yourself," she asked, needing to take her mind off MacNeil.

Silence greeted her question, and for a moment she thought she would have to return to her sad thoughts.

"I was born to the laird of my clan," he finally said, "and voted in when my father died four summers ago."

"Did you know your mother?"

"Aye. I lost her this past winter after Iona disappeared." He clicked the horse into a trot.

His gruff voice should have given her an inkling that he didn't wish to talk, but she pressed onward. "I never knew my mother. MacNeil would never talk of her other than to say I look like her."

Something she had said must have disturbed Conall for he had withdrawn from her, and it set her mind to worrying. She had put her faith in him from the beginning just as Iona had asked, and the thought that he couldn't be trusted wrenched her stomach.

"Have you ever heard of the Druids?" he suddenly asked.

"Druids? Nay. What are they?"

For several heartbeats he stared ahead, and she thought he had refused to answer when he said, "They are healers, seers and the like. Some say they hold the magic of Scotland."

"You speak as though you must say those words yet you don't seem to believe them." She regretted her words as pain flashed through his eyes.

"Rest," he commanded, and pushed her head against him.

Emotions, strange and unmistakable in their intensity, raged within her. But one question stuck out—was Conall her savior and the man Iona had mentioned or another jailer?

The image of a tall, beautiful woman wearing a white gown with blonde hair and green eyes beckoned her. Glenna blinked and the image vanished as quickly as it had come.

* * * * *

Conall waged a war within himself. The Druids already called to her, but if she never knew she was a Druid, he wouldn't have to break a vow. Of course, the mere fact he was thinking this way didn't bode well for his honor.

They would come for her. Unless she refused them.

His mind latched on to that thought. If she refused them, he didn't have to protect her and his honor would stay intact. All he had to do was turn her against the Druids, which wouldn't be hard since he was still upset at their refusal to help find Iona.

His thoughts turned to his clan. He had to keep Glenna safe. Not just from the Druids but from his own people. They would take one look at the MacNeil plaid and God only knew what would happen next. The hostility from his own soldiers had grown instead of lessened as he had hoped.

There was no deception in her golden-brown eyes. Only honesty and truth resided there, but his clan wouldn't see that.

She sighed and nestled closer to him, and his body screamed to taste her lips, her body. He knew she was untouched, and the fact no other had tasted her only made him burn stronger for her. Her hips moved to find a more comfortable position, but all they did was rub against his heated, aching cock, inflaming his growing desire.

It was such a strong craving that it took all his will to tamp it down. No woman had ever held such power over him, and that's exactly what she had, though she didn't know it. And wouldn't know it if he had any say in it.

"Conall."

He looked over his shoulder to see Angus rein his horse next to his. His friend's forehead was lined with worry, and that wasn't a good sign. "Something amiss?"

"Aye," his friend said. "The men want revenge for the trap."

"In other words, they want Glenna."

Angus nodded. "I've told them ye'll do what's right, but hatred for the MacNeils runs long and deep."

"So it has, but when has any man from the MacInnes clan ever laid a hand on a woman? It won't start now, either. Make sure of it. If anyone harms her, they'll answer to me."

Angus smiled and turned his head to spit. "I've been waiting for that MacInnes temper to show itself. Felt it was safe with the lass asleep?"

Conall rolled his eyes heavenward and prayed for patience. "You'd drive a saint to madness."

"I do try." Angus' expression turned serious. "I've never known a lass to willingly turn herself over to the enemy. Ye don't think the MacNeil is using her as a spy, do ye?"

"There's no deceit in her."

"So yer gift comes in handy once again, aye?" Angus chuckled.

Conall reached over and punched him in the arm. "Enough."

"I don't know why ye keep it secret," Angus said, and rubbed his arm.

"There's no secret. I don't have any type of gift, so leave it be."

Angus *tsked*. "Yer mother told me ye'd deny it. It's been in yer family for generations. Don't fight it. Yer sister didn't."

It only took one look from Conall to silence any more words Angus might have.

"I'm not going to apologize. Ye need to talk about it," Angus stated. "I just came to tell ye I'd make sure the lass was safe when ye couldn't."

"I knew I could count on you."

Angus spun his horse around. Conall knew he would take the end position to watch the men. Damn. He glanced at Glenna. At least she hadn't heard any of the exchange with Angus.

A gift. He snorted.

He didn't have a gift. It was a curse. As far back as he could remember his mother had told him and Iona tales of the Druids and their ways. Magical tales — and it had filled his head with thoughts a lad shouldn't have.

He had even grown up thinking he would be a Druid priest as well as his clan's leader. Fate, it seemed, had other ideas for him. But Iona had only one dream — to become a Druid priestess.

Every year she and their mother would venture into the woods and not come out for weeks. Iona's entire life had been centered around the Druids while his had been on the clan.

His father even advised him to marry a Druid to make his line stronger. All would have gone as their parents planned if Iona hadn't disappeared, and the very people she sought to follow refused to help him.

The drivel the Druids had told him about her fulfilling her destiny only made him want to gnash his teeth. It went beyond comprehension why the Druids couldn't just say what they meant. Nay, everything was said in verses that would take the average man years to decipher.

Anger stirred within his heart until they crested a hill and he pulled up on the reins. Home.

The MacInnes castle had been built four hundred years before, and with every laird a new section had been added to the already considerable size. From the original donjon to the two square and four round towers.

He should be finishing the stone walkway his father had wanted from the castle to the loch and finding a wife. Instead, his only thought had been of Iona and the vow to his mother.

From his vantage point atop a hill he had a clear view of the surrounding land and castle. A swift glance told him no enemy was near. Yet.

He raised his hand and motioned for his men to follow as he nudged his horse. The quick step of the horse jarred Glenna awake.

"We're home, lass."

Chapter Four

Glenna sucked in her breath at the brief view she had of the castle. It had been built into the cliffs, which aided in its defense as well as the loch that surrounded two sides and gentle, rolling hills on the other two.

Now she knew why the MacNeil wanted it. Not only was it beautiful, it was well defended. No one could attack without being seen by the guards from the castle. When Conall nudged his horse into a walk, she settled herself more comfortably to ease the ache in her legs. The sky had begun to darken. She hadn't realized she had slept that long.

It wasn't until the horse veered right that she asked, "The castle is straight. Where are we going?"

"You'll see," was all he said.

So she focused on the spot between the horse's ears to detach herself from the excruciating agony and told herself it was just a little longer before she would be off the beast.

A droplet of water landed on her hand and brought her out of her daze. Darkness met her gaze and an abyss opened its mouth as they entered.

"It's just a cave," Conall said, his voice low and soothing as if he had felt her fear.

Just a cave. Ha. "I can't go in there. Don't take me in there," she pleaded as she turned around until she almost faced him. She hadn't even tried to hide the fact she was terrified.

The thought of spiders dangling from the ceiling as they waited to crawl over her stopped any pretense she might have tried to use. She was petrified, and she must make Conall understand that to bring her in the cave would be bringing her into a living nightmare.

His eyes stared hard into hers. "With the threat of your father, I must take precautions. Entering through the caves is one of them. It's not very far to the other side."

She glanced over her shoulder at the yawning hole of shadows. "I'm not going in there," she stated.

"Aye, you will."

Gone was the soothing tone and in its place a voice hard as steel. There was nothing she could say to this man to change his mind, and she knew attempting to run would be stupid with her legs aching as they did.

Her stomach clenched in apprehension. She shivered at the thought of all the spider legs that would be crawling on her. Fear seized her as its clutches wrapped themselves around her. Her body began to shake as she tried to see into the darkness.

"I give you my word nothing will happen to you."

Strangely enough she knew he would try to protect her. She let him right her in the saddle and took hold of his hand, determined to act more courageous than she felt.

"I'm going to hold you to that vow, MacInnes," she said, and hoped she would be able to get his sword unsheathed before the first spider landed on her.

He wrapped an arm around her waist and held her tight against him. Just before they reached the entrance to the cave he whistled, and Angus ran his horse to the front to take the lead.

"If there's anything in there it will get Angus first," he whispered as they entered the darkness.

She smiled at his jest while his breath warmed her neck and made her breasts tighten, temporarily setting aside the trembling. His arm, wrapped so snugly around her waist, touched the undersides of her breasts.

Without the glorious Highland landscape to distract her, she grew conscious of every inch of her body that touched his. She sucked in her breath and closed her eyes as each new sensation swept violently through her.

His long legs had rather handsome knees, if one could call knees handsome. Thick, muscular thighs helped to hold her securely onto the horse and molded her against a hardness that had been pressing into her back for some time now. Arms so solid, so strong she was sure they could fell an ancient oak with a simple push held her gently but firmly. Muscles in those mighty arms flexed as he moved the reins.

A soldier behind them slapped at something and muttered about a bug. She tensed, expecting to feel hundreds of hairy legs swarming over her, but there was nothing. Nothing except Conall and his muscles.

She forced herself to lean back against his shoulder before her head began to ache and was surprised to find his hand grazed her throat then moved to her cheek.

"See. I told you there was nothing to fash yourself about," he murmured into her ear.

She smiled. He was an arrogant laird.

"Ah. A smile. It's good you trust me."

"You gave me your word and, despite what I should be feeling, I somehow know you'll honor that vow." She turned her head toward his, only to find her lips grazing his jaw sprinkled with a day's growth of beard.

The spiders were forgotten as she concentrated on the feel of his face against hers. His head moved slightly and she wished for some light, for she was sure it was his lips she felt for an instant against hers.

"You are my prisoner, and while at my home I'll protect you. I always protect what's mine."

An ominous mood overtook her at his words, but she didn't think more about them as they rode from the cave. Light blinded her as they emerged and she quickly covered her eyes with her hands. Cheers erupted around her at Conall's safe return until his plaid fell away to expose her MacNeil plaid.

The silence was deafening.

She couldn't look at the people staring at her with such open hostility so she looked around the bailey. To her left was the massive two-story gatehouse, flanked by two square towers, which projected outside the wall from what she could see. A stairway from the bailey led to the gatehouse. Two posterns, or secondary doorways, were visible in the curtain wall that formed a rectangular bailey.

The curtain wall itself was made up of cut stones that made up the battlements of alternating solid parts and spaces, merlons and crenels they were called, but to her they looked like square teeth.

To her right was the main castle itself, the chapel and the well where many of the occupants gathered. All in all it was a very impressive castle. Not just in its structure, but in its size.

"The MacNeil set a trap," Conall's voice called out. "I know now that they're responsible for Iona's disappearance. I have MacNeil's daughter until they return my sister."

Voices once again rose to praise their laird, but he wasn't done. With one raised hand he silenced them.

"Whatever we may feel for the MacNeils, I want no harm to befall Glenna. She's under my protection until I return her."

Return me?

That hadn't been her plan, but then again she had put herself in Conall's hands.

To get to MacNeil, not to return me to him.

Either she would have to convince Conall of another way to have Iona returned or she would have to escape from him. And she had a dreadful feeling that escaping from Conall wouldn't be easy.

She looked out over the MacInnes' people as they stared back at her. Most were curious while others had hatred sparkling in their depths. She couldn't blame them. If the positions were reversed, she would probably feel the same way.

Coldness surrounded her when Conall dismounted. Without him behind her she felt vulnerable and suddenly very scared. She knew if she attempted to walk she would fall on her face, but she could not, and would not, tell him that as he reached for her. She had already acted the fool about the cave.

She slid into his arms. Instead of being set on her feet, he began to walk to the castle with her in his arms. When she raised her eyes to his, she found him staring straight ahead, his jaw clenched.

"Thank you," she said, and focused on his plaid instead of the faces that watched her. She would survive this. She had made it through the caves. And who knew how many spiders had lain in wait for her?

Once they entered the castle, she looked around to find it filled with beautiful, ornate tapestries as well as swords, shield, maces and other weapons. She longed to look around and explore everything. It was such a colorful and happy place compared to her home. And clean.

She had grown up thinking a castle was meant to be dirty but had refused to let her own chamber, small as it was, be filthy. Now she knew it was simply her home that was dirty and not something that was commonplace.

Conall's steps didn't slow as he turned and mounted the stairs. He stopped at the first landing and carried her down a hallway before entering a chamber.

He walked to the bed and gently set her upon it. "Have a bath drawn immediately," he said, and a servant Glenna hadn't seen scurried away to do his bidding.

"A bath?"

"Your muscles are overtaxed. The heat from the water will soothe them."

Now she couldn't wait for her aching body to slip into the scalding water. Maybe afterward she would be able to walk again. "Thank you."

"Why didn't you want to go into the cave?"

She had thought he had forgotten about her terror, but it seemed she had fooled herself once again. "It was nothing."

"It was most definitely something. Are you afraid of the dark?"

"Nay," she said hastily, and realized her mistake. It was better to say she was afraid of the dark instead of spiders.

"Then what?" he prompted.

"Nothing." She stared at him, daring him to probe further. One corner of his mouth lifted in a smile.

He nodded and turned to go but stopped at the chamber door. "I'll have supper brought to you. I'm sure you've no wish to have everyone ogling you on your first night here."

And before she could express her gratitude, he was gone. She didn't trust her legs to hold her to inspect the chamber so she waited for the bath, which, thankfully, didn't take long.

Once the servants departed, she hastily disrobed and threw the MacNeil plaid onto the bed. She had to nearly crawl to the tub, but once she sank into the heated water, her muscles began to relax.

The water and serenity, along with the bottle of wine that had been left beside the tube, put her at peace. She found herself drifting in and out of sleep with passionate silver eyes haunting her.

* * * * *

Conall opened the chamber door and halted in midstride. Glenna reclined in the wooden tub before the fire. Steam had drifted around her, moistening her skin, and the flames from the nearby fire set it aglow. Her hair was in a knot atop her head and several strands had escaped and now stuck to her neck and sides of her face.

All he wanted was to get into the tub with her. He closed his eyes and took deep, calming breaths. But it didn't help. That image was now burned in his memory.

St. Myrtle's hairy fingers.

He looked at her again, her face turned toward him as she sighed and opened her eyes. If she was surprised to see him, she didn't show it.

For long moments they simply stared at each other, and all he could think of was the brief touch of their lips in the cave. It had been an accident, but one that had scalded him to his very soul.

"Laird."

Her voice, husky from the relaxing water and sleep stirred his body. Then he saw the empty ewer of wine and realized why she wasn't screaming at him for seeing her in her bath.

He should feel grateful to whatever servant had left the wine, but right now he needed a strong drink himself. Finally he found his voice. "The water is improving your legs?"

"Aye. Although I don't think I'll be able to walk for another sennight," she said, a grin pulling at the corner of her lips.

"Do I need to carry you to bed?" As soon as the words left his mouth he saw himself doing just that, but he didn't leave her to sleep. He made love to her.

Mine, a voice said. He shook his head and pushed the voice aside.

Her soft laughter floated around the room. "I think I could sleep right here if only the water would stay hot."

This conversation was getting out of control, but apparently he was the only one who thought so. He turned his gaze to the floor. "I just came to see how you were faring."

"You shouldn't be in here. Not while I'm at my bath."

Finally a sane thought. "I wondered if the wine had sped common sense from you."

She laughed again, the sound bringing a small tilt to his own lips. "I've never drank so much wine before, and I don't think I shall again. I'm fairly certain I should be demanding that you leave immediately."

"And why aren't you?" What devil prodded him to ask that he would never know, but now that it was asked, he wanted to know the answer.

She sighed and put a hand to her forehead. "It doesn't matter," she said, her eyes leaving his, but not before he saw the desolation.

He wanted the mischievous grin back, but he had a feeling she was sobering rapidly.

"Am I to be kept in this room?"

He raised his eyes to find her gaze on him. "If I wanted to imprison you, I'd have put you in the dungeon. I'm not a monster."

"I know. I simply wanted to know of your plans."

He shrugged and ran his hand through his hair. "I haven't thought about it really, but I don't plan to confine you to this chamber."

"What if I told you I wanted to explore outside the castle walls?" she asked, and leaned up.

For a moment he forgot to breathe, forgot her question, forgot everything except the water that beaded on her heated skin and rolled down her bare neck and shoulders. He wanted to follow those droplets with his tongue and nibble her skin while she squirmed beneath him.

He blinked and focused back on her face. "If you want to explore, then I'll take you."

A bright smile illuminated her face. "Really?"

"Aye."

"Would it be sacrilege if I said I didn't want to be returned to MacNeil?"

"No one wants to be returned to a monster, even if that monster is one's father."

She pulled her knees up and wrapped her slender arms around her legs. "You have much hatred for MacNeil. Tell me what he's done."

"You'll learn a lot about your clan while here." His body burned hotter with every inch of skin exposed. He didn't know how much longer he could stand there without yanking her from the tub and tasting her.

"Clans are always at each other's throats and stories get distorted."

"We don't lie," he ground out between clenched teeth. He couldn't blame her. He had been thinking the same thing. Still it stung.

"All I know is this feud has gone on for generations. Who even knows how it began?"

"I know," he said, and watched her eyes grow round. "As you'll soon find out. Your father took the feud to a new level when he became laird."

"How?"

He heard the fear in her voice, but he couldn't stop the truth from leaving his lips.

"He isn't called a butcher for nothing."

Glenna sat back in the water after Conall departed and thought over his words. Her mind buzzed with questions about her father and clan, but she really didn't want to know. If what Conall said was true, then it was no wonder his clan had such hatred for her.

The peace of the water eluded her as her wine-addled brain sobered. She stepped out of the now-tepid water and quickly dried off. The heat of the fire kept the chill from sinking into her bones but not from her soul.

What had prompted her to act like the wanton? She could blame it on the wine, but if she were honest, she would admit to liking the fire that kindled in Conall's eyes.

Now that the wine was wearing off, she was mortified at what she had done. When she turned back to the bed it was to find a simple white nightgown lying at the foot. She hobbled to the bed and wiggled into the gown.

She had just sat down when she noticed a small blue jar sitting beside the bathtub. It hadn't been there a moment ago. With a sigh she stood and slowly made her way back to the tub. With great effort she bent down and retrieved the jar. Once she was again seated, she opened it.

Inside she found a brownish-colored cream. She sniffed and the smell of mint filled her senses. It was a healing cream she held, and there was only one thing wrong with her. With a shrug, she pushed up the hem of her gown and rubbed the cream into her legs.

After her legs had been thoroughly doused with the cream, Glenna began to feel restless. It was a strange feeling since she was used to long periods in her chamber at home, but here it was different. Ever since she had left MacNeil Castle, she had had an unmistakable sense that there was magic surrounding this land.

Whatever it was must be absent from her home. She chuckled, the sound bouncing off the walls in the chamber. She stood and found her legs didn't ache as they had just a short while ago.

The window beckoned and she peered outside. The night cascaded with stars as clouds fluttered across the moon's path. A flash caught her attention. It was outside the castle walls in the forest. She strained to find it, and was about to give up when she saw it.

It was a light so bright it shown white in its intensity. It wasn't large, no larger than a man, but Glenna still couldn't make out what it was.

Magic, the night seemed to whisper.

Aye, it was probably magic, for it had been magic that brought Iona to her and freed her from MacNeil. A special magic beat in the heart of Scotland, and she wondered why it was so strong here and nonexistent at MacNeil's?

Regardless, she was determined to find out what the white light was and delve deeper into the mystery of this magic land.

* * * * *

The two Druids stared at the castle. "Did it work?" the man asked. "Did she see?"

"Aye, Frang," the woman answered. "She's come home at last."

They turned when the Fae being approached them. "You don't have much time."

"Glenna will be ready, Aimery," the woman stated.

Aimery smiled. "Glenna already feels the magic here. She will come to you eagerly, Moira. Make sure she learns all that she needs to know for MacNeil will challenge her."

Frang shifted and peered again at the castle. "How much do you think we should tell her about her parents?"

"Nothing," Moira hurriedly answered. "Not yet."

"She needs to know," Aimery said. "Without that knowledge, she cannot battle the evil."

"Then she will know," Frang said, and put his hand on Moira's shoulder.

"Until next time," Aimery said, and disappeared in a flash.

"Moira," Frang began, but she shook her head.

"I don't want her to know."

"She must," Frang insisted. "The Fae know much more than we do. It's they who bestowed Glenna her powers. Who are we to question them?"

"Who indeed?" Moira repeated while she stared at the castle. "She watches us even now though she cannot see."

"She sees what the Fae want her to see."

Chapter Five

The next day Conall strode into Glenna's chamber and said in no uncertain terms, "You'll spend the day by my side."

"By your side?" she asked stupidly when he handed her a simple yellow gown. "You're laird and have many things to do. The last thing you need is to have me in the way."

"It'll get your legs moving to work out the soreness, and my clan will become accustomed to seeing you."

She opened her mouth to protest but quickly closed it.

He raised a black eyebrow. "Have you something to say?"

Her throat tightened. Would he punish her as MacNeil did for speaking her mind? It was a chance she wanted, nay needed, to take. With her heart in her throat, she said boldly, "I'd prefer to spend the day in my chamber."

"And I'd prefer you with me. I'm concerned about your safety."

"In other words, you don't trust your clan?"

"I trust them with my life." He paused and crossed his arms over his chest. "However, their minds are clouded with hate and they will turn it on you."

"While your clan will see me I'll be with you so you can protect me."

A slow, sensual smile crept across his face. She was sure that smile had left many a maiden with broken hearts.

"Aye," he said. "But there's one catch."

The grin she had worn slipped. Why must there be some sort of catch. Here she thought he might be a good man who had her welfare in mind. He lowered his arms and stared at her fixedly, his silver orbs fierce and uncompromising. She knew whatever he had to say would be final and no amount of arguing would budge him.

"Keep the MacNeil plaid if you must, but you won't wear it here."

She blinked. She hadn't expected to be asked so little. Setting aside the MacNeil plaid wouldn't be difficult since she had never been a part of the clan. Actually, she was grateful to set it aside. She had wanted away from that clan for many a year. She had the chance and wasn't about to pass it up.

"I'm asking this for your benefit," he continued, unaware that she had eagerly set aside the plaid. "My people react harshly to the sight of the MacNeil colors."

Let him think she wanted to keep it, she thought. He was making this very easy on her, but was it in her best interest to let him know that? "Give me a moment to change."

He stopped and pointed to the blue jar. "Where did you get that?"

"I don't know. I thought you brought it. I found it after my bath last eve."

He shook his head but said no more about the jar. He stepped out of her chamber and she quickly shed the MacNeil plaid, folded it and placed it in the small chest in the corner.

She slid the gown over her head and was surprised to find it nearly fit her perfectly. It was just a wee tight across her chest. It was also a little long, but she could tell it had been hemmed.

It wouldn't be difficult to keep from stepping on the lovely gown. It wasn't new, but she was determined to make sure it was returned to the owner in this same condition.

She took one step, expecting her muscles to scream in agony, but there was only tightness with slight soreness. Whatever was in that jar worked wonders to work out the stiffness, she thought.

With a shaky breath, she masked her pain and opened the chamber door to find Conall lounging against the opposite wall as if he had all the time in the world. He nodded his approval and held out his arm.

She noted his wound had been tended and it didn't seem to bother him in the least.

"Who do I thank for lending me this gown?" she asked as they began to descend the stairs.

"Iona."

Glenna's knees buckled. She briefly saw the stairs fast approaching, but her mind had frozen at hearing Iona's name. Strong hands grabbed hold of her waist and jerked her up. Her breath stopped as she looked into his silver depths.

"Are you all right?" he asked, a mixture of irritation and concern in his voice.

She swallowed hard and nodded.

"I forgot about your legs," he said, and wrapped an arm around her for support.

She hastily blinked away her tears and continued down the stairs, her mind turning to Iona. Their time together had been brief, but they had become fast friends. But she wasn't given long to reflect on her days with Iona as she entered the hall with Conall. His soldiers turned and stared angrily at her.

She waited to feel their hate. Her lungs squeezed, but it wasn't near as debilitating as before. She contributed it to the fact she wasn't wearing the MacNeil plaid, either that or the fierce scowl on Conall's face. It didn't matter what stopped them, she was just delighted that something worked.

Conall didn't stay long in the hall and ushered her outside. Once they were in the bailey, he placed her next to the wall. "Stay here," he ordered, and turned to begin to practice with his soldiers.

She became mesmerized by the play of his muscles in the morning sunlight as he swung his sword as if it were an extension of his arm. He moved with the grace of a horse and the strength of a lion.

It took only seconds to best his men yet there were no harsh feelings when he did. She couldn't stand there and not compare this training to MacNeil soldiers. There, the MacNeil commanders would ridicule and torment anyone who couldn't disarm them.

There was hardly a day that went by that a soldier wasn't killed during their so-called training. Her legs began to ache from standing so long. She slowly lowered herself to the ground with the help of the wall and was surprised to find this gave her a better view of Conall.

The sound of someone approaching drew her attention. She grudgingly dragged her gaze from Conall to find a very old man standing beside her. His beard was matted and what hair was left on his head was solid white. He had also seen battle by the scar that ran across his face. She followed the scar and found half his ear gone.

"Like that scar, do ye?" he asked, a sneer on his wrinkled face, showing toothless gums.

She swallowed. "It looks as though it caused tremendous pain."

"Do ye know who put it there?"

"Nay." And she didn't want to know.

"The MacNeil hisself, though he was just a lad at the time. His father was still alive. It wasn't until after he became laird that he slaughtered my family."

Bile rose in Glenna's throat. What had made her think she wanted to know what MacNeil had done? "I don't wish to hear any more."

"I'm sure ye're wantin' to know how I know it was him." He cackled and pointed a gnarled finger at her. "Because I watched him do it. Me wife was heavy with child and my two sons were just babes. Just babes," he cried.

She scooted away from him, her heart screaming for him to stop. But he wasn't through.

"What kind of man kills women and babes? A butcher. That's who. Yer da's a monster, same as ye!"

"Enough," roared Conall as he came to stand beside her.

But she couldn't take her eyes off the old man. He still wore his grief, and she could well understand why. How she wished MacNeil wasn't her father. She would do almost anything to change the past.

"Glenna."

She jerked her eyes from the old man to Conall. "Why did you stop him? I thought you wanted me to learn what my father has done."

"Not like this," he said after a pause. He held out his hand to help her stand. "Come, it's time I dealt with some clan business."

She waited while he dunked his head in the water trough and splashed some children with water. It amazed her that he was so gentle and kind to the children. MacNeil had never even spared one a glance.

Could everything she had been reared to believe be wrong? She knew in her heart that Conall was a good man. Anyone who treated children with such decency and honesty had to be a good man. Even the animals liked him, and didn't they have the ability to know when someone was evil?

She had already seen vast differences between Conall and MacNeil, and she knew there were many more. Conall gestured for her to follow. Her feet were heavy as she trailed him into the castle to the great hall. When two men came in and began to haggle over a pig, she let her mind drift.

Until an older woman walked up with a warm smile. Glenna smiled back, eager for a friend. The woman walked with a slight limp, and Glenna saw that she was missing her left pinkie finger.

"I wondered if I'd get a chance to talk to ye," the woman said, her smile soon replaced by a sneer.

Glenna's gut pooled with dread. She knew before the woman opened her mouth she had no wish to hear what she had to say.

"You're the MacNeil's brat. Finally you're here so I can slit your throat like he did my husband. I'm not sure if I could get one of the men to rape you like he did me."

"Please," Glenna begged, desperately wanting her to stop.

"Please?" the woman gasped. "I begged him, and all I got was my finger cut off, my belly full with his child and my entire family to bury all because the laird's mother chose another man rather than the MacNeil's father."

Glenna swallowed the bile in her throat. "You had his babe?"

The woman cackled. "I wouldn't bring the devil into the world."

"You killed an innocent child?"

"Nothing that comes from the MacNeil is innocent," she spat. "Your time is comin'. Our laird may have put you under his protection, but there are ways of going around that."

Glenna watched her walk away and tried to calm her breathing. A hasty look around confirmed others had not only heard the woman but also agreed with her.

She shook from fear but sought to appear calm. The woman was right. There would come times when Conall wasn't around, and she knew they would kill her even if she was innocent of any crimes.

Not totally innocent.

She ignored her conscience and the people around her to focus on the soothing lilt of Conall's voice as he solved the many problems of his clan. It wasn't until the day was almost gone and she once again stood outside while Conall inspected some horses that she noticed a little girl with beautiful black hair staring at her.

Glenna offered a smile and was surprised to find the child walking toward her. When the girl stopped in front of her, Glenna went down on her haunches and bit her lip to stop the cry of pain she almost let slip. She gasped when she found herself staring into familiar eyes.

"Hello," the little girl said. "My name is Ailsa."

"What a lovely name. I'm Glenna."

"I like that name," Ailsa said. "Where did you come from?"

Glenna looked down at the small hand on her arm. "From far away," she finally answered.

"Are you staying here now?"

"For a time." Movement caught Glenna's eye and she looked to find Conall talking with Angus. When she looked back at Ailsa, the little girl had backed away.

"Where are you going?"

"I was told to stay away from the laird."

"By who?"

Ailsa lowered her eyes and shrugged her shoulders.

She took hold of Ailsa's hands. "Who told you to stay away from Conall?"

"Glenna," Conall called.

She looked to him then to Ailsa. "Have you ever met him?"

"Nay," Ailsa shook her head of raven curls. "And I mustn't."

Determination filled her. Conall didn't know he had a child, and there was no mistaking those eyes. Ailsa was his, and she was going to make sure he knew it. Today.

"Do you trust me, Ailsa?" she asked, holding out her arms.

After a moment's hesitation, she answered, "Aye."

"Then come with me." She lifted Ailsa in her arms and strode to Conall, ignoring the agony in her legs.

He smiled as she neared. "I see you made a friend. What's her name?"

Glenna's breath came faster and faster, her heart beating fiercely in her chest. "Ailsa."

"What a pretty name for an adorable child," he said, and tweaked Ailsa's nose.

She squealed with laughter before ducking her head in Glenna's neck.

"Look at her," Glenna told him.

"I have. She's a sweet child."

"Nay. *Look* at her," she said again, and raised Ailsa's face. "Take a look at her eyes, and tell me why she was told to never to go near you."

Glenna heard his sharp intake of breath when he gazed into his own eyes. "God's blood," he hissed, and took Ailsa into his arms. "Who's your mother, lass?"

Ailsa shrugged. "I made her die."

Pain flashed in Conall's eyes when he looked at Glenna. "Come," he told her and Angus as he carried Ailsa into the castle.

She was surprised at Angus' silence, but one look at his slack-jawed face let her know no one had known of Ailsa. She followed Conall into the solar and took a chair opposite him. Ailsa slid from his grasp and climbed onto her lap.

"Ailsa, you've got to tell me your mother's name," he begged, anguish deepening his voice as he braced his elbows on his knees.

"Mary MacBeth."

He closed his eyes and let his head drop. "Well, I know who told you to stay away from me," he murmured.

Glenna enfolded Ailsa in her arms. "Why did they want you to stay away from Laird Conall?"

"They'd never tell me."

Haunted silver eyes rose to Glenna. "I owe you," Conall said before he turned to Angus. "See to it that Frances MacBeth is told that I now have my daughter, and she'll be reared here. I also want to know why they kept her away from me."

"I'll send someone to get Ailsa settled," Angus said before he left the solar.

Glenna gave Conall a smile to let him know he was doing the right thing, but it wasn't until a servant came for Ailsa that he spoke.

"For five summers I've been deprived of my child. Why would they do that?"

"I have no idea."

He rose and paced the room before stopping in front of the narrow window to look out over the bailey. "I don't think I can ever repay you for seeing what others haven't."

But she knew of one way he could. "Don't return me to MacNeil."

Conall's dark head slowly turned her way. "You ask the impossible."

* * * * *

Glenna's day didn't end after Ailsa's discovery as she would have liked. She had hoped to have another quiet supper in her chamber, but Conall had other ideas. He had requested her presence, and the thought of having to endure another round of hatred wasn't something she intended to do.

"Nay," she stated, and walked to her window.

His eyes burned like liquid silver. "You will sit beside me this night. No more hiding in this room."

"I've been by your side all day, just as you requested, and I have no desire to have my life threatened again."

"Who threatened you?" he asked, the worry and anger evident in his creased forehead.

She stopped short of rolling her eyes. What had gotten into her? She had a rebellious streak women weren't meant to possess, and years with Alisdair MacNeil had tamped down any resistance she might have. Until she had met Conall. Never would she have dreamed of talking this way to MacNeil.

"It doesn't matter," she finally answered.

"It does or you wouldn't have mentioned it. Now tell me."

He was a man used to getting his way, and it was time someone refused him. "I made it up."

Immediately he took the last remaining steps to stand in front of her. "You didn't lie, and whoever did it scared you mightily."

The fact he had hit upon the truth stunned her. The fight went right out of her when she saw the concern in his eyes. She lowered her eyes and shrugged her shoulders.

"Tell me about the feud between our families?" she asked, needing a change of subject.

He sighed. "It seems your grandfather was constantly looking for a wife. Your grandmother died giving birth to your father."

"I never knew that. MacNeil never talked of anything to me."

"For years your grandfather searched for a wife. He fell in love with another woman, but she chose the laird of the Sinclairs. After that, your grandfather just wanted a wife. He asked for my mother's hand, but she refused. The feud began when he heard that she had chosen my father."

There were no words that would ease the pain of seeing fellow clan members die.

"Let me stay here."

"Nay. I need for the clan to see you."

"Don't you even care what I want?"

"I will protect you."

Pigheaded. "You aren't always near."

He smiled and it nearly melted her heart. "Which is why I will keep you beside me."

Glenna knew she could stand here all day and argue but she still wouldn't win. He had set his mind on it and would do whatever was needed to see it through. She took his offered hand.

She inhaled deeply and raised her head as she stepped into the hall. Conall guided her to the dais and sat her down beside Angus while he took the other chair. She had just taken her seat when people began to file in.

The hall overflowed with the MacInnes clan and every eye turned to her. She was on display, and if she thought the effect of the forty MacInnes warriors who had leveled their hatred at her was dreadful, then she was sure she would die this night.

Loathing. Disgust. Hatred.

The emotions directed at her pinned her to the chair, unable to lift even a finger. Her chest pinched painfully and the room began to spin, but she tried to make her eyes focus.

She scanned the room for the one who directed the most hatred, but there were too many people. With a crowd this large the roar of conversation would have been deafening, but there were no boisterous laughter or curses.

Whispered words and looks thrown her way greeted any person who ventured into the hall. Blackness began to close in. She concentrated on her trencher in an effort to keep it at bay.

Conall sighed and knew he shouldn't have made Glenna sup in the main hall, but he had liked having her beside him. He had been surprised at her refusal, but liked the idea that she wasn't afraid to speak her mind.

He looked over his clan and was ashamed. Glenna wasn't the villain, but being the daughter of the villain made her as much of one.

An elbow in his ribs drew his attention. He turned and found Gregor glaring at him. "What the hell is wrong with you?"

"Are you so blind you don't see what's happening to Glenna?" he asked, appalled. "Again."

Conall studied Gregor for a moment before he turned to Glenna. Her skin was nearly gray and a fine sheet of sweat covered her face. He had seen her look this way once before.

"Glenna," he whispered. He kept his head down so as not to draw attention to her.

"Please. Get me. Out. Of. Here."

In one movement he was out of his chair with her in his arms. She needed air and privacy. He raced to the battlements. Once there he rested his hip on a crenel. He leaned against the solid part, or merlon, and shifted Glenna so he could move the hair from her face.

A soft breeze cooled her skin, but her pallor remained gray. "Glenna. Talk to me. What's happening?"

"The hatred," she mumbled, her eyes tightly closed.

Gregor had been right, he thought. She was affected by his clan's hatred, he just hadn't realized how much until this eve. And his stupidity had nearly killed her.

"What do I need to do?"

"Keep me. Out here." She paused, and said, "Please talk."

And so he sat with her in his arms, her hair dancing around them. With the aid of the moon and a nearby torchlight he was able see the color return to her little by little.

"I talked with Frances MacBeth earlier. She said it was her daughter's wish for me not to know, though I don't believe it."

He saw the faint smile on her lips and rejoiced.

"Mary was quite taken with me, you know," he teased.

"Arrogant."

The faint whisper made him chuckle. "Frances had the gall to demand Ailsa be returned to her. I will get answers from her. No one denies me."

She slowly opened her eyes and attempted a weak smile.

"You should've told me that happened to you." He smoothed the hair from her face.

She licked her lips. "I couldn't. It built until I couldn't move."

"Are you saying you couldn't have stood and left?"

"Nay. The hatred was so strong, especially from one source." She sighed and nestled closer to him.

He found his gaze drawn to her plump mouth and hastily jerked them back to her eyes. "Who?"

"I couldn't find them. The hall was too crowded."

"You're safe now," he whispered, and found himself lured by her parted lips and half-closed lids. The sound of a lute reached him, the music sensual and romantic as it floated on the night's breeze.

A longing filled him to taste the nectar from her mouth, to quench the thirst racking his body. He lowered his head until their lips were breaths apart. His eyes found hers. A part of him said to take her. She was his prisoner. His.

Mine.

Aye, she was his, and he knew she wouldn't push him away. He saw the hunger burning just below the surface of her eyes. And words from his father he hadn't recalled in years came to mind.

"A Druid always knows his mate, lad. And even though ye aren't destined to be a priest, the Druid blood courses through yer veins."

Mate? Was something telling him Glenna was his mate? That couldn't be. For if he kissed her, if he let himself feel anything, then he wouldn't send her back to the MacNeil. And he wouldn't have Iona returned.

He brushed aside a dark lock of hair. "I love your hair down. You look wild and untamed."

"Yet I am anything but those two things."

He smiled for he knew better. "You just don't know it yet."

* * * * *

Moira turned and looked at Frang when he approached. The elder Druid chuckled when he spied what she looked at.

"It seems Glenna and Conall will find their love on their own."

"He's fighting it," Moira said, and turned back to the couple.

"She'll help him see the way."

Moira nodded and continued to watch as Conall helped Glenna to her feet. "We could release him from his vow to us."

"What? And make it easy? You know Aimery wouldn't like that at all."

She sighed loudly. "I'm not sure I can do this, Frang. I'm not as strong as you think I am."

He patted her shoulder and gave her a fatherly smile. "Aimery wouldn't have given you such a task if he didn't think you could accomplish it. Have faith in yourself, lass."

"I feel something in the air."

Frang chuckled, his long, gray beard moving in the breeze. "It's desire."

"Nay. Something else. Something that shouldn't be."

Frang stilled and raised his face to the moon. "Aye, you have the right of it. We'll have to keep a close eye on Glenna and Conall. So much rides on them."

Moira took one last look at the couple before she followed Frang back into the stone circle. Her back tingled along her spine and that meant there was great evil, greater than MacNeil, who was out to destroy their plans. But who?

* * * * *

The Shadow moved deeper into the woods. He would have to be careful. Frang and Moira had almost seen him. He hadn't expected to find them spying on Glenna and Conall as well, but it proved just how much was at stake within the Druids.

He laughed softly and quietly made his way to the castle. He had plans of his own, and with the help of a certain lass it would be carried out swiftly. Then he could have Moira. Frang was old — too old to stop him from getting what he wanted. He had waited long enough and been denied too many times. It was his time now.

No more waiting.

Chapter Six

The morning had begun perfectly. Ailsa had run into Glenna's chamber and demanded to take her exploring. Glenna had readily agreed, eager for the innocence of youth to wash away the pain and confusion that grew steadily in her heart. She never stopped to think what Conall would say, and she didn't want to know.

They had just stepped into the noisy bailey when Glenna spotted Conall training with his men. She had been hard-pressed to continue on with Ailsa instead of watching Conall's rippling muscles strain and flex with each trust and parry of his sword.

Her stomach tightened when she remembered the heat from his eyes when he had almost kissed her the night before. With the stars shining overhead, the music from the lute lulling her and his full mouth just breaths away it had been a magical night.

Aye, he had been close, but something had stopped him, much to her disappointment. She had often wondered what it would be like to be a wife and mother, but no man had made her dream of being kissed. Until Conall. He made her think of things that would bring a blush to a nun's face.

She had wanted his mouth on hers more than she had wanted anything. The gentleness of his hands as they swept the hair from her face, and the intensity of his eyes had haunted her sleep. She would have like to know if he tasted half as good as he looked.

"If you'd rather stare at the laird instead of exploring with me, I ken. All the women say he's a fine man."

Glenna smiled. With Ailsa around she was never bored. The child said the oddest things. "Of course I want to go with you."

But Ailsa's comment caught her attention. She looked around the bailey and saw the many women, young and old, who stood and gawked at Conall. It made Glenna uncomfortable that they stared so openly until she realized she did the same thing.

Although, it was a beautiful, red-headed woman who ogled him so wantonly that brought up Glenna's ire.

With the firm resolution to ignore Conall and his magnificent body, she took Ailsa's hand and was about to set out when a velvet-smooth voice she had come to recognize stopped them.

"And just where are you two going?"

Glenna's stomach fluttered when she heard Conall's smooth lilt. She turned and found him smiling at his daughter. "We're going exploring."

"Want to come?" Ailsa asked then quickly ducked her head. "Never mind."

Conall's brow furrowed as he looked to Glenna, but she shrugged her shoulders. "You don't want me to come?" he asked Ailsa.

Ailsa raised her head. "You're laird and don't have time for m...anyone."

Glenna tightened her grip on Ailsa's hand. The child had been told Conall didn't have time for her. It brought painful memories of Glenna's own childhood to mind. If Conall didn't agree to come, she was going to give him a swift kick in his shins.

"As a matter-of-fact," Conall said, and went down on his knees in front of Ailsa, "I don't have anything to do today. I'd love to come if you still want me."

Ailsa's face lit into a huge smile as she flung herself into Conall's arms. "Oh aye, I want you to come."

Glenna rejoiced quietly. Conall continued to do things so unexpected from what she was used to, but she didn't mind. It just proved to her there was love in this world.

They set out after Conall washed the grim from his body. Ailsa ran ahead and led them down the path to the loch while Glenna and Conall walked side by side.

"I'm surprised you're not keeping everyone in the bailey," she finally said when Ailsa was too far ahead to hear.

Conall looked at her with his silver eyes. "There's no way MacNeil can get to us here. On the other side of the forest is a sheer drop off the mountains. The only way to reach my castle is through the path we took here."

"And the soldiers from the gatehouse towers can spot them far in advance."

"Exactly." He reached over and plucked the basket of food from her hand.

They ceased talking when Ailsa declared she had found the perfect spot. She ran along the edge of the loch, picking up stones as she went. Glenna yearned to go with her but didn't feel comfortable with Conall near. She didn't want him to know how much this meant to her because he might refuse to let her come again, or worse, make her return to the castle immediately.

"What are you waiting for?" he asked.

His words stunned her. Could he know her deepest, darkest desires? "Excuse me?"

"You came to explore with Ailsa yet you aren't doing any exploring."

"Then I'll leave you here alone," she said quickly before he could change his mind.

Without a backward glance she trailed after Ailsa. The fresh smell of the loch infused her senses. The sun warmed them from the cool weather that wouldn't loosen its hold to spring, and the songs of the birds added to the magic.

It took Glenna some time to navigate her steps through the rocks that lined the loch so she wouldn't twist her ankle, but she quickly caught on with Ailsa's help. Conall watched his daughter and his captive as they practiced skipping rocks on the water. It had been quite a while since he had laughed so much in one morning.

If the situation were different he could almost think it was his family he observed. It pained him to think he might never know what it was like to have a wife and family. Thanks to the Druids, he would never be able to marry until he found his mate. It would be a cruel twist of fate to finally find his mate only to have to lose her.

He put aside thoughts of revenge and his vows and allowed himself his first free day as he gazed upon Ailsa and Glenna as they explored. Their carefree laughter brought back memories of his childhood playing in the loch.

It wasn't until his neck began to cramp from not moving that he looked up and found the sun high above him. The morning had sped past and the noon hour was upon them. He dug in the basket and found a banquet. The cook, Tess, had given them one of the first wedges of cheese of spring, fresh loaves of bread and milk that he placed on a plaid that had been packed.

He called to Glenna and Ailsa, and they sat on either side of him. He listened while Ailsa explained their part of the Highlands to Glenna. After several glances, he noted that Glenna wasn't eating because she was so enraptured at Ailsa's words. He hid a smile and pushed Glenna's food to her mouth.

A laugh escaped as Glenna took a small bite of bread and put down the food. It was clear to him then just how much she had missed being kept within MacNeil's walls. It was odd seeing a child teaching an adult, but that's what was happening right before his eyes. As he listened to Ailsa's descriptions of the loch in winter, the falcons that soared above them and the taste of fresh snow, he realized he had come to take things for granted.

Ailsa was oblivious at just how much her words meant to Glenna, he noticed. She went about eating while she talked. "Just there," Ailsa pointed over her left shoulder, "is my favorite pine."

"You have a favorite tree?" Glenna asked, eyes wide with amazement.

"Aye. I come here nearly every day to visit him." Ailsa then pointed to a spot of earth. "Very soon a clump of wild hyacinth will sprout. If you look close you can see the leaves just coming up."

Conall learned so much about his daughter and Glenna, and he had said not two words the entire time. Every once in a while Ailsa would raise her eyes and smile at him, as if making sure he was still there.

Glenna was hungry for information and Ailsa was a willing teacher, but he knew the time drew near for them to head back. He packed the rest of the food and watched as they squatted together while looking at the hyacinth Ailsa had pointed out.

He raised his face to the sun. The afternoon had flown by. He hated having to tell them it was time to leave and spoil their fun. "It's time we head back," he called.

Ailsa frowned. Glenna stood, and said, "Go on then. We'll be up later."

He almost laughed. No one told him nay, much less his prisoner. He understood why she didn't want to return, but the point was he had given an order. "We'll all return together."

Glenna bit her tongue when she realized she had spoken so harshly, and by the hardness of his eyes she knew she had spoken wrong. She decided to try another tactic.

"You said yourself we were safe here."

"I know what I said, Glenna. You'll be returning with me," he said, and turned to walk up the steep path to the castle.

And for the first time in her life she acted like a petulant child and stomped her foot. Ailsa gasped and ran after Conall. Glenna raised her eyes and found the hem of Conall's kilt smoking as flames shot up.

"Conall," she called as Ailsa reached him and began slapping at bottom of his kilt.

He turned and, seeing the flames, quickly jumped into the loch. When he rose from the water, Glenna knew real fear. His steely eyes roamed the area around them.

"How did my plaid catch fire?" he asked her.

She shrugged her shoulders and marched up the hill to the castle. The last thing she wanted was to explain to him how things seemed to catch on fire when she got angry. Nay, better to leave that out for now and control her temper so it didn't happen again.

They had just entered the bailey when a guard yelled, "Rider approaching."

Glenna jerked her eyes to Conall. Trepidation pooled in her belly and grew like an unwanted weed. Her mind screamed nay, for she knew it was a MacNeil who approached.

It's too soon. I don't have my answers.

But now everything had come crashing down around her. She placed Ailsa in Angus' arms and caught up with Conall before he reached the steps leading to the battlements. "Did you expect them so soon?"

"Aye. I anticipated them yesterday."

His flat tone and hard eyes told her much. This was the man that went into battle. It sent a shiver down her body and almost made her miss a step as she climbed the stairs. An image of his sword raised against the MacNeil flashed in her mind. She stopped and closed her eyes in hopes of seeing more, but the vision faded. Her eyes opened to find Conall had already reached the top. She raced after him and came to stand by his side.

A low growl sounded from his throat. "He sent only one man. I'd have thought he'd be here with his army."

"You'll yet have your chance to fight him, laird," she said as she looked down from the battlements at a young lad she had seen once or twice at the MacNeil holding.

She ventured a glance at Conall and found his eyes boring into her. "How do you know that?" he asked.

"I just do." She shrugged while trying to find the words. "I can't explain it other than to say I saw it while we walked the stairs."

"Glenna," he began then stopped and struggled with something he wanted to say.

He turned back to the MacNeil waiting below.

"I've a message for the MacInnes' laird," the lad called.

"I'm laird of the MacInnes," Conall answered. "What message do you bring?"

"Laird MacNeil has requested you return Glenna immediately, and he'll let you and your clan live. If you don't, you'll be responsible for your clan's devastation."

She watched as Conall gripped the stone so hard his hands turned white. "As you can see, Glenna is here and well. I'll return her as soon as the MacNeil returns my sister Iona."

That surprised the rider for he was at a loss for words. "I'll give your message to the MacNeil," he finally said, and wheeled his horse around.

Glenna watched until the rider disappeared from view. When she turned back to Conall, she knew he wanted to ask what she knew of Iona, and she prayed for some reprieve. She wasn't yet ready to divulge everything to him.

"There's one question I've been meaning to ask you," he said.

She swallowed hard and bit her tongue to stop herself from begging him not to ask. A shout from a guard drew his attention. His handsome face turned red with ire. "By the saints. She wouldn't," Conall hissed, and pushed pasted her.

She watched while he flew down the steps and confronted a woman with long flowing blonde hair. She was stunningly beautiful, even from a great distance. Jealousy sharp and true sliced through her.

It had never occurred to her to ask if Conall was married. No woman had come forward when she had arrived and none had sat with them while they supped. But seeing the enchanting creature arguing with him, made her realize he had asked the woman to stay away while she was here. She sighed deeply and felt something take her hand.

Ailsa. The child had an uncanny knack for knowing when she needed comfort.

"The laird doesn't like her," Ailsa said.

"She's beautiful."

"Aye. We rarely see them anymore."

"Any of who?"

Ailsa didn't answer but pointed instead. Glenna looked up and found Conall and the woman staring at her before he pointed for the woman to leave.

The music Glenna had heard began again as the woman departed. Every fiber of her body urged her to speak to the woman and propelled her feet forward. It was then she realized it was the woman from her vision.

She managed to reach the bailey before Conall stopped her. "Where are you going?"

"Who was that?" she asked, and looked around his broad shoulders for another look at the woman.

"No one."

The music dimmed until there were only the voices of the people around her.

"Please," she begged as she looked at him. "Who was that?"

His jaw clenched in agitation. "Her name is Moira."

"Is she your wife?"

"Saints no," he spat, and turned his head to look at where Moira had been. He looked back to her, and said, "I don't have a wife."

She had seen him have such hatred in his eyes only once before, and that was for the MacNeil. Whoever that woman was, he despised her. But why?

When he turned on his heel and stalked away she didn't stop him. She needed to be alone and the battlements would offer some privacy. She made her way back up the stairs by the wall and tried not to notice how people avoided her like some plague.

It had been the same at MacNeil Castle, but there they had a reason to treat her like that. She reached the top and nodded to a soldier as she walked to a secluded spot where she could look over the landscape.

The loch was still as stone, not a ripple in the water, and to her left, nothing but beautiful, rolling grassland. In the distance, but not too far away, the mountains rose up and showed their snow-covered peaks, some mist-shrouded.

If there was a more peaceful, stunning place in which to live, she had never seen it. And it probably could be her home if only she wasn't who she was and there wasn't Iona.

Before Iona had left MacNeil Castle she had given Glenna a warning. "There will come a day when you'll need to confess all. It will seem the darkest of days but a light shines through the clouds."

Iona had always talked in riddles, never answering directly. Glenna still had no idea what she was referring to unless it was to tell Conall what she knew of Iona and…everything else.

"It's very lovely to look upon," Gregor said as he came to stand beside her.

She looked over and was surprised he wasn't wearing his usual leather vest but a saffron shirt instead. "Aye."

"Do you know how long I stayed at the MacNeil's?"

She was surprised he had come out and asked her so quickly. "Nay, but that doesn't surprise me. I knew very little of what went on there."

"You were hidden away."

"Aye," she said, and looked away from his dark, probing eyes. "I'm not sure why the MacNeil was ashamed of me. I've never done anything to him."

"Does Conall know how the MacNeil used you?"

Her head whipped around to look at him. "What are you talking about?"

"I was there that day MacNeil wanted to show you the Mackenzies."

She felt the blood leave her face as she recalled that day well. She had rejoiced to learn she would leave the castle for the first time, but that had quickly turned to fear when she had been taken to battle. "I...I..."

"Did MacNeil never tell you that you did it?"

She closed her eyes and heard the Mackenzie clan screaming while their homes burned around them. "I didn't do that."

"Why else do you think MacNeil wanted you by his side?"

"He said he wanted to show me the cruelty of other clans," she said, and opened her eyes to stare into his black ones. "Just how do you know so much about my clan?"

He lifted a shoulder. "I listen. Fathers want to protect their children from the harshness of war, not bring them to the fight."

She had thought the same thing, but when she had asked MacNeil he had become so angry she hadn't pressed further.

"The Mackenzies had taken a boy from our clan and hung him. They left him for the world to see."

"That was a Mackenzie lad. And your clan hung him."

Her knees threatened to buckle. The enormity of what she had done weighed heavily on her heart. She still saw the desolation in her dreams. Nothing she could say or do would forgive her for the destruction of the Mackenzies.

"To have the ability to control fire is a great gift," Gregor continued, his eyes intent upon her.

"But I can't control it."

"Why do you think Iona was sent to you?"

That thought had never occurred to her, but now that she thought of it, Iona had asked her many questions about fire. "She wasn't able to teach me everything."

He ran his hand through his blond hair. "You've learned just enough to be dangerous. MacNeil didn't want you knowing too much. You were a pawn to be used."

Nay, her mind screamed. She knew her father had done horrific things, but surely he wouldn't have used her like that. She narrowed her eyes and took a step closer to him.

"How long where you at the MacNeil's?"

"Too long," he murmured, and quickly lowered his eyes. When he raised his gaze, the shields to guard his feelings were back in place. "MacNeil doesn't know I'm here. Not yet anyway."

"What are you proposing?"

"I can get you out of here. Conall trusts me."

"I didn't figure on you being loyal to the MacNeil."

"I'm loyal to only one person, Glenna. Me. Don't fool yourself into thinking I'm doing this out of the kindness of my heart," he said, his face dark and menacing.

She looked deep into his black eyes and saw kindness there. A thick stone wall hid it, but it was there. What ever had happened to him had scarred him terribly.

"I'm not leaving," she finally answered. "Whatever haunts you won't go away with the MacNeil's help."

Gregor's mouth held the barest hint of a grin. "Are you trying to warn me?"

"Aye."

"Do you think I'm afraid you'll tell Conall what I've offered?"

"There's nothing to tell."

His face became as serious as death. "As long as MacNeil doesn't come after this clan. If he does all the angels and saints in Heaven couldn't help you."

She watched him stride away and knew what he said was true. His offer hadn't been to take her back to MacNeil. It had been to simply get her out of here because he knew, like she did, that if she stayed and MacNeil came there'd be nothing left of the MacInnes clan.

Her eyes found Conall who stood head and shoulders above other men. His thick, raven hair was held back at the nape of his neck by a leather thong, and she found herself wondering just how long it was.

She couldn't leave. Wouldn't leave.

No matter what lengths she had to take to stay out of MacNeil's sight, she would do it. Leaving this castle, this land…Conall just wasn't something she could do.

Not when the answers Iona had promised were so very close.

* * * * *

Moira walked into the stone circle and motioned to Frang. "It isn't going to be easy to gain access to Glenna," she told him once he reached her.

"What happened?"

"Conall refused me entry and refused to let me talk to Glenna. He wouldn't even let her near me."

Frang nodded and walked to the bowl of sacred water that rested atop one of their smaller stones. He gazed deep within it and swirled the water with his finger. Several moments later he raised his head and sighed.

"Conall's hatred for us has intensified. He won't open his heart to the truth."

"What are we to do?"

"Only time will tell. We'll carry out our tasks and pray Glenna has enough fortitude to break through Conall's barriers."

* * * * *

Conall cursed long and low. Just what were Gregor and Glenna discussing? He told himself it was out of fear for her safety, but for whatever reason, he couldn't go but a few moments without seeing her with his own eyes.

When he had spotted her atop the battlements with Gregor, suspicion and envy ran rampant through him. He was no fool. The women around the castle had fallen all over themselves to gain Gregor's attention. What made Glenna any different?

But their conversation had been heated. Even from a distance he had been able to see both had gotten angry at some point. And it made him wonder if he could trust Gregor as much as he had first thought.

Which brought another thought. Gregor had said he was at the MacNeil's on business. But just how long had he been there? Gregor could very well know something of Iona and he hadn't asked.

Something he would have to remedy soon. Like now, he thought when he caught sight of Gregor striding into the stables.

Chapter Seven

The smell of horse and hay, a favorite of Conall's, greeted him when he walked into the stable. His horse stuck his big black head over the stall door and blew loudly.

He rubbed the black's soft nose and watched as Gregor saddled his horse. "Going somewhere?"

There was just the smallest hesitation of his movements at hearing Conall's voice.

"Just to rid myself of some energy. Want to join me?"

"Aye, I think I will." Conall opened the stall door and quickly saddled his mount. After a glance at Gregor, he swung himself up on his horse. "The exercises I put my men through must not be enough for you."

Gregor slanted him an annoyed look before he mounted and kicked his horse into a run. Conall smiled and clicked to his mount. They thundered into the bailey, through the gatehouse and out of the gates, the ground blurring beneath the horse's hoofs.

They raced until the horses' sides heaved and sweat glistened their coats. Conall pulled up when they reached the stream. He waited until Gregor turned his horse around and trotted back to him.

"What do you wish to talk about?" Gregor asked as he slid from his horse to let it drink and rest.

"You come right to the point."

"There's no sense skirting the issue."

Conall had to agree. As much as he hated to admit it, he couldn't prevent his respect for Gregor building. "What were you talking to Glenna about on the battlements?"

Gregor turned and looked him in the eye. "I asked her if she wanted me to take her away."

"Why?" he asked through clenched teeth. He took a deep breath and forced himself to calm. "I'm not mistreating her."

"Nay? There's much you don't know about Glenna. You're hurting her, and you don't even know it. You tease her with a life that she should have only to give her back to MacNeil. That is beyond cruel."

Conall advanced on him. He grabbed Gregor's shirt and fisted it in his hands. Anger boiled just beneath his surface and he jerked Gregor against a tree. "What do you know that I don't? What are you keeping from me?"

"We both know the monster that MacNeil is," Gregor said, his voice cool, but his eyes heated with fire at having Conall's hands on him. "Even if Glenna doesn't admit it yet, she doesn't deserve to be sent back to him."

Conall loosened his hold and stepped back. "Are you in love with her?"

Gregor barked with laughter and smoothed his shirt. "There's no such thing as love, Conall."

"If you don't love her, then why would you want to help her?"

"She's seen too much pain. Everyone deserves a little happiness in their life."

Pain flickered in Gregor's eyes, and Conall knew when a man had secrets he wanted kept hidden. He didn't press Gregor on that front. "What do you know of Iona?"

He needed to know the answer before it killed him.

Gregor let out a long sigh and sat. "I was there when she was brought to the MacNeil holding. I could tell she'd been taken from her home."

"Was she hurt?"

"Bruised a bit but nothing fatal. I asked her many times where she'd been taken from, but she declined to tell me."

"What do you mean?" Conall sat when he legs refused to hold him. He couldn't understand why Iona wouldn't have sought help in returning home. "Why wouldn't she tell you she was a MacInnes?"

Gregor shrugged. "She'd been stripped of her plaid. All she'd tell me was that she was there to fulfill her destiny."

Conall didn't think he could stand to have another person tell him it had been Iona's destiny. He squeezed his eyes closed and dropped his head into his hands. "What did they have her doing?"

"She was taken to teach the Druid ways. Can you not think of someone who needed the teaching?"

Conall raised his eyes as everything fell into place. "Glenna."

"But the MacNeil wouldn't allow Iona to finish her teaching. He stopped it very soon and spent the rest of the time trying to gain information about your clan."

"Is she still alive?"

Gregor looked at his hands. "That I cannot answer, for I don't know."

Conall had seen the grief flash in Gregor's eyes. He reached out with his powers and probed Gregor's mind. Usually he didn't need to focus this hard to gain the information he needed, but Gregor had closed himself off to everyone and it made it more difficult.

Finally Conall broke through and found that Gregor had told him the truth. The effort had cost him though as his head began to pound fiercely.

But if Gregor couldn't tell him what happened to Iona maybe Glenna could.

*****

Glenna watched from the battlements as Conall and Gregor raced from the castle. She longed to go with them, but the thought of climbing back on a horse stopped that idea quickly enough.

Her life here, for however long that might be, was much improved. Even though some of the clan had threatened her life at least she had been noticed. At her home even the servants barely spared her a glance. Fear and hatred were brethren in her clan.

She had always been ignored, and then later feared, it seemed. No one would talk to her, not even when she would seek them out. It had gotten so unpleasant that she had taken to eating her meals in her chamber after she had retrieved the food from the kitchens herself because the maid was afraid of her.

Why everyone had been anxious she hadn't known. Until today. Just knowing she had killed innocent people twisted her stomach into thousands of painful knots. To everyone in her clan she was a murderer just like MacNeil.

And they were right.

Her eyes closed tight at that thought. She spun on her heel and walked swiftly down the stairs to the bailey. Her chamber would offer her solace and allow her to gather her thoughts.

A monster is what Conall's clan had called her. Here she had thought to make a new start once she found her answers, but that didn't look to be the case. The clan didn't ignore her, but the hatred was worse.

She had thought God had punished her by setting the barn on fire when she had become angry with her father. The little boy who had been badly burned had haunted her since, but now…that sin was nothing compared to what she had done to the Mackenzies.

The only brightness in all this gloom was Conall. It disturbed her to realize just how much she trusted him and how easily that trust had come. She had learned long ago to never trust anyone until she had met Iona. Yet it had never been a question with Conall.

Had Iona known it would be Conall who would come for Glenna? Had she known Conall would have such an effect on her? Had she known Conall would turn her thinking and her world upside down? Somehow she knew the answer to those questions was a resounding "aye".

Iona had changed many things in Glenna's life. She had looked forward to meeting the man who would free her. That man was Conall. He was everything MacNeil wasn't and more. He was a good, honest man who didn't deserve what MacNeil had done to his clan. He didn't deserve what she had brought with her, either.

The castle door was but a few paces from her when something knocked into her shoulder and nearly sent her to the ground. She raised her eyes to find the woman from the night before.

"I told ye I'd find ye alone," the woman cackled.

A shiver of apprehension crawled down Glenna's spine. With her mind screaming for her to run, she took a step back and spun around. The sound of the woman's laughter faded as her feet raced away.

She made her way to the gatehouse and was slightly surprised when the guards didn't question her as she walked out the gates. She walked down the rocky slope and glanced back at the intimidating castle to see if anyone followed her. It appeared no one even cared. It had always been thus, why should it bother her now?

If she wished, she could leave and never look back. But that isn't what she wanted. She wanted to venture on her own, to see what she could find, to see what this land would offer up to her, to see if there really was magic, and if it would show itself to her.

The cluster of trees ahead held her attention, and the hauntingly beautiful music reached her ears once again. It came from the forest, she was sure of it, and she hurriedly made her way to it. She entered the woods and the music grew louder. Her breath quickened in excitement at the thought of finding where the music came from. Her feet took her near giant oaks and tall pines that had been around for centuries. Birds and butterflies flew around her as if she were one of them, their chirping mingling with the music. Through the canopy of trees she spotted a falcon soaring overhead, his cries echoing around her.

She reached a small clearing with an array of wildflowers blooming in the spring air. She would have been content to sit there all day and soak up the beauty. A twig snapped. Her head jerked toward the sound and her mouth fell open in awe.

Before her stood a massive stone circle, the kind Iona had described to her. The stones had to be at least twelve feet tall and three feet wide, and from where she stood she couldn't guess how many there were.

Touch them.

Glenna reached out her hand to touch a stone but was stopped by a voice. "I wondered when you'd finally venture here."

Her mouth dropped open for the second time. It was the woman from the castle. The one Conall wouldn't allow to enter the bailey. "You know me?"

"Aye, Glenna. I've been waiting for you for some time," she said, and smiled warmly.

"You're Moira."

Moira laughed. "I see Conall at least told you that."

"You came to see me earlier?"

"Aye. Conall refused."

Anger heated Glenna skin. How dare Conall. "What would you want with me?"

"She wants to tell you lies," Conall said as he came into the clearing.

Glenna turned and looked at him and found his eyes fastened on Moira. Glenna looked from one to the other, and asked him, "Why won't you let me talk to her?"

But he ignored her words. "Come back to the castle, Glenna."

Moira turned her green eyes to Glenna. "You can't stop destiny, Conall, no matter how hard you try."

"Aye, I can," he thundered, and took hold of Glenna's arm. "Stop calling to her, Moira. I don't want to lock her in the castle."

"You couldn't if you wanted to, Conall. What of the prophecy," Moira said.

Glenna looked from one to the other. "What prophecy? And why couldn't you lock me in the castle?"

"I don't know what you're talking about," he told Moira.

"You were told many years ago," Moira said, and bent to pluck a yellow wildflower. "Could you have forgotten so easily?"

Glenna was awed by Moira's beauty and spirit. She was picking flowers in the face of Conall's anger. Glenna didn't have that kind of daring.

"You don't need her. Let her be," he said, and turned to leave, pulling Glenna with him.

"You made an oath, Conall. You can't ignore that." Moira's voice reached them as they walked away.

*****

The Shadow smiled and mulled over the new development. He had known Conall disliked the Druids, but he willingly kept a powerful Druid priestess from them. It wasn't something he expected the laird of the MacInnes, sworn to protect all Druids, to do. This could well work to his advantage. If only MacNeil would hurry and arrive.

He should have known better than to mix himself up with the likes of MacNeil, but he had been the only one who had the mentality it took. He hated to see Moira upset. He could easily kill Conall for distressing her, but killing Conall wasn't going to be easy. Iona had put a protection spell on him before she had been kidnapped.

But he hadn't found that out until he had tried to kill Conall. Iona's magic had been strong. Not as strong as his, but still strong enough to keep Conall safe. That was fine though. There were other ways to get to him, the Shadow thought with a smile. But it was growing late. He needed to return before he was missed. He had been careful so far. No need to ruin it now while he stood here and gloated.

* * * * *

Gregor rubbed the heels of his hands against his eyes and leaned back against the tree once Conall had ridden away.

It had finally happened.

He had begun to feel again, and that didn't settle well in his gut. In order to survive, he must keep all feeling as far away as possible. And it would have worked if he hadn't met Glenna and Conall.

Gregor grunted. Conall had offered him friendship without question or hesitation. Conall had even brought him into his home and welcomed him into the clan. For the first time in years he had yearned for his clan and the comfort of its colors. Glenna's vulnerability pulled at him where his heart used to be. She was an innocent who had done something against her will and her entire clan condemned her for it.

She also reminded him of his sister. The agony he had kept control of swooped in and clamped itself firmly around him. If he gave in to the pain he would be destroyed.

With deep, slow breaths, he pulled away from the anguish and righted his world again. It gnawed at him to know he would eventually have to hurt these people, but that was his way.

Had always been his way.

Would always be his way.

Which is why he kept all emotion and anyone who tried to be a friend as far away as possible. He hoped he would be able to pull this off. If not... He didn't want to think what would happen.

* * * * *

Glenna waited until they left the woods before she asked, "Why do you hate Moira?"

Conall increased his steps until she practically had to run to keep up with him. They walked around the castle until they reached the loch, her breath ragged and sides heaving from the trek.

He stopped, his breath shallow and sweat sheening his skin. His hand dropped from her arm and she took a quick step back. She had seen that look in her da's eyes and it usually earned her a smack on the jaw.

A glance back at the castle told her they were far enough away that they couldn't readily be seen, and she wondered what Conall had planned. A loud splash echoed in the silence. She turned and found him gone. A few moments later his head emerged from the water.

"You can swim?" she asked, hating the awe in her voice.

"Aye." His eyes had lost their hard glint. "I needed to cool off. I always do after a talk with Moira," he muttered.

"She's a Druid, isn't she?"

"Aye," he answered, and dove under the water before she could ask more.

He rose up, water running down his bare chest and arms that bulged with rippling muscle, down his sculpted belly to...forbidden places.

She swallowed and tried to look away, but her gaze hungered for more of him. The more she saw the more she wanted.

One corner of his mouth tilted up. "Come join me."

"I cannot swim."

"I'll teach you, then."

Did he know what he offered? Could he possibly know how he tempted her? She licked her lips and looked at the castle.

"We're too far away for anyone to see. I'll turn my back until you're in the water," he offered.

Her mind screamed for her to do something rash. *I just did something rash. I left the castle.*

Aye, but swimming with a man is definitely what I'd call rash.

Her conscience was right. Conall was nearly naked...or naked. By the saints, she hadn't thought of that. This was something she would never have done while at the MacNeil's.

But you aren't with the MacNeils anymore. Grasp this opportunity with both hands because you never know when it'll come your way again.

"Turn around then," she said, not believing her own ears.

By the time she had shed her gown, shoes and wool stockings she was so excited she had to bite her bottom lip to stop the giggling. All that remained was her shift, and she was not taking that off. Just the thought of being that near to Conall naked sent her heart to beating rapidly and her breasts to tingle.

With her arms folded over her chest she walked to the water and poked one toe in. It was cool but not nearly as cold as the stream they had stopped by. She looked for Conall but didn't see him. Before she lost what little courage she had, she quickly marched into the water until only her head was visible.

Her breath came out in a whoop when Conall's hands clasped around her waist. She hadn't heard him move.

"I've got you," he said into her ear from behind.

Bumps rose on her neck where his warm breath grazed her sensitive skin. Her body responded instantly to his touch and craved more. She wasn't given long to think of that as he took her into deeper water.

His mouth moved next to her ear, and whispered softly, "Are you afraid?"

She shook her head and wished she could see his face. She didn't know what he planned to do, and it unnerved her. In the next heartbeat he turned her around and held her against his hard body.

The angry reply dissolved from her lips. His eyes burned molten as the heat of his silver gaze melted her. Her body burned, but for what she didn't know. All she knew was that she wanted him to touch her.

If she had thought he had nearly kissed her last night, she had been wrong. But she knew she was about to get her first kiss by the uncontrolled desire that lit his eyes.

"You shouldn't have come into the water," he said, his gaze fastened onto her lips.

Her breath came out in a whoosh at his words. He was dangerous, but only to her heart if she wasn't careful. In truth, she wanted to throw caution to the wind when he was near. "I know."

His eyes rose to hers. "I don't know how much longer I can resist you."

Glenna suddenly became afraid. There was no way she could give any amount of herself to Conall. He deserved much better than someone as much a monster as her father. Not to mention once he learned what she knew of Iona, he would hate her.

With every ounce of her strength Glenna pushed away from him. When her feet didn't hit bottom as she had expected she didn't panic. She didn't try to reach the surface. If she died this way Conall would never know of her sins and his view of her wouldn't change to one of hatred.

She feared that more than death.

With a vicious yank she was jerked out of the water and deposited on the bank of the loch. She inhaled deeply and gazed at the clouds dotting the blue sky. She knew Conall loomed above her, but she couldn't meet his eyes, knowing there would be concern in their silver depths.

"If you didn't want me touching you that's all you had to say. There's no need to drown yourself."

"That wasn't it at all," she said, and focused her eyes on anything but him. Until he rose up and leaned over her as water dripped from his face on to her.

"Then why did you almost drown yourself?"

Chapter Eight

Conall's body hummed with desire. He could still feel Glenna's ample breasts pressed against his chest, her legs against his and her arms wrapped around his neck while her hands plunged into his hair.

The need to kiss her had been overwhelming, and had she not moved, he would have done just that. He had promised himself not to get close to her, but his body obviously wasn't listening.

And he had taunted her to learn to swim. Ye saints! His brain was addled this day. Actually, he had been addled from the first time he had seen her. Her beauty alone had outshone any women he had ever seen.

He looked down at her, her breathing still labored as she stared at his chest. Something was wrong. She wore her feelings for all the world to see, and she was troubled. It wasn't the episode with Moira. It was something else.

He reached out with his powers and felt her desolation and fear. Then he knew. Iona.

He had put off questioning Glenna because deep down he knew she held the answers. It wasn't something he could delay any longer. He rose and began to dress.

Once his plaid was fastened he turned back to Glenna and found that she too was dressed and sitting on a rock, running her fingers through her wet hair. She had such abject misery radiating from her that he hesitated in questioning her.

"You have some questions for me," she said.

Her face was devoid of emotion and it unsettled him. Her news wouldn't be good. "Tell me all you know of Iona."

"She was brought to the castle about a year ago. MacNeil told me she would teach me…things."

"What things?" he prompted.

She glanced warily at him. "Does it matter?" After a moment's silence she continued. "I only saw her for about four hours a day and guards were always in the chamber with us. I asked her several times why she had been taken."

"Well? What was her response?" he asked more harshly than he intended.

"That it was her destiny."

"St. Christopher," Conall growled, and stood to pace some of his energy off. "Go on."

"One day she didn't come. When I asked the MacNeil, he said I no longer needed Iona. I never found out what happened to her."

Conall's heart squeezed painfully and his feet stopped in their tracks. He had pinned all his hopes on Glenna giving him the answers he needed. He didn't know where to go from here.

She turned and looked into his eyes. "I didn't know she was your sister."

Now he knew why he stopped himself from kissing her. Deep down he had known she knew something, was somehow involved with Iona's disappearance.

He had to get away from Glenna. "I need to get back to the castle."

With a heavy heart, he started up the steep path and didn't wait on her to follow. Part of him wanted her to run so he wouldn't have to keep her around, reminding him of what he couldn't have. But the other half…desperately wanted her to follow. That part of him needed her as he had never needed another person, and it scared him.

How could that be possible? I don't really know her.

You do know her.

Conall stopped and looked over the loch. It had been Iona's favorite place, other than the stone circle. Nay. He couldn't let Glenna go free. She was his prisoner. His.

Mine.

He turned and saw her still sitting on the rock, looking out over the calm loch.

"Glenna."

She twisted and gazed at him with haunted eyes. She still kept something from him, of that he was sure. "Come," he ordered.

He waited until she neared before he continued up the path. If something had happened to Iona, if she was dead, he had to decide what he would do with Glenna. Sending her back to the MacNeil wasn't a possibility.

But neither could he allow her to live here. As it was, if she stayed near him another minute he would give in to the temptation and taste her lips, her skin, her soul.

Once they entered the gates and reached the castle doors, he told her, "Go to your chamber until I send for you."

It was the only thing that would keep her safe from his desire. That and the knowledge she was a Druid, a MacNeil. That in itself should be enough, but his rod had been hard since that first contact in the water.

"She told you."

Conall raised his eyes to find Gregor standing in front of him. "Aye."

"Is that all she told you?" Gregor asked, eyes hard and arms crossed over his chest.

Conall narrowed his eyes. Whatever Glenna continued to keep from him, Gregor knew also. "I know she's hiding something from me. I haven't asked what, but I don't think she'll tell me as easily as she told me of Iona."

"And after all those questions you still aren't closer to knowing anything, are you?"

"Tell me, Gregor. Just how long were you at the MacNeil's?"

"Too long," he answered, his eyes never wavering. "I don't have a clan. I'm a mercenary. Hired out to whoever pays the most. Have I answered all your questions yet?"

"Why is it MacNeil soldiers didn't know who you were? One was about to kill you."

"I was rarely there, and then only a select few knew of my comings and goings."

"Just what were you hired to do?"

Gregor's black eyes turned a shade darker. His jaw clenched. "Gain your trust. Take over your castle and clan."

Conall drew his sword and pointed the tip at Gregor's throat. All the men in the hall armed themselves, waiting for a word from him.

To give Gregor credit he didn't blink at the sword pressed into his neck. "Go ahead, Conall. It would be a relief to die and end this miserable life."

But Conall couldn't do it. Beneath the hard exterior he *felt* Gregor was a good man. "You've gained my trust. Do I need to lock you in the caves to keep you from taking my castle and turning my clan over to the MacNeil?"

One blond brow cocked itself. "You think I'll tell you the truth?"

Conall almost laughed. Gregor had no way of knowing of his gift, and he intended to keep it that way. "Aye."

After a lengthy moment of silence Gregor let out a long breath. "Nay. You've nothing to worry about from me."

Conall reached out to read Gregor but couldn't get through this time. His gut, however, told him Gregor could be trusted.

"I'll tell you truthfully," Gregor continued. "The MacNeil wants you dead. He'll stop at nothing. Especially since you have Glenna. She's precious to him."

"I know," Conall said, and lowered his sword. He motioned to his men to do the same. "Tell me what she's keeping from me?"

Gregor shook his head. "That isn't for me to do, and you know it. When she's ready, she'll tell you. Don't be too harsh in your judgment of her though," he warned.

Conall didn't like the fact Gregor was warning him, but what irritated him the most was that he was doing it on Glenna's behalf. Regardless of what Gregor had said, Conall couldn't help but think he and Glenna had known one another at MacNeil's. It would explain how Gregor knew so much about her.

Gregor snorted. "How many times must I tell you Glenna had never seen me before the day you came to MacNeil Castle?"

Conall watched him walk away, his thoughts heavy. How in the saints had Gregor known what he had been thinking? Was Gregor a Druid as well?

* * * * *

Glenna sat on her bed and stared into the fire. Conall hated her now. It had been inevitable, but she had hoped the fantasy would go on a little longer before it came crashing down around her like everything always did.

Fate hadn't been kind to her.

It had been crueler still to Iona.

Iona. She had been Glenna's first and only friend. Iona had even kept silent about where she had come from, never telling Glenna the MacNeil had taken her from her home. She mourned her friend's absence and prayed she was still alive.

A gust of wind howled through the narrow window and swirled around Glenna, sending her hair into her eyes.

Glenna.

She jumped off the bed and looked around the room. Someone had said her name, yet she was alone. What magic was this?

Glenna. It's Moira.

"Moira?" she asked, and smoothed hair out of her eyes. "Where are you? I don't see you."

Laughter filled the room. *Think, Glenna. Iona was sent to teach you of your power.*

"I don't have powers," she whispered as chills rose on her skin, the wind lifting her skirts. Well, that wasn't entirely true. Gregor, after all, had seen what she was capable of.

Aye, you do. Fire. Mine is wind. I can control it just as you'll be able to control fire. Given time and training your powers will grow.

Now she was intrigued. "Powers? I have more than one?"

You can foresee the future. That gift is one many Druids have. Another is the gift of healing in which I have.

"Iona never told me any of this."

She couldn't. She fulfilled her destiny, Glenna. Now it's your turn.

"What destiny?"

You are one of three chosen before they were born to fulfill an ancient prophecy. Time is of the essence, and you have much to learn. Come to me, Glenna.

"I cannot. Conall has forbidden it," she said. The wind grew weak. Moira was leaving, but Glenna had many more questions.

Come, Glenna...

"Don't leave me," she begged, but it was too late. Moira had left. And Glenna knew she had to learn more, even if it meant gaining the ire of Conall. The Druids were the ones who would tell her all she needed to know. Iona had been a Druid and she hadn't lied to Glenna.

Highland Mist

* * * * *

Moira collapsed against the oak true, her breath coming in great gulps, but a smile was on her lips.

"Well?" asked Frang, the Druid high priest who had reared her.

"She'll come. The MacNeil almost beat all of her spirit out of her, but she still has some. Her curiosity will get the better of her."

"If she defies Conall he's likely to lock her in a tower," he warned, and leaned on his tall staff.

Moira looked at the Druid elder and smiled. "He'll try, but her powers are greater than we realized. Such strength courses through her, yet she has no idea."

"Then it's good Conall took her from the MacNeil before more damage could be done."

Moira seethed at what the MacNeil had used Glenna for. Many innocents had perished, but she didn't intend for that to happen again. Once Glenna learned to control her powers, the MacNeil wouldn't be able to use her again.

"Conall doesn't know he's fulfilling his destiny. He's turned his back on his Druid blood."

"He's trying," Frang said, and ran a hand down his long white beard. "But he cannot deny what's been given to him. With Glenna's help he may yet come around."

Moira rose and stood next to the man who had reared her after her parents' death. He had taught her everything he knew. "Do you think he'll fight his feelings for her?"

Frang cackled, the sound echoing around the stone circle. "He's been fighting it since the first moment he laid eyes upon her. He may yet set her aside."

Moira squared her shoulders. "Then I'll have to make sure he doesn't put up much of a fight."

Chapter Nine

ഌ

The morning dawned crisp and sunny. Glenna eagerly waited until she heard Conall training with his men before she walked from her chamber. Her eyes found the guards that roamed the battlements. There was no need for them to ride the hills awaiting the MacNeil. The way the castle stood atop the cliff no one could ride toward the castle and not been seen many leagues out.

There was no way the MacNeil could launch a surprise attack, which was why she felt safe enough to venture into the forest, though the way her heart beat so fast and loud she was sure everyone around her could hear it.

She circled around Conall and his soldiers. The people still hadn't accepted her yet none stopped her when she left the castle nor when she walked through the gates. She should have been elated yet part of her was miserable. Once again she was being ignored. Would there ever come a time when she meant something to someone, anyone?

The music had woken her and continued to play as she broke her fast, until she could no longer deny the tug of the music. It pulled at her soul, urging her feet faster until she stood outside the stone circle.

Moira stepped into her line of sight. There were so many questions Glenna wanted to ask, but they would wait. For now she was content to watch and learn as Moira held out her hand.

Glenna walked with her until they reached a solid wall of stone. She looked to Moira and waited.

"Do you believe in all I've told you?"

Glenna nodded. "I know what Iona taught me. I know that innocent people have been harmed because—"

"Because when you get angry or upset fires erupt," Moira finished. "Iona was brought to teach you that you bring about fire during high emotion. I'll teach you how to extinguish one, how to start one and how to control it."

"You can do that?"

She smiled. "I'm a Druid."

"Is that what I am?" Iona had been right. She was finding answers, and she would find herself here.

Moira nodded. "A very powerful one at that. Do you believe?"

Glenna looked from Moira to the stone wall. Moira was trying to tell her something, but she couldn't figure out what. "Aye, I believe."

In that instant the stone wall disappeared to show a luscious green meadow with a waterfall. It was like a dream. Everything was in bloom, and she had never seen so many different birds in all her life.

"How," she whispered, unable to believe her eyes.

"It's called a *fe-fiada*, an invisibility cloak. We make this invisible to anyone who doesn't believe in us. They cannot see anything other than the stones themselves."

"So what if someone lied and said they believed?"

"It doesn't work that way. If one truly doesn't believe then they'll never see anything other than the stones."

Glenna followed her inside the circle. Something powerful and strong blossomed in her body. She was home. Her spirit was lighter, freer.

"Welcome home, Glenna," said a man with thick, white hair that flowed down to the middle of his back and a white beard that hung past his neck.

He walked with a long, solid stick, but his eyes weren't those of an old man. They were powerful in their intensity, and they bore into her soul as if they searched to see if she was worthy.

"This is Frang," Moira said. "He's the Druid high priest."

"Hello," Glenna said, and was relieved when he smiled at her, showing a mouth full of white teeth. He might present the world with the old-man guise, but she soon realized he was anything but ancient.

Frang walked to her and held out his hand. Glenna looked down and saw a dagger. A ruby the size of her palm was nestled into the hilt and beautiful scrollwork etched into the blade.

"This was to be presented to you at the time of your birth," he said, and handed it to her.

Glenna grasped the dagger, amazed at its weight, though it felt good in her hands, as if it belonged there. "Why wouldn't the MacNeil let me have it?"

"Because he isn't your father."

Her eyes jerked to his. "You lie," she said, not believing her ears. It couldn't finally come true after years of wishing. It was too cruel.

"I do not lie," he said, his blue eyes soft and kind. But there was great sadness there as well. "I know this is hard for you, but it's the truth. MacNeil took you from your parents."

Glenna saw the truth shining in his eyes and her knees buckled. Moira caught her and wrapped an arm around her for support.

A lump formed in the pit of her stomach. "And who is my father?"

"A great laird named Duncan Sinclair. He was well known throughout the Highlands, and his death was mourned deeply."

"He's dead?" *Nay*, her mind screamed. *He cannot be dead after I've just found out about him.* "My mother?"

"Catriona. A fairer woman I've never met. She had more grace in her little finger than any queen."

Glenna couldn't believe her ears. There were so many things she wanted to know about her parents. Her stomach churned in dread for fear of the answer, but she took a deep breath, and asked, "Where is my mother?"

Frang and Moira shared a look before he said, "She's dead as well. They died together."

"I need to know how."

"Come," Moira urged. "No more questions."

Glenna jerked her arm from Moira's hand. "Nay. For too long I've lived with lies. Tell me."

Moira closed her eyes and turned away. Frang smiled despondently. "Aye, you deserve to know. MacNeil killed them two days after you were born."

A knife plunged in Glenna's heart as she let his words soak in. Nay. It couldn't be true. But she knew it was. "Why?"

"Your parents were Druids. MacNeil feared them."

"Yet he raised me. I don't understand."

"He wanted to use you."

"And he did," she said forlornly, thinking of the Mackenzies.

"Don't," Frang said, and placed a hand on her shoulder. "Don't let distressing memories weigh down your heart. You were not to blame for the Mackenzies."

But she couldn't believe his words because it had been her who enflamed the entire clan.

Moira placed her arms around her. "This has been a lot for you today. Now you must turn your mind to learning the Druid ways. We have little time for you to prepare."

Glenna looked from Frang to Moira. "Prepare for what?"

"The prophecy is soon to come to pass. You have much to learn before then if you are to succeed."

But Glenna wasn't able to think past one single thought—her life had been a total lie, and she would exact her revenge against MacNeil for what he had done.

* * * * *

Conall wiped the sweat from his brow. He had trained harder and longer than usual this morning, and it still hadn't taken a certain dark-headed temptress from his thoughts.

Her body, wet and warm was still vivid in his memory from their swim in the loch. Her full lips still begged for his kiss, and his body demanded to sink into her until they were one.

He desperately needed a woman, but not just any woman.

His sword raised in time to stop Angus' downward thrust. With a step and a pivot Conall relieved him of his weapon. The big man stared dumbfounded at his weapon thirty paces away.

"Och, Conall. After all these years, how are ye still able to manage that one on me even with yer mind elsewhere?"

Conall laughed. "You weren't expecting it."

Apprehension tickled his skin. He looked to Glenna's window. She wasn't in the castle. He didn't ask how he knew, he just *knew*.

"Finish the training, Angus," he called as he ran out of the gates to the forest and the circle of stones.

As much as he hoped Glenna wasn't with Moira, he knew it was futile. It had only been a matter of time until Moira reached her, and if he would have kept a closer eye on Glenna he might have kept her away a bit longer. He had been a fool to think he could keep Glenna and the Druids separated.

He slowed his steps and crept close to the stone circle. He had only been inside once, when he was a small child, but it had lived with him forever.

The Druids walked in pairs while the Druid warriors, Druids who defended other Druids who didn't have powers, stood guard. Conall snorted. He hadn't even ranked a Druid warrior.

"It's glad I am to see you again, Conall. It's been a very long time."

Conall whirled around to find Frang standing behind him. He lowered his head and rubbed his eyes. "Must you always do that?"

"As long as you sneak up on my people," Frang said with a wide smile. "I've been waiting for you."

Conall straightened and flexed his hands. "Why?"

"I knew you would come for Glenna, but you must let her train."

It was on the tip of Conall's tongue to tell Frang why he didn't want Glenna with the Druids, but he changed his mind.

Frang sat on a nearby rock. "Oaths are funny things."

"How so?" Conall asked. He crossed his arms over his chest and waited for the high priest to share whatever wisdom he thought Conall needed.

"People can make too many oaths. When they do they put their honor at stake, or at least they think they do."

"Why don't you just tell me what you want to say and quit talking in riddles?"

Frang cocked his white head to the side and grinned. "But I am, Conall. You just aren't listening."

Glenna's voice reached him, and he turned to see her standing beside Moira. She looked more relaxed than he had ever seen her, and it pained him to know he was going to try to keep her from them.

It's only for a wee bit. Then she can spend eternity with them if she wishes.

"It doesn't do to lie to yourself."

Conall turned to give Frang a piece of his mind only to find he was no longer there. "I hate when you do that."

Frang's laughter echoed around the forest. He waited while Glenna trained with Moira until they walked from the circle. With a quickness that had saved his life several times, he ducked behind a tree and watched while they said their goodbyes. His feet barely touched the ground as he followed Glenna until she was safely inside the castle walls.

He yearned to interrogate her but knew he couldn't allow himself to get close. He might throttle her for not obeying him and then not gain any answers.

Still, he had to admire her gumption. The MacNeil liked women meek and timid, but Glenna had shown him she had fire since she had been here. And it was something she would need if she were to be Highlander's wife.

Wife? Now where did that come from?

He thought of finding Glenna naked and sprawled atop the covers, waiting for him while the drapes hanging on the bed gave him tantalizing glimpses of her body. Just that simple image caused his desire to flare. Painfully.

A swim in the loch was just what he needed to cool his rock-hard cock. He nearly ran to the loch, ignoring Angus' calls as he did. He quickly shed his kilt and dove into the chilly water. But it didn't help.

The water swirling around him only reminded him of her silky legs and how well they would fit around his waist as he filled her. She would be tight and hot, but she would have as much passion for loving as she did for living. He would just have to coax it out of her.

He had to take his mind off Glenna and her tantalizing lips. He dove under and stayed until he thought his lungs would burst. His head cleared the water and he sucked in a deep breath. Then heard the splash.

* * * * *

Glenna couldn't resist the temptation of the loch. It had beckoned once she had left Moira, and after informing Angus where she was headed, her feet moved swift and sure. She still didn't know how to swim, but at least this time she could remove all her clothes and enjoy the delectable feel of the cool water against her skin.

She ventured out until the water was to her waist before she stopped and crouched down. She leaned her head back to gaze at the clouds racing across the sky as she wondered at Angus' smile when she had told him of her destination.

It must have been a ripple in the water that alerted her. She wasn't alone. She turned and saw a naked backend as someone went under the water. For several heartbeats she sat and waited when her mind screamed for her to run.

When she had finally convinced herself to leave, a man burst from the water. Conall. Her breath wedged in her throat as she caught sight of his body. It was then she became aware of his lack of clothes.

Water dripped from his unbound hair that hung past his shoulders and ran down his chest. Muscles flexed in his chest as he raised his arms to wipe the water from his face. One droplet of water held her attention as it wound its way through his black chest hair to his hard stomach and trim waist to disappear into the loch.

She should have felt ashamed for her disappointment at not being able to see the rest of him, but no such emotion flowed in her. He was quite handsome with a body most women would die to run their hands down, and she had to admit she was one of them.

She was so caught up in the glory of his body that she lost her balance and fell backward. Water splashed around her face and she looked up to find him making his way toward her. Without thinking she gasped and stood. He stopped in midstride. His eyes left her face to drift hungrily over her body.

Her breasts tightened and an ache began between her legs. The urge to have his hands on her heated her body. A low growl, one that could only come from a man burning with desire, resonated from Conall. She looked down and groaned before quickly covering her breasts and sinking into the water.

How could she have forgotten she was naked? *Because you were held captive by the hunger in his eyes.* Just to make sure she hadn't imagined that hunger, she chanced a look. Instead of desire, anger radiated from his molten depths.

Fear gripped its steely manacles around her stomach. She hastily backed into deeper water until she was on the tips of her toes with her chin barely above water. He reached her in a blink and wrapped his big hands around her arms. She barely had time to gasp as he dragged her into deeper water. He held her away from him, his jaws clamped tightly together while he glared at her.

"Conall," she said, but his look hardened even more.

"What were you doing away from the castle?"

"I told Angus I was coming here."

"I know where you've been." His eyes glistened with the sun's reflection off the water.

How did he know she had been to see Moira? It seemed she couldn't keep anything from this man. "If you know, why are you asking?"

"I told you I didn't want you near Moira."

She had to make him understand. "I have no control over it. I'm drawn there by an unknown force, something I can't ignore just as I can't ignore the breath that fills my lungs."

"You didn't try very hard."

"Please," she beseeched. "I've learned so much today. I feel as though I've found part of myself that's been missing. Don't take that from me."

"I cannot let you go back."

"Aye, you can."

He sighed and she didn't like the sadness that entered his eyes. "There are reasons. If you value your freedom, don't return to them."

Anger consumed her. How dare he refuse her the very people who had given her answers and filled the holes in her life? How dare he refuse to allow her to live as she should have.

She lifted her feet and with all her might she shoved against him, sending herself into the deep, dark water. It was much darker than she remembered and she tamped down the panic at not being able to find the bottom.

Try as she might she couldn't reach the bottom. She had thought she had her back to the shore, but she had been too intent on Conall to pay much attention. And now she would pay with her life. Now that she didn't wish to die but live.

Fate once again laughed at her.

She looked up to see the sunlight filter through the water, but didn't see any sign of Conall. Her lungs burned and her hands clawed for the surface to no avail. She wasn't moving either up or down.

When she tried to kick her legs, they wouldn't move. She looked down to find them ensnared in weeds. Since she had done this before, she wouldn't blame Conall if he let her drown this time.

The more she struggled, the more the weeds wrapped around her legs as if they were alive. A shape loomed in front of her and she forgot about her legs. She wouldn't drown—she would be eaten by a sea creature.

But it was Conall's face that soon came into view. His hands immediately began working on the weeds, but it wasn't quick enough. She tried to keep still so he could free her legs, but fear had settled firmly around her and all she could think about was getting loose. A couple of times she thought Conall might have freed her only to discover more weeds had wrapped around her.

Her time was running out, as was the air in her lungs. She clawed at his face, begging him to get her some air. Abruptly Conall placed his hands on her face. She opened her eyes as his mouth covered hers. Precious air flowed into her lungs. Had she not needed the air she would have thought more about the fact he had his mouth on hers.

He pulled away and shot to the surface. He returned and worked on the weeds, but only managed to untangle a few of them. Once again he had to give her his air, but this time his tongue touched her lips.

She had long since stopped being afraid for she knew Conall would eventually free her. The heat from his body warmed her as he offered her air. He drew back and looked into her eyes. With a smile he shot to the surface.

It him took two more trips for air before he was able to break all the weeds from around her legs. In an instant she was jerked out of the water and onto rock. Except it wasn't rock but Conall's chest. She wound her arms around his neck and held on for dear life.

She eased her grip somewhat when she felt his arm around her waist. "Th...thank you."

He pulled her away from him enough to see her face. "That's the second time you've tried to drown yourself. Why? I would never harm you."

The hurt in his eyes was almost more than she could bear. "I wasn't intending to drown. I was going to shore, but I didn't pay attention to how far we'd come out."

Her hand slipped and her body moved across his. Her nipples hardened. She sucked in her breath when she felt his arousal, hard and hot against her leg.

She gazed deep into his eyes and saw the desire burning there. His arms pressed her naked body tight against his, and the yearning that always consumed her when he was near spread like wildfire through her.

Her fingers touched his unbound hair. He was just heartbeats away, and her gaze dropped to his wide, firm mouth. His arm urged her forward. She leaned close, their lips touching briefly. He groaned and held her tighter.

She gave in to her body. She had wanted this for a long time and she wouldn't deny herself. His lips moved over hers, nipping, tasting and learning.

His tongue ran along her lips, urging her to open for him. She did and nearly died from the pleasure when his warm tongue swept in and swirled around hers. His tongue touched every part of her mouth, giving her everything of himself and demanding the same in return.

Her first kiss was fiery hot, passionate and wanton. A taste of what it would be like having a man such as Conall as a lover. The ache between her legs intensified as his rod rubbed against her when he shifted her more fully in front of him.

He groaned and buried his hands in her hair. His lips trailed hot kisses across her jaw then back to her mouth where he claimed her with a kiss so full of fervor and wanting that it touched her soul.

Her hands left his neck and wound in his hair as the kiss deepened and intensified. His hands slide down her back to cup her derriere and pull her against his cock. She moaned as passion heated her body, sending waves of pleasure through her. She wanted to run her hands over him as he ran his over her, to know him as he learned her.

He left her mouth and trailed hot kisses down her neck to her throat as his hands came up to squeeze her breasts. His calloused palms ran across her nipples, and she cried out from the pleasure. Instinctively she rubbed her hips against him.

Conall was going to die from the desire flooding his body and rod. Once he had tasted her sweet mouth there had been no turning back. He had to have her.

All of her.

She was like a wine he couldn't get enough of. Her breasts, fuller than he had realized, filled his hands. He ran his thumb over her nipple. It hardened as she leaned her head back and brought her hips against him.

He wrapped her legs around his waist, and the heat of her seared him. His cock jumped at the contact and by sheer will alone he didn't plunge into her.

She lay back in the water, her dark hair floating around her, her breasts thrust forward, waiting for him. He leaned over and took a nipple in his mouth and swirled his tongue around it.

Nails raked his shoulders and arms as she cried out in pleasure when he sucked. He held on to her back with one arm and with his other found her sex.

She was slick and hot and moist. He moved aside her woman's lips and found her pearl. While his thumb rubbed around it, he slowly slid a finger inside and she nearly came out of his arms.

Take her.

He had never desired a woman so much in his life. Had never had one match his own passion so equally, but he couldn't have her. This had to stop before he took her right there. He wrapped his arms around her and kissed her deeply before taking her under the water with him.

The sensation of the water surrounding them as their mouths melded heightened the kiss. He brought them to the surface and made his way to shore with her legs still locked around him as their mouths joined.

He laid her on the shore, the water lapping around them. Her golden-brown eyes were glazed with desire and her lips swollen from his kisses.

"Why did you stop?" She reached to stroke his face.

You deserve better than being taken your first time like this.

"It should never have happened."

"Why do you fight what's between us? I may be an innocent, but surely what's between us isn't common."

Conall ignored her words that cut to his heart. "I swore to my mother I'd get Iona back."

Her eyes, just moments ago filled with passion and longing were now filled with doubt and mistrust as his words sunk in. She rolled from underneath him. He watched as she dressed and walked back to the castle.

He flipped onto his back, his arms out wide and gazed at the sky. Just moments before the sun had been shining, but now dark, ominous clouds rolled in. Quite fitting for his mood.

* * * * *

The Shadow narrowed his eyes on Conall. Damn him, he thought. Conall had stepped over the boundaries with Glenna. He had given her his protection, but now things had been taken to a new level.

On silent feet the Shadow crept back to the castle. He would fix Glenna once and for all. Conall was a powerful warrior, and he didn't want to fight Conall. All of his plans had been well thought-out, but he hadn't thought about Conall falling for Glenna.

He growled. He had to stop this before Conall claimed her body as his own. But he would have to watch himself. The Druids had been active of late with the Otherworld beings. The Fae were meddling in human lives as they hadn't done in an age.

The Shadow crouched behind a tree as Conall walked past. He sucked in his breath as Conall stopped and listened. With slow movements, the Shadow eased his dirk out of his sleeve in case Conall ventured any closer.

But Conall walked on and the Shadow was able to hurry back to the castle to put his next set of plans into action.

Chapter Ten

The main hall buzzed with conversation. The sounds of knives scraping trenchers and goblets banging on tables would make anyone think everything was normal. But it wasn't.

Glenna could *feel* their eyes on her.

Ire simmered just below the surface, but she was determined to keep it hidden. She had refused to stay in her room. She had stayed hidden her entire life. No more would she hide from the world because they didn't want to see her.

Well, they would just have to get used to seeing her. She had made up her mind after she left Conall at the loch that she had everything to live for now. Knowing she wasn't a MacNeil helped to heal some of her wounds, but she would exact her vengeance against him.

Maybe then she could think of finding someone she could grow old with, have children with even. She didn't think too long on that, though, because she was afraid. Fate would take that from her as well.

Thunder rolled in the distance as the rain continued to fall. She was glad for it. The rain cried the tears she refused to shed. After the tender way Conall had touched her in the loch, it was hard to bear his cold treatment now, if he acknowledged her at all.

He had been furious when she had declined to stay in her chamber. Oh, he had used what happened with the clan's hatred as an excuse, but she had a feeling he didn't want to see her.

She rose from the dais to sit with Ailsa before the fire when the pain hit. It brought her to her knees and she clutched her chest as the hatred seared painfully through her.

Gregor and Conall were at her side in an instant, but she paid them no heed as she frantically searched the hall. The woman was easy to find. She didn't try to hide. She stood against the wall, her dark red plait falling over her shoulder as she stared at Glenna, hatred forming an aura around her. It was the same woman who had looked so longingly at Conall the other day in the bailey.

"By the saints, Glenna. I knew you should've stayed in your chamber," Conall whispered in her ear.

"Who. Is that?" Glenna managed to ask him as walked her to the fire.

"Who?"

She gasped for air, silently begging for some reprieve from the intense pain. Finally, slowly, the pain began to ebb. When she looked back to where the woman was, she was gone.

"Who?" Conall asked again, his silver eyes clouded with worry.

"She's gone now. She's very pretty with red hair."

"Effie," Conall said, a sigh leaving his lips.

Gregor gently turned her head to him, his black eyes filled with worry. "Are you all right?"

She tried to smile to reassure him, but knew she failed miserably. "I think I'll be fine."

He nodded and walked off.

She watched him, wondering about his concern for her when Conall said, "Is there something going on between you and Gregor?"

She almost laughed. Instead she shook her head. "I met him the day you took me from the MacNeil. You know more of him than I do."

He seemed satisfied with that answer and helped her over to the fire so she could sit with Ailsa. Before he could leave, Glenna took hold of his arm. "Why does Effie hate me?"

"For a brief time we were lovers. She thought to be my wife even though I never gave her any reason to think that."

"How long ago was this?"

"Almost two years ago."

* * * * *

Glenna thought about what Conall had told her as she situated Ailsa on her lap. The child had asked for a story before bed and she had agreed. She had never been around children before, and she wasn't about to pass up this opportunity.

After the story had been told, one with a beautiful princess, Fae folk and a handsome prince who saved the day from the wicked villain, Ailsa was taken to bed.

Glenna stayed by the fire. She sat alone in one of the massive chairs, but she preferred it that way. The hostility from the clan had lessened, except for a few, and she could handle the pain their hatred caused from this distance thanks to Moira's teaching.

The fire crackled and hissed, its yellow, orange and red flames drawing her deeper into her thoughts. As she gazed into the flames, she saw herself in a chamber lying naked on a bed. Hands, big and strong, came around her and drew her back against a chest of solid muscle.

Conall.

She leaned her head to the side to grant him access to her neck as his mouth and tongue found spots on her skin that drove her wild with longing. Her hips rocked back against his, his rod hot and hard against her back. He rolled her over and took a nipple in his mouth as he guided her hand to his shaft and closed her fingers around him.

Glenna moaned. He was velvet smooth and so hot he seared her hand. She couldn't take her eyes off her hand as it encircled him. Liquid beaded at the tip of his rod. She moved her finger to catch it and brought it to her lips.

With a deep growl he drove into her, filling her with his hardness. She moaned and moved her hips in time with his. Pleasure so intense it took her breath away engulfed her. Her only thought was of him and the passion between them.

Her breath came faster and faster as he pumped in her, bringing her closer and closer to…something.

The sound of wood splintering jerked her out of her vision. She swallowed and tried to control her breathing. She looked around the room to see if anyone watched her when her eyes found Conall.

Even from the great distance separating them she could see the molten desire burning in his eyes, and her body pulsed with a need so strong it almost brought her to him. It was almost as though he had seen her vision.

Her breasts tightened in response, and she knew she had to leave the hall. She stood, and with shaky legs made her way to her chamber. She had just closed the door when it opened, and Conall filled the doorway.

"Is everything all right?" he asked with one hand braced against the door.

"I'm fine. Just tired," she lied, her body throbbing with need.

For him.

His eyes roamed over her, sending a thrill down her spine. He wanted her. It shone brightly in his eyes, but he was fighting against it.

Conall gripped the chamber door in an effort to keep from walking into her chamber and kissing those full, pink lips. The vision he had below of them making love had brought his already-aching cock to a state of need like he had never experienced. It was made worse when he realized she had not only seen his vision but shared it as well. When she had looked at him with her lips parted and chest rapidly rising and falling, he had nearly taken her right then.

He didn't know what had prompted him to follow her, but now that he was here, he couldn't leave. He didn't want to leave. He wanted her. On the bed. Naked. And willing.

"Tell me what Moira has told you." He had to take his mind off loving her or they would end up on the floor in matter of moments.

"She told me the MacNeil used me," she said, and looked away from him.

For a brief moment a flash of sadness had shone in her golden brown eyes. "There's more. Tell me," he said, and walked into the chamber to stand beside her.

Her head jerked up and he saw the anger radiating from her just seconds before the flames in the fireplace roared to life. He looked from the fire to her. She had caused it to do that. Her powers were great.

"Have you always been able to do that?"

She sat on the bed, her face bleak. "I cannot control it."

"My plaid the other day. Was that you?"

She smiled sheepishly and lowered her head.

"I gather you learned something of yourself today." He hated the fact the Druids had gotten to her and now compromised his oaths, but he had seen her there. She belonged.

He didn't think her face could become any more desolate, but he was wrong. She blinked away tears, her mouth trembling. "MacNeil isn't my father."

Conall sat next to her, stunned. This had been the last thing he had expected to hear. "I'm sorry."

"I'm not. I'm relieved," she said as hatred heated her gaze.

"If MacNeil isn't your father, who is?"

"A man named Duncan Sinclair."

The room tilted around him as memories poured in. It had been eighteen years since Sinclair and his wife had been murdered along with their three daughters. The infant had never been found and it was assumed she had perished with her family. No one had thought she had been taken. And the prophecy Moira had spoken of rang clear and true in his head.

In a time of Conquering
There will be three
Who will end the MacNeil line
Three born of the
Light, Harvest and Beltaine
Who will destroy all at the
Feast of the Dead

He raised his eyes and looked to Glenna. "What happened to your parents?"

"MacNeil killed them."

"What else did Moira tell you?"

"That I was part of a prophecy. One of three Druids who will fulfill that prophecy."

"And the other two?" he asked, his throat thick and tight.

"I...haven't asked," she said, her head bowed. "I was trying to learn all that I could of my past."

"All these years we thought you were dead."

"What?"

He recovered himself and stood. Discord brewed inside him and he needed time to think. "Good eve, Glenna."

Without another word he left her and climbed to the square tower overlooking the loch. The tower had always offered him solace. He inhaled the clean night air deeply, filling his lungs with its freshness from the recent rain. The stars and moon sparkled off the still waters of the loch, but the war continued to rage within him.

His Druid side urged him to bring Glenna to Moira to finish her training so the prophecy could come to pass. But his other half wanted Iona returned as he had promised his mother.

The oaths he had given hung around his neck like a noose. He had to get Iona back. If he didn't he would fail his mother. And if returning Glenna to MacNeil could achieve this, then he would do it.

He had to.

"I can't," he whispered, and lowered his head to the cool, damp stones of the castle. The thought of handing her back to the MacNeil turned his stomach. Not to mention if the prophecy wasn't fulfilled all of Scotland could be lost.

But he would have to make his decision soon. The MacNeil and his clan would arrive any day. If only he would have gotten reassurance that Iona hadn't been killed.

* * * * *

"Go," urged the Shadow to the young serving maid. He had seen the way she eyed Conall during the evening meal and it had given him a way to drive a wedge between Conall and Glenna.

The maid, Lorna, turned and gave him one last look at the door to Conall's chamber. "Are you sure he asked for me? He's never paid me much attention."

"Aye, I'm sure, lass. He awaits you now."

* * * * *

Conall groaned and tried to find a comfortable position in his bed. His body needed to find a woman, and until he did he wouldn't get any sleep. But the thought of searching for a woman just for the night didn't appeal to him.

He knew he could go to Glenna, but he had put himself in a tight spot anyway after kissing her. He didn't need to make it worse by bonding their bodies.

A knock on his door brought him out of bed. He wrapped his kilt around his hips and stalked to the door. He swung open the door and found one of the serving maids, Lorna, standing before him.

"Can I help you?" he asked, wondering what brought her to his chamber.

"I thought...I," she began, but stopped. She quickly stepped under his arm and into the room.

Conall blinked and turned to find her standing naked. His body, already in a state of such need that it was painful, flared.

Lorna walked to him and grasped him under his plaid. Her warm hand around his shaft brought out a groan. He didn't desire her, but his body desperately needed her. He didn't stop her when she unhooked his plaid. She rubbed her body against his and brought his hand up to cup her breast. His body took control as he pulled her against him.

Her hands brought his head down for a kiss, but as soon as her mouth touched his, he knew he couldn't do this. She wasn't Glenna, and that was who his body wanted. He began to pull away when he heard a gasp at the door.

Fool that he was he hadn't closed his chamber door and standing there was Glenna. Her wide eyes moved from Lorna to him before she turned and fled down the hall.

"Damn," he muttered before he picked up his plaid and hurried after her.

He opened her door to find her sitting on her bed. "Glenna—"

"I shouldn't have been there. I'm sorry," she said, but she wouldn't look him in the eye. "It won't happen again."

Conall knew it was foolish to try to explain what had happened. He would be better off leaving things as they were.

Glenna waited until Conall shut her door behind him before she covered her face with her hands. Seeing him with that woman had sent a bolt of jealousy through her that had been so strong that for a split second she had thought of doing the woman harm.

She had fooled herself if she had thought for a moment there would be any hope for her and Conall. Even though their bodies wanted each other, his heart wanted his sister more.

And who could blame him for that?

Chapter Eleven

ಸಿ

Glenna basked in the morning sun on the shore of the loch as the birds chirped noisily. The previous night's rain had washed the earth clean and everything sparkled around her. Even the scent of heather was more powerful than normal.

She covered her mouth to stifle the yawn. She had gotten little sleep thanks to the vivid vision she had had of Conall making love to her then his visit to her chamber. Disappointment had filled her when he had hastily departed after finding out about MacNeil, and she didn't allow herself to think of him with that other woman. It was just too painful.

Could the fact she wasn't MacNeil's daughter be the reason he had avoided her so cleverly this morn? Not that she sought him out, but usually he wanted her very near him. Then Angus had come for her, and she had known something had upset Conall.

A laugh escaped her as she watched Ailsa play near the water with the other children. The child had begged her to come, and Glenna hadn't been able to refuse those big silver eyes. Would Conall ever look at her like that?

She shook her head and pushed thoughts of him out of her mind. Or at least she tried.

Angus sat beside her to protect her from the clan. She had to laugh. She wasn't the one who needed protecting. The others did from her uncontrollable powers. With Angus by her side all morning she had been unable to leave the castle and visit Moira for more of her training. She was sure Conall had seen to that, but she was just as sure that she would eventually return to the stone circle and Moira.

She was going to have to find other means of getting to the stone circle. There was much to learn about the Druids and her abilities, and if Moira was right, little time in which to do it.

A cry sounded from the castle. Angus jumped up and called for everyone to run for safety. Glenna grabbed Ailsa and started for the steep stone steps that lead to the castle.

She touched a stone as she walked past. The image of Ailsa running toward Conall and an arrow imbedded in her small back flashed in Glenna's mind.

"Angus, we must keep Ailsa with us."

The big man turned, his red eyebrows drawn together. "What's wrong, lass?"

"I'm not sure. I must get to Conall."

Without another word Angus gathered Ailsa in his arms and strode toward the castle. Glenna ran to keep up with him. Once they reached the safety of the castle, she put a hand on the wall to steady herself and gulped in air.

When she looked up, Ailsa was gone. "Nay," she screamed, but Angus stopped her.

"It's all right, lass. I've sent Ailsa with a servant for safekeeping."

Relief washed through her. As long as Ailsa was kept safe, she didn't need to worry about any stray arrows. Then a thought occurred to her. Just who was arriving at MacInnes' castle that would put everyone on alert?

But she knew.

MacNeil.

Dread pooled in her stomach and rose to choke her. She was angry and scared in turns. She wanted to confront the MacNeil and ask him why he had killed her parents, but she couldn't. He could very well use her as he had in the past.

"Glenna."

She turned and found Conall standing beside her, his silver eyes intent. "It's MacNeil."

"Aye."

Gregor strode up, bow in hand. "I hear we have company."

"I expected him sooner," Conall said as he turned. Over his shoulder he said, "Glenna, I need you standing beside me. I want the MacNeil to see you."

Glenna's eyes met Gregor's startled black ones. "Nay," they said in unison.

Conall whirled around and glared at them, his nostrils flaring. "Aye, you will. It's a fine time for you to be wanting to argue, Glenna."

A sob choked her as she thought of his clan dying. She turned to Gregor, silently asking him for his help.

"She can't," Gregor said, and looked to Conall. "MacNeil will use her like he has before. You and your clan won't stand a chance."

But Conall wasn't convinced. He turned his gaze to Glenna. "I'm going to get my sister back. That means you must return to the MacNeil, and these lies won't prevent me from returning you."

She reached out and grabbed his arm. "You don't understand. If he sees me, he wins. I need to be somewhere I can't see or hear him."

"Tell me why. Give me a reason."

"I don't have time to explain. Please. Trust me," she begged.

Gregor stepped forward. "The destruction the MacNeil will cause will be great if you make Glenna stand beside you. It's no lie, Conall."

Glenna watched as Conall's forehead creased and he stared hard at Gregor and then turned to her. He shook his head as if to clear it and it was obvious something bothered him.

"There's nothing the MacNeil can do from down there. You'll be by my side," Conall finally said.

She couldn't hold back the tear that escaped. But the sound of a child's voice reached her ears. Ailsa's voice. She turned and watched as the child raced toward Conall, calling for him.

And Glenna knew.

Her vision would happen before her eyes.

* * * * *

The Shadow gave Ailsa a smile. "Go to your father, little one. He wants to see you."

"I'm not sure. Angus and Glenna wanted me kept safe."

"You can't get any safer than in the arms of your father." The Shadow almost patted himself on the back at those words. Ailsa didn't hesitate as she raced toward her father.

He turned to Effie. "Now's your chance. You only get one, so make sure you hit the target." He watched as Effie pulled back the string of the bow and let the arrow fly.

"It starts now," he said as he heard Glenna scream.

"Finally," Effie said, and hurried to hide the bow. "I'll comfort Conall as he mourns the loss of his daughter."

"You're quite the bitch, Effie, but then that's what brought me to you. You do have your uses."

* * * * *

Glenna had been wrong to think that Ailsa would be hurt during the heat of battle. With her mind intent on saving Ailsa she raced toward the child. Glenna looked up and spotted the arrow just before it was released.

She dove at Ailsa. She tucked the child against her body and took the brunt of the fall as they hit the hard earth, the hiss of an arrow whizzed by her ear. When they had stopped rolling, she continued to lie there. Ailsa's sobs reached her just as hands took hold of her shoulders and another set grasped Ailsa.

Glenna looked up into Conall's startled eyes. "Is she hit?" she asked.

He moved to show the arrow stuck in the ground with her gown attached. He quickly grabbed Ailsa and pulled her against him for a fierce hug.

Angus ran up. "By St. Brigit, lass. It's glad I am ye knew something was going to happen."

"What?" Conall asked. He let Angus take Ailsa and yanked the arrow from the ground, freeing Glenna.

She rose and dusted herself off. "I had a vision of Ailsa being struck by an arrow while she ran toward you. What I didn't see was that it would be someone in the castle."

Conall narrowed his eyes and looked at the arrow. Glenna was right. The arrow had come from the castle. He didn't need this. Not now. Not with everything else going on. Besides, why would anyone want to kill his daughter? She was just a child.

"It seems we have a traitor among us." He turned to Gregor. "I don't think the MacNeil should know you're here. Take Glenna to the caves and keep her safe."

He waited until they disappeared in the cave entrance before he looked at Angus. "What have I done?"

Angus clapped him on the back. "Ye did the right thing. Ye made an oath to keep the Druids safe."

"And what of my oath to my mother? If the MacNeil doesn't see Glenna I'll never convince him I have her, and I won't get Iona back."

Angus' usually merry eyes turned sad. "My gut tells me Iona is dead."

"Don't," Conall warned his friend. He refused to give up, and he wouldn't have anyone speaking what he thought about in the dark of night.

"Ye can't tell me ye haven't thought about it."

"I don't have time to talk about this. The MacNeil is approaching." He stalked to the battlements before Angus could argue anymore.

He spotted the MacNeil clansmen making their way toward the castle. He didn't have long to wait for the MacNeil to break from the group and run his horse to the castle gates.

"Where is Glenna?" MacNeil shouted up.

"Safe."

"You expect me to take your word for it?"

Conall laughed. "You don't have a choice."

"I need to see her. You could've killed her for all I know."

Conall ground his teeth. "Show me Iona and I'll let you see Glenna."

The MacNeil cackled, the sound booming around them. "She didn't want to come."

Fury ripped through Conall. "Did you think you would be able to hide the fact you took Iona? Did you think I'd never find out?"

"Nay. Why do you think I invited you within my walls?" He laughed again. "I didn't figure you for a witless laird, Conall, but only a fool would've taken my offering."

"You tried to kill me. I'm still standing here, as is every one of my men who entered your gates that day."

MacNeil nodded. "That's true enough, but not for long. I've long wanted your castle, and I'll wait no more for it. Show me Glenna."

"Nay."

A bellow of rage erupted from the MacNeil.

Conall rejoiced in MacNeil's anger. Angry men didn't fight rational. They made mistakes. "Many clans larger than yours have tried to take siege on this castle and not one succeeded."

"I'm not leaving without Glenna."

"Glenna isn't going anywhere until Iona is returned."

MacNeil drew his sword. "Iona has no wish to return home. She told me to tell you to send Glenna home with me."

"Iona would never have said that."

"Are you sure?" MacNeil asked. "People do change. Especially when every one of my men has had her."

Conall's vision turned red with rage. He bellowed the MacInnes war cry, revenge running rampant through his veins.

* * * * *

Glenna huddled inside the cave. She hated the darkness where she couldn't see her hand in front of her face, but Gregor had said they needed to stay hidden. Suddenly a vision of Conall walking out the castle gates with sword in hand ready to fight the MacNeil flashed before her. But he was attacked and killed from behind.

"Gregor," she called.

Instantly he was by her side, holding the torch so he could see her face. "What?"

"You must stop Conall. He's going to fight MacNeil, but he'll die. MacNeil has a man hidden behind a boulder to kill Conall when he walks from the gates."

Gregor turned and ran from the cave without another word. Glenna sank to the ground, her thoughts of Conall. All she could do was pray she had seen the vision in time.

"Moira," she called. "Moira, I need you."

Several moments passed without any sound then a whoosh of wind whipped around her.

I'm here, Glenna.

"I've seen Conall's death. You must help him."

I'll do what I can, she said, and then was gone.

Glenna wrapped her arms around herself. She prayed for another vision, anything to let her know what was going on, but nothing happened.

Instead, she had only the darkness and her thoughts for company.

* * * * *

Conall walked from the castle gates, Angus' harsh words ringing in his ears. Angus hadn't wanted him to leave the safety of the castle, but he didn't have a choice. He had to avenge Iona.

He stood ten paces from the MacNeil when the sound of footsteps approaching from behind made him turn around. "What are you doing?" he asked Gregor.

"Saving your arse." Gregor walked around a large boulder and returned with a dagger held to one of MacNeil's clansmen.

Conall turned his eyes to the MacNeil.

MacNeil shrugged. "I never said I fought fair."

Conall circled around MacNeil, his sword raised. He brought it down hard on MacNeil's. MacNeil pivoted and thrust his sword, but Conall anticipated the move and smiled when his elbow connected with the bastard's nose.

MacNeil wiped the blood from his broken nose and sneered. He charged, his sword swinging in a downward arc. Conall parried and tried to duck MacNeil's fist.

The metallic taste of blood filled his mouth. He spit and swung his sword around before he launched another attack. This was his chance for vengeance, and he refused to fail.

He was fierce, giving no quarter. He slashed MacNeil's chest and blood soaked the front of his plaid. After ducking a weak swing to his midsection, Conall lunged and delivered a nasty cut to MacNeil's arm. Blow after blow he hammered MacNeil until the older man's arm begin to weaken.

Triumph soared through him. He had MacNeil backed against a boulder. This was it. With one flick of his wrist MacNeil would be gone from this world. His father would be avenged, Iona would be returned and Glenna would never have to worry about returning. And all of Scotland would be safe from this murdering bastard.

Conall raised his sword but a piercing pain stopped him. MacNeil's wicked cackle reached his ears. He looked down to see an arrow sticking from the top of his arm. Out the corner of his eye he saw MacNeil raise his sword.

Fool that he was, he had turned his back on MacNeil and now he would pay with his life. Conall's thoughts centered on Glenna and how she would fare once he was gone.

Before MacNeil's sword penetrated his skin a vicious wind whipped around them. The wind howled loudly, and Conall could barely open his eyes against it. He raised his arm to shield his eyes and saw MacNeil running toward his horse.

"Another day," MacNeil called as he mounted his horse and he and his men rode away.

Angus and Gregor reached Conall as the wind died down to nothing. "Shall we go after them?" Angus asked.

"Nay. If we leave the castle he wins, and he can never win MacInnes Castle."

Conall looked toward the forest and raised his face to the cliff. Gazing down at him was Moira. Only one other time had he ever witnessed her control over wind. She had helped him. It gave him pause, but he refused to give her the upper hand.

"This doesn't mean I'll allow Glenna to come to you," he whispered, and knew she heard every word.

Chapter Twelve

Glenna trembled in the dampness of the cave. Gregor had taken her so deep she couldn't hear anything but the constant dripping of water. She bit her lip and moved to her left. Bugs. She just knew there were bugs crawling on her. She hated bugs, but she hated spiders more. And once she thought about a spider, every place on her body felt as though hundreds of tiny legs crawled on her.

At first she tried to ignore it. She couldn't. She moved her hair out of her face, but the sensations steadily became worse. Her skin and scalp tingled just thinking of those nasty spiders. Every sound was those eight legs crawling on her.

It was too much. She jumped up and ran in the general direction she thought Gregor had taken her. It didn't matter how many times she told herself she was being silly for running from something she wasn't sure she had felt, the fact was that there might have been something. Her fear was too much. She chided herself for not paying better attention after running into a couple of walls.

But then it was hard to notice when there was nothing but blackness around with the occasional torch to guide her. Her eyes had become accustomed to the dark, but not enough so she could really see. She would have to talk to Conall about that. How did they expect a person to walk in this blackness?

Then she went face first in a spider web the size of a castle.

She shrieked as she struggled to get the web off her. Had anyone asked, she would have sworn she could hear the spiders crawling toward her. Her heart pounded and the more she tried to get the web off, the more it clung to her. Hysterics set in. Something touched her side. She screamed and banged into a wall as she jumped.

Her hair clung to her face with sweat, and it wasn't until she brushed a strand away from her face that she felt it.

A spider.

The unmistakable feel of eight legs crawled rapidly over her finger and it was all she could do not to faint. Her mind told her to fling it off her hand, but her body refused to move. She stood frozen in terror. But when it sank its fangs in her, she let out a scream and viciously flung the spider off. Then she flipped her head over and swung her hair around to make sure there weren't more of them hiding in her hair.

Unfortunately, spiders were drawn to her, and the one she had flung off came right back toward her.

*****

"Where the hell is she?" Conall demanded.

"I left her right here," Gregor said, and held the torch higher to shed more light.

"She must have ventured off."

"Unless she can become invisible, I think you're right." Conall tamped down a groan as blood trickled down his arm. "She could be anywhere. These caves go deeper than I've ever explored, even as a child."

"I knew I should've stayed with her," Gregor mumbled.

They both stopped and stared at each other when the scream reached them.

"Glenna," they said in unison, and ran in the direction of the scream.

*****

Glenna stopped running when her lungs begged for breath and a stitch started in her side. She had no idea how far she had gone, but it was definitely not the way to the castle.

All she saw when he looked around was never-ending walls of stone. She wished for a torch so she could be sure the spiders were no longer following her.

A flicker of light caught her attention. She quickly followed, hoping it was Conall. Instead she found Moira.

"I wondered how long it would take you."

Still gasping for breath, Glenna asked, "What are you talking about?"

"I wanted to see if you could find your way without hearing the music. You did. Your Druid powers are more than I expected, especially at how little you've been taught." With that Moira turned and walked away.

Glenna stared stupidly after her. Had she really found her by herself? "Moira?"

"Remember the way," she called out, her image fading in the darkness. "This is where I will meet you. This cave leads to the stone circle."

Glenna's mouth dropped open. Was it coincidence she happened upon this route?

"Go, Glenna. Conall is coming."

She followed Moira's urging and turned back to retrace her steps. She hadn't gone far when Conall and Gregor rounded a corner.

"There you are," Conall said, and rushed toward her as he held up the torch. "Are you all right? We heard the scream."

She nodded. "It's silly, really. I hate spiders."

"You ran because you saw a spider?" Gregor asked.

The torch shed enough light to let her see they both thought she was daft. "It wouldn't leave me alone. I think it was upset because I ran into its web." She shivered and rubbed her hands along her arms.

"Did you kill it?" Conall asked.

"I couldn't. Gregor reached you in time I see." She was anxious to make sure he was unharmed, to know her vision helped.

"Aye."

It was the slight wince that drew her attention to his shoulder. She spotted the blood and the hastily wrapped bandage around his upper arm. The thought of him injured sucked the breath right out of her.

She gently laid her fingers on his arm. "You're hurt."

"It's only a scratch. Angus tended to it."

"It doesn't look like a scratch. What happened?"

"A soldier tried to prevent me from killing the MacNeil."

"Oh, is that all," she said, anger making the words harsh.

How could he be so nonchalant about it? There was blood. He was in pain. Not to mention she hadn't had a vision about someone trying to kill him. How would these visions help if she couldn't have one when it counted?

"This isn't the first time I've been wounded, nor do I think it will be the last. Now tell me. Did you have another vision?"

She shrugged. "It seems I've had a few of them lately. But I didn't see this," she said, and again touched his arm.

He turned her face to his with a finger under her chin. "You saved Ailsa's life as well as mine this day."

It was the sadness in his voice and his eyes that told her what she had been dreading. Tears she couldn't control ran down her face. "He didn't bring Iona, did he?"

He shook his head and wiped her tears away.

She yearned to scream her anguish. Instead she put her trust in Conall. "What will you do now?"

He put a hand on her back and urged her to walk. "I've some thinking and planning to do. He's made it known he wants MacInnes Castle. He'll do whatever it takes to get it. He was mighty upset at not seeing you."

"I thought he might," she said. "I'm sorry he is such a bad man. I never knew."

"No one should be reared by a man like that."

"Where is the MacNeil? Does he wait outside your walls?"

"He and his army are gone. For now. They'll be back with more men, I'm sure."

"But you'll be waiting for them."

He stopped and stared at her. "Aye, I will. I aim to kill him."

Glenna started to speak when the torch went out. A sound came from farther down the cave and she just knew it was the spider. Anger and fear welled up inside her. "I need light. I can't stand this darkness. The spiders will come."

"I know the way," he said, and put his hand on her back.

But Glenna didn't move. Fear had frozen her again. She closed her eyes and wished with all he might for some light.

The torch blazed again. She opened her eyes and found Conall looking from the torch to her.

"You did this?"

She shrugged. "I don't know. Maybe?"

"She did," Gregor said.

* * * * *

Conall ran his hands down his face and stared at the mead flask sitting between him, Gregor and Angus in the now-empty hall. His arm throbbed, but the cream he had found sitting on the table in his chamber had lessened the pain and stopped the bleeding.

He didn't even want to know how Moira had gotten to his chamber to leave the healing cream without being seen. Aye, he knew it was she who had left the cream. Her healing abilities were legendary, but why she would want to help him after everything he had done to her was a mystery.

Angus cleared his throat. "We can go after the bastard."

"His men outnumber us." Conall rubbed his eyes as weariness set heavily on his bones.

"What are you thinking?" Gregor asked.

Conall shrugged. "I'd been planning his death for some time now, but I won't leave my people defenseless. This castle has withstood many sieges from lairds hungry for our land. It will again."

"MacNeil has a weapon you don't know about."

Conall raised his eyes to Gregor. "And just what weapon is that?"

"Glenna."

If one of the Fae people had suddenly popped in front of him Conall wouldn't have been more surprised. "Explain yourself."

Gregor lifted his goblet and drained its contents. "It's why she didn't want to be able to see or hear MacNeil. Iona taught Glenna just enough..."

"To be dangerous," Conall finished. "St. Joseph." He rose and began pacing. "Just how dangerous is she?"

"How is Glenna dangerous?" Angus asked.

Gregor raised his black eyes. "She wasn't lying, Conall. Your clan would all die."

"Surely there's a way to get the clan out," Conall said.

"How is Glenna dangerous?" Angus asked again, his face becoming red in his agitation at being ignored.

"Fire," Conall and Gregor said at once.

Conall slid into his chair. "Fire is her power."

"She's got no control over it?" Angus asked Gregor, his eyes wide with confusion.

"She doesn't know how to," Conall answered for Gregor. "That's why Moira was so insistent to get to her."

Gregor nodded and poured himself more mead. "What are you going to do?"

"I don't know," Conall answered, and looked up to find Ailsa walking toward him. "What are you doing out of bed?" he asked with a smile.

"I wanted to tell you what happened today," she said in a small voice.

Conall picked her up and put her in his lap. "I know what happened today. Glenna saved your life, but don't worry we'll find who did it."

"A man told me you wanted me. That's why I left the castle, but I think he tricked me."

Conall raised his eyes to Angus and Gregor. Their shocked expressions mirrored his own. "What did this man look like?"

"I'm not sure. He had a cloak on and it covered his face."

"You didn't see anything else?"

She shook her head. "All right," he said, and set her on her feet. "Off to bed with you. We'll find this cloaked man."

After Ailsa was gone from the hall, Conall ran his hands through his hair. What was he to do now that there was a cloaked stranger in his castle?

Gregor whistled through his teeth. "Finding a cloaked man shouldn't be hard, but I've a feeling he wore the cloak only to hide himself from Ailsa."

"You've the right of it," Conall agreed.

"What are ye going to do?" Angus asked this time.

"I don't know," Conall said, and walked from the room. He needed time to think.

Alone.

*****

Glenna sat on her bed and stared through her narrow window at the sun making its descent, waiting for the time she would meet Moira. She had made sure she remembered her way through the caves when Conall had walked her back.

Excitement coursed through her. She hated deceiving Conall, but she was a Druid. She couldn't ignore the yearning within her. Still, the thought that she was doing something she wasn't supposed to sat heavy on her heart, but she couldn't deny that ever since she came here she was finding herself, little by little.

She rose and left her chamber. The castle was busy with the evening meal as she made her way down the stairs. A glance told her the hall was full, which would occupy Conall. He had left her alone this night, and she was sure he would continue to do so. She quickly made her way outside.

Once in the bailey, she kept to the shadows and headed for the cave. When she was in the cave, she grabbed a torch and took a deep breath before heading into the darkness.

Before she knew it she had come to the spot where Moira had been. After a deep breath, she forced her feet to move and soon found herself in the forest, the stone circle ahead of her. She couldn't believe no one had stumbled upon this before.

"They cannot see what they don't believe," Frang said from behind her. "And we don't discourage the ones who do believe. We've nothing to hide here, Glenna."

She bit her lip. "You read thoughts?"

"I could tell by your expression what you were thinking."

She laughed, relieved that she didn't have to guard her thoughts. Moira stepped forward then and offered her hand.

"Are you ready to learn more of the history of the Druids?"

Glenna willingly went with her and sat while Moira's words began.

"The Druidic philosophy of balance between spirit and flesh is oneness between the physical and spiritual. This is a unity we hold as a natural, healthy and necessary state."

Glenna closed her eyes. There was magic around her and she eagerly opened herself up to it.

"We also recognize a oneness with this world and the Otherworld," Moira continued, her voice soft and smooth. "The Otherworld is a substantial place, just like ours. Though the laws of time may differ in as much as they don't age like we do, their magic is more powerful and commonplace."

"Magic," Glenna whispered.

"The realm of the Otherworld is made of earth, water and wind. It's energized by fire."

Glenna's eyes popped opened. "What are these Otherworld beings?"

Moira walked closer and peered deeply into Glenna's eyes. "They are the Fae. It's they who gave us the prophecy that you are a part of."

"Don't all Druids hold powers?"

"Nay. You are different, special. You were given those powers because you were born on a Druid festival, Imbolc, that is marked by fire and water."

"And the other two?"

Moira lowered her green eyes. "One was born on Lughnasadh, the celebration of life, and the other was born on Beltaine, the return of the sun."

A chill raced down Glenna's spine. She glanced around and saw the Druids dressed in masks and scantly clad. Her eyes jerked to Moira. "Tonight is a feast."

"Aye. Beltaine."

"I want to see."

"It isn't time," Moira stated, and turned away. "This is the most powerful night for the Druids. The veil between worlds runs thin this night. You don't know enough to understand and you could be hurt."

Glenna refused to listen. How could Moira tell her these things but expect her to stay away. She kept her thoughts to herself and concentrated on learning of her power.

For the next two hours she began to learn to control the fire. It took immense concentration, and she was attempting to create a fire when Conall's voice boomed around her.

"Moira! Moira, I'd speak to you now," he demanded.

Glenna jerked her eyes to Moira. "How did he know I was here?"

"He doesn't," she answered. "He wants to talk to me about you. I've been expecting him since MacNeil left. Stay hidden," she said before walking to him.

Glenna ducked behind a huge pillar so she could see Conall. He stood outside the circle, the moonlight surrounding him in its glow. His hair hung loose around his shoulders, giving him a primal look, and the memory of its silky feel heated her skin.

"What brings you here so late?" Moira asked him.

His jaw flexed. "Why did you help me earlier?"

"Because Glenna asked it of me."

He nodded and crossed his arms over his chest. "Do you know where Iona is?"

Moira's head bowed and her hands fisted at her sides. "Nay. I wanted to tell you, but I knew you wouldn't listen even though you could've easily used your gift."

"Gift," he bellowed. "It's not a gift but a curse."

"How can you say that? You've used it often enough. You should know yourself if MacNeil is lying."

He waved off her words. "Why didn't you help Iona?"

"I...we couldn't, Conall. It was her destiny. She knew it for years."

"Explain yourself," he said, and took a step toward her.

Glenna became afraid for Moira but a hand on her shoulder stopped her. She turned and found Frang beside her.

"Don't, lass. Moira can take care of herself," he cautioned.

Glenna doubted it for she knew how Conall fought, but she didn't argue.

Moira took a deep breath. "I've no need to explain. You know what I speak of for you were told of your destiny as well."

Conall snorted. "You're mistaken."

"Do you hate us so much that you've turned against what is in your blood?" Moira asked, incredulous. "I knew you hated me, but I thought it was because of Iona. But it isn't just me, is it?"

He neither denied nor agreed with her assessment, but by the silver glint in his eyes Glenna knew Moira had struck upon something painful.

"It's your oath."

Conall turned his head away from her and stared into the trees. "A man is made or broken by his oaths."

"But you made another oath," she said softly.

Glenna wished she could see Moira's face. Whatever she had remembered seemed to change many things. But Glenna's heart when out to Conall as he struggled with his anger and resentment.

Conall chuckled, but it lacked humor. "You knew I did. You were sitting beside my mother. Did you forget so easily?"

She didn't answer him. "So that's why you don't want Glenna here."

"I knew it wouldn't take you long to figure it out."

"You cannot deny what is inside you forever. Even now you're fighting against the inevitable."

"By the...what's that supposed to mean?"

Glenna was surprised to find that Moira turned and looked at her.

"Are you expecting Frang to help you?" he asked, and began to pace.

Moira smiled and turned back to him. "You must remember what was told to you. If you don't all could be lost."

He raised his head and looked around. "Moira? Come back. I wasn't done."

Glenna blinked and Moira had disappeared. Conall glanced one way then the other, demanding Moira show herself. Moira came to stand beside her. "You must go back now. He'll be headed to your chamber. And, Glenna, stay there tonight. Don't venture out."

With Moira's warning ringing in her head, Glenna rushed into the cave. She didn't stop running until she had reached the bailey, and it was only then she realized she had entered the caves without a torch.

The chants of the festival reached her and she knew she wouldn't return to her chamber. She wanted to see what went on. She wanted to be a part of everything. Surely taking a peek wouldn't hurt anything, she thought and walked out the gates.

The castle and bailey were deserted, but she didn't wish to be spotted. So when she found a cloak near the gatehouse, she quickly slipped it on and pulled up the hood. It wasn't hard to find the celebration. The fires could be seen from the castle.

Glenna hastened to the forest where the largest fire roared, sending its orange glow high into the trees. She ducked behind a tree as a couple came into view. Both wore masks and naught else. Their passion was palpable, and Glenna had no wish to alert them to her presence.

With silent steps she walked closer to the fire, hidden behind a huge stone. Moira and Frang stood by the fire, their hands raised to the sky while other Druids danced around a large mound of earth.

Glenna had never seen anything like it before. She pushed back the hood of her cloak to see better. Grass, greener than any she had ever seen, covered the mound. Something pulled at her soul and she closed her eyes.

Magic.

Magic flowed pure and fierce from the mound. Her eyes opened at a hissing sound. Bright white light poured from a slit that suddenly opened in the mound. Then many colored lights flew from the slit.

The colored lights soared fast and furious around the Druids and forest. The brightest came to stand in front of Moira and Frang. The white light surrounding the being diminished and Glenna could make out a human form.

The woman was more beautiful than mere words. Her hair glowed like gold that hung past her hips. Her face was perfection, as though an artist had created her. A glance around showed Glenna the bright lights had weakened to reveal many more beautiful beings. This is what Moira had told her about. These beings were from the Otherworld where magic was a way of life and didn't need to be hidden as it did here.

Glenna wanted to speak to one of these beings, to ask...she didn't know what she wanted to ask. She just wanted, nay, needed to be near one.

Chapter Thirteen

Leaves rustled in the darkness. The shadow of an owl swooped down from his perch high in the trees to catch his prey. But Moira didn't return.

Conall stood alone by the stone circle yet he knew he wasn't alone. The presence of others could be felt, but he couldn't see any Druids. They had cloaked the circle somehow. And there was only one reason for them to do that to him.

Glenna. She had been there. Aye, she had probably run as soon as he had bellowed for Moira.

He cursed long and low. Moira drove him daft. He should have known better than to try to gain answers from her, but he had found out something. She knew no more than he did of Iona's whereabouts, but it did little to ease his mind.

The moon, no more than a slit in the inky night sky, hovered above him. He stared hard at it and pondered Moira's words. What prophecy had she spoken of? Oh, he knew of the prophecy surrounding Glenna, but Moira had made it seem as if there were more.

Something kept nagging at the back of his brain, something he should know, but he couldn't grasp it firmly. He needed to talk to Glenna. She would clear his head.

Talk? You don't want to talk. You want to ravish her.

Ah, it was true. Every time he thought of her he imagined her silken skin against his and her mouth open and willing. His cock came to life instantly.

Damn. He couldn't—and wouldn't—go to her in this state. There was no telling what he would do if he did.

The sound of chanting reached him. Beltaine. How could he have forgotten this all-important Druid festival, the most powerful night where the Otherworld could be seen?

The last time he had witnessed Beltaine he had been but a lad of fourteen and had snuck out of the castle. He could still recall the desire that flowed so freely on that night.

His rod swelled. He had Druid blood and powers. He had shunned Beltaine and the other feasts for many years. Maybe it was time he took part.

He might be able to learn something of Iona.

And maybe, just maybe, he might retain some of his honor when all this was over.

With the decision made his legs quickly carried him to the nemeton, a sacred clearing in the midst of a wooded grove, and the Faerie mound.

* * * * *

Glenna's body hummed with a need she didn't understand. Everywhere she looked couples were entwined together while a few Druids stayed by the mound and talked with the Otherworld beings.

The cool caress of the moon on her skin was mystical. The shadows in the forest offered her a promise of primal secrets and mystery. She briefly wondered where Conall was and if he had indeed went to her chamber to seek her out, but those thoughts quickly faded as the fires of Beltaine roared high enough to reach the sky.

Her eyes couldn't stray for long away from the Fae who stood next to Moira and Frang. One man and one woman, but it was obvious by their clothes they were very powerful. The other Fae had ventured off with the Druids into the woods as sounds of moans reached her.

Suddenly the male Fae turned and she could have sworn he looked right at her, but surely that wasn't possible. She was hidden behind many trees. She closed her eyes as the chants of

Druids around the fires peaked. Her soul blossomed and spread its wings. She was home, and nothing Conall could say would change her mind. She was destined for this world and the power it held, and she would fulfill the prophecy or die trying.

* * * * *

Conall felt the pull the closer he came to the nemeton. Sacred fires lit the way to the mound for the Sun on his return from the dead, or winter. For the first time in days Conall could *feel* his power. He stood in the shadows and stared at the magical Fae and Druids, and he had to wonder why he had never ventured here before.

No wonder the Druids found this place so special. The magic radiating from the Faerie mound was strong, and the trees made a natural barrier so the spirits were free to frolic and interact with the Druids.

A giggle to his left signaled a couple mating. Conall's feet took him toward the mound and the stunning Fae who conversed with Moira and Frang, but a naked figure stepped in front of him.

His cock demanded release, and Conall could no more deny himself than he could stop the Druids. Slim, elegant hands reached for him, but it was the blue glow from her eyes that signaled it was a Fae who wished to mate with him.

He opened his mouth to speak, but she held up a hand and shook her head.

No words, he heard whispered in his head.

She leaned closer and pressed her body against his. Her magic engulfed him as she traced her hands down his bare chest.

* * * * *

Glenna turned at the sound of her name. Except no one had spoken. She had heard it in her head. Standing before her was one of the beings who had come from the mound.

He smiled and held out his hand. Without hesitation she accepted it and allowed him to remove her cloak. He then led her deeper into the trees. Her body pulsed with growing need, and when his fingers lightly skimmed her arm, she almost cried out from the pleasure of it.

"What's happening?" she asked, but he wouldn't answer her.

He covered her eyes with his hand and walked behind her. He pulled her back against him. Glenna offered herself up to the magic that flowed through her. It beat strong and sure and she gloried in it.

You are destined for something great, Glenna. Always follow your heart and it will lead you.

His words penetrated her mind. She opened her mouth to speak the same time he removed his hand from her eyes. Her words were forgotten as she stared at Conall embracing a very naked female Fae.

Slowly his head raised and his eyes locked with hers. He turned away from the naked creature in his arms and took a step toward her.

He wants you.

She didn't need her Fae to tell her that. It showed brightly in Conall's silver eyes, eyes that promised pleasure beyond her wildest dreams. His feet moved toward her, her body waited for his touch.

With her heart thundering in her chest, Glenna turned and ran as fast as she could to the safety of her chamber. She slammed the door and leaned against it, the chants of the Druids coming through her window.

She jumped at the knock on her door. She knew it was Conall. She turned on shaky legs as the fire crackled and hissed. She took a deep breath and opened the door.

Conall filled the doorway. He was still bare-chested with his kilt wrapped around his waist. She couldn't catch her breath once she saw the desire in his eyes. He stepped into her chamber, his gaze holding hers firmly. She backed away until she bumped into the opposite wall. His hands came up on either side of her face, stopping any retreat she might have thought of making.

But she wasn't afraid.

His head lowered until he looked her in the eye. "You shouldn't have left the castle."

Glenna blinked. "Wh...what?"

"I didn't expect to find my prisoner so willful. I'd heard MacNeil kept his women meek."

Her mind raced at his words. "He does like his women meek."

"Why did you leave the castle?"

"I have questions that need answered."

He raised a dark brow. "Really? So that makes it all right for you to disobey me? This wasn't a night for you to venture out," he said softly, and ran a finger down the side of her face.

Her knees shook, but she was determined to put up a brave front. Never in her life had she seen a man look as Conall did. It frightened her, but it also thrilled her. His eyes almost glowed, but he was so gentle when he touched her. Her breasts tightened and the ache between her legs grew.

She licked her lips and saw his eyes travel down to her mouth. "Will you lock me in the dungeon now?"

"Nay," he said after several long, agonizing moments. "I'll have your word you won't return to the Druids." He leaned forward and placed a hot kiss on her neck.

Glenna's body cried for more of his touch, and she struggled to keep her hands to herself. "I cannot offer you what would be a lie. Moira is a good woman who does nothing that would harm you."

"This isn't about Moira. It's about you accepting yourself as a Druid," he said, and lowered his head.

As she gazed upon his tormented face she yearned to comfort him. The urge to ask him about his oath to his mother was strong, but she didn't want him to know she had listened in on his conversation with Moira. He needed someone to care for him, and she could easily do that simple task.

Yet it wasn't for her to do. This would never be her home. Oh, she wanted to stay, yearned to stay, but knew she couldn't. If she stayed her feelings for him would become known, and he had already made it clear he didn't want her involved with the Druids. Nay, it wouldn't work. She was a Druid.

He hated Druids.

"I ask once more. Give me your word," he said as he raised his head.

She looked into his silver depths and wanted to cry tears of despair. "I cannot."

"Why the hell not?" he thundered.

"Do what you must, laird, but given the chance I will go to the Druids again."

"Give me one good reason why I shouldn't lock you in this chamber," he said, but his eyes were once again fastened to her lips.

"MacNeil will return, and when he does, I need to be ready."

His gaze jerked to her eyes. "Of course he'll return. He's made that perfectly clear. I'll need something better than that."

"You know why."

And Conall did know why. "Because you're a Druid."

"Aye," she said, tears shining in her eyes.

He could never stand to watch a woman cry. He pushed away from the wall and paced. "And if I lock you in here?" But he knew.

"I'll go to the Druids. MacNeil will never be able to reach me there and your clan will be safe."

And I'll never be able to reach you.

He stopped pacing and looked at her. He never tired of staring at her. Her long dark brown hair hung in waves almost to her waist, and her golden-brown eyes showed such sorrow it nearly broke him in two. "You could always turn your back on the Druids. I can fight MacNeil."

She tilted her head to the side and smiled. "I can't change what I am, Conall."

"I'm not asking you to."

"Aye, you are. Tell me the real reason you don't want me with the Druids."

"I am."

"You aren't. How can you expect me to understand you when you won't share the truth."

The fire roared, sending sparks shooting up the chimney, but he didn't look at it. His eyes were on Glenna and the glow of her skin from the light of the fire.

Of their own accord, his feet walked to her. She licked her lips. He couldn't stop the groan that came from his mouth at seeing her pink tongue, and all the feelings that had flooded him in the nemeton came back in a whoosh. She was going to be the death of him.

He raised his arm and ran his thumb along her lower lip, and nearly fell to his knees when her tongue darted out to touch his thumb. Her chest rose and fell rapidly, and he found his own breathing irregular.

Her eyes burned with intensity. His hand wandered to her neck to thread his fingers into her thick hair. With his hand cradling her head he urged her mouth toward him. The Fae had told him to take Glenna, to make her his. Glenna took that last step that brought her against his chest. The impact of their bodies touching brought a rush of blood to his cock and made his balls jump in anticipation. He wanted to devour her, to love her until the sun peaked across the horizon.

His body screamed for him to take her, to make her his. After all she was his prisoner.

Mine.

Chapter Fourteen

ಬ

Conall pushed his thoughts aside and let himself feel as he brought his other hand to her tiny waist. Her lips parted, waiting for him, her breathing harsh and her heart beating rapidly.

He couldn't stop the satisfied male smile at seeing her thus without touching her. But his body was on fire and he needed to quench it before they both went up in flames.

"Glenna," he whispered, and lowered his head until their lips almost touched. She wrapped her arms around his neck and pulled his head down.

His body sizzled at her kiss, her tongue touching his lips tentatively. He was stunned by her actions but quickly took control of the kiss. He slanted his mouth over hers again and again, sweeping his tongue inside and cupped her buttocks to bring her against his aching rod.

She whimpered when he rubbed his cock against the juncture of her thighs and it only hardened him more, if that was possible. She entwined her fingers in his hair. He groaned as her fingers brushed across his heated skin. Her innocent touch was devastating.

He spotted the bed. Without another thought he backed her up until her legs hit it. She fell back, her dark locks spread out around her.

"Och, lass, you've no idea how beautiful you are."

"Nay. It's you who are beautiful," she said, her eyes shining the truth.

She held out her hand, but he wanted to be sure she knew what she was doing.

"Glenna?"

"Don't," she stopped him. "I don't want to stop feeling like I do at this moment."

It was all the urging he needed. He let her pull him atop her and heard her intake of breath. "Am I hurting you?"

She smiled and shook her head. "I just didn't know you'd feel so good lying on me."

He sighed and laid his head in the crook of her neck. Aye, she was going to be the death of him. Her lips began placing kisses along his neck and jaw. He lifted his head and looked into her eyes. "I cannot let you go."

She only smiled and snuggled closer. Her body was so soft, so tiny that he thought he might hurt her, but when he started to roll off, she stopped him. Desire swept through him swift and sure. He claimed her mouth and her body as his own. His hand found her breast and squeezed through her gown.

Her nipple hardened and his mouth was on it instantly. He didn't lessen his assault until she was writhing on the bed, calling his name. He raised his head and saw her swollen lips and flushed skin, and all this while she still wore her gown.

Saints, he had to stop this. He couldn't do this to her. She needed better than this.

"Nay," she cried when he began to rise from her.

He realized just how bad off she was, probably as bad as himself thanks to the Beltaine. He couldn't leave her like this, and even though it was going to kill him, he would see it through. He raised her gown to her hips while he took her mouth in another kiss.

She sobbed and arched her back when his hand cupped her sex. She was hot and moist, ready for him, but he controlled his raging cock and slipped a finger inside her.

Her hips rose and rubbed against him. He withdrew his finger and slowly entered her again. She moaned and grabbed the covers. His thumb found her most sensitive spot and began to rub as he increased the tempo of his finger.

She clenched around him and cried out as the climax hit her, but he wasn't done. He continued until she was completely drained. Only then did he raise his head. Never before had he wanted only to please a woman, but somehow Glenna changed things.

His body thirsted to plunge into her, needed her with a desire he had never experienced. With his breath coming faster and faster as he controlled his passion, she gave him a smile and traced his lips with her finger. That simple touch nearly sent him over the edge.

Glenna's soft, innocent touch only ignited his passion higher. His tongue yearned to pull her finger into his mouth, to taste more of her flesh. Instead, he closed his eyes and prayed to keep his body under control. When he opened his eyes, he found her fast asleep, a hint of a smile on her sweet lips.

He arranged her gown and shifted her until she was lying on the pillow. He covered her and left before he sank into her and rode her as he had dreamed of doing. He strode to his chamber, and with every step wished he could have stayed with her.

Outside the castle, Beltaine still thrived and would until morning. His chamber door clicked into place, echoing in his lonely chamber. He dropped into his favorite chair and gazed into the fire while his thoughts turned to Glenna.

"A drink, laird?"

For just a moment he thought it was Glenna. He jerked around and spotted Effie. His eyes narrowed. "What are you doing in here?"

"I used to come every night, laird," she purred, and ran her hand along his shoulder.

He stood and faced her. At one time he had thought her pretty, but now there wasn't anything attractive about her. Her once-merry eyes were now tinged with cruelty.

"I didn't invite you."

Her gaze strayed to his crotch. "I know when a man needs tending, laird, and you most certainly need it."

His body screamed for release, but the thought of lying with Effie turned his stomach. "It's been a long time since you warmed my bed. You're the one who refused me."

She shrugged and tossed her head, sending red hair falling around her. "I've changed. I wanted marriage."

"You still want to be married."

"True," she smiled, and licked her lips.

Two years ago he would have had her on the bed already, but a lot had happened during that time. For one he had come to know Effie had one thing on her mind....marriage.

To him.

"Why are you here?" He crossed his arms over his chest and gave her his most stern expression that he saved for his soldiers.

"I've missed your touch. Isn't that enough?" She ran her hands wantonly down her body and walked toward him.

"Nay. I've no need for you in my bed this night."

Instantly her demeanor changed. Gone was the seductress. In her place was a woman scorned. Her lips peeled back in a sneer, and her eyes flashed angrily. "You don't know what you're missing."

He walked to the door and held it open. "Don't come here again without my permission," he said as she glided past him.

A shiver ran down his body. His mother would have called it a sign of something bad coming, but he knew it was nothing more than Effie's cold nature.

But in the back of his mind he wasn't so sure.

He slid the bolt into place. Why all of a sudden did Effie want him again? After a year of her practically ignoring him? He ran his hand through his hair and sat. The fire crackled and sparked and reminded him of Glenna. He blew out a breath and stretched his legs out to cross them at the ankles.

She wanted to live with the Druids. But there was no way he could let her go. He didn't want to think about why he didn't want her to go.

Mine.

Aye, she was his. His body told him that whenever she was near. He longed for her touch, to have her run her hands down his body, to have her surrender herself completely to him.

He would just have to convince her that the Druid way wasn't her way. It would be difficult since Moira would make sure Glenna was reminded that the Druids were in her blood.

His thoughts crept to Moira's words of a prophecy. He searched his memories but could only remember one. The centuries-old prophecy of three Druids bringing about the downfall of the MacNeil had been known to him since he was a lad.

When he had realized he couldn't be a Druid priest, he had shut out everything he had been told, even going so far as to not use his skills. But now he needed to remember everything he had been told.

Something told him it was vitally important that he remember. In the meantime he needed to figure out a way to keep Glenna near. And then it came to him. She had saved Ailsa and himself as well as his entire clan.

He laughed. She didn't even know what that meant to a Highlander, but she was about to find out.

* * * * *

Aimery grinned and stretched his arms above his head. His all-knowing power had picked up on Conall's decision.

Finally the Highlander would admit his soul was mated to Glenna. It had taken him long enough, Aimery thought ruefully.

His smile slipped. But there were still many obstacles to overcome, and some they may falter over. He sighed and rubbed his eyes. How long would he allow his Fae to sit back and watch the humans make the wrong decisions?

Not long. The Druids depended on the Three to save Scotland and their way of life. Time was fleeting in this, even for a Fae.

His eyes narrowed as he picked up on the evil stalking MacInnes Castle. Aye, it was time the Fae investigated this evil.

* * * * *

Glenna stretched and rolled out of bed to find she still wore her gown. Memories of the previous night flashed through her mind and she sank back on the bed. Her heart raced at what she had done, but she wouldn't take it back. Conall had showed her something she hadn't dreamed could be achievable.

She had also seen something she had never thought possible. Faeries had touched her, talked to her. Magic flowed in her veins, and with a little work she would be able to control it so innocents would no longer be hurt.

She smiled and rushed to freshen up, ignoring the sun shining bright through her window and the chatter of birds. She splashed water on her face and brushed her hair before plaiting it.

A look out her window showed Conall training with his men. Then, as if he knew she was looking, he raised his head and smiled at her. Her stomach fluttered, and she turned away before she embarrassed herself. The smiled stayed on her face while she straightened her chamber. She spotted the fireplace and the ash that still smoldered. She drew everything she had learned and concentrated. A spark fluttered and for a moment she thought it would erupt into a hearty flame. Instead it left only a thin trail of gray smoke that wafted up the chimney.

After she had brought Conall's torch to life in the tunnel, she should be able to start this small fire. She squared her shoulders and tried again. Nothing. Not even smoke this time. She rose and stared at the ashes.

Frustration coursed its way through her. How could she be one of three great Druids when she couldn't use her powers? She plopped down on the bed but jumped right back up as fire erupted, sending sparks everywhere.

She grinned. It wasn't exactly as she had planned, but it was a start. Now if she could only learn to put it out.

* * * * *

Gregor leaned his head to the side until he heard his neck pop then he arched his back to stretch out the kinks from sleeping on earth packed with rock.

The Beltaine feast had been impossible to ignore. Something about the Druids and the mystery surrounding them had brought him out.

He had heard tales of how the Beltaine affected people, but he hadn't been prepared for the sight of all the naked glory. He had caught a brief glimpse of Conall and wondered if he had found such a willing bed partner as the one who lay next to him with a grin upon her face. Gregor had eagerly followed her into the woods, but if he had hoped to feel anything more than physical release he had been disappointed.

The woman moaned and rolled onto her side, her red hair ablaze in the morning sun. What kind of man had he become if he wasn't disturbed that the woman had whispered Conall's name instead of his?

This wasn't the life he had hoped for, but what else could be expected after his family had forsaken him, and his clan turned against him? This was as good as it was going to get. He had better realize that instead of becoming concerned with Conall and Glenna's feelings.

* * * * *

Ailsa waited for Glenna in the great hall when she walked down to break her fast. "How did you sleep?" the child asked.

"Wonderful," Glenna answered, and was mighty glad she wasn't prone to blushing.

"Did the laird tell you what I told him?"

"About what?"

"When MacNeil came and I ran into the bailey. There was a cloaked man who said the laird wanted to see me. It's why I ran toward him."

Glenna sat with the bread halfway to her mouth. A cloaked man? There was an enemy inside Conall's castle. She continued to eat and listen to Ailsa chatter about nothing in particular when suddenly Glenna found she couldn't move.

Her stomach clenched and rolled as though it was about to lose its contests. She swallowed and tried to breathe evenly. Panic threatened to envelope her, and knowing Conall wasn't nearby to lend his aide made it worse. Whoever had such hatred for her was very near.

Her eyes drifted around the hall. It was empty except for a lone woman. Effie stood about ten paces from them. And to Glenna's amazement, Effie wasn't looking at her. She stared at Ailsa.

There was no way she would sit and watch Effie harm Ailsa. Glenna thought back to Moira's words and how she could control her body's reaction to the hatred. With every ounce of strength she had, she rose from her seat. Effie's eyes darted away from Ailsa and it freed her.

Glenna grabbed Ailsa and ran from the hall. Once outside, she took in huge gulps of air and leaned against the wall still holding Ailsa's arm.

"Glenna?" Ailsa asked. "Are you all right? You look almost green."

"I'll be fine in a wee bit." She tried to smile but didn't think she managed it by the look of doubt on Ailsa's face.

Without another word Ailsa turned and ran. Glenna started after her and gasped when Ailsa ran through the middle of the training soldiers to Conall. A few words spoken to her father and he strode to Glenna with Ailsa in his arms.

"She tells me you are ill," he said, and gave her a quick look. "You're pale. What happened?"

Glenna moved her eyes to Ailsa, and Conall nodded. He set her down and told her to go play. He straightened. "Did someone say something to you?"

She shook her head. "I began to feel sick and knew someone was close by. When I looked up, Effie was standing near us. Except she wasn't looking at me."

His eyebrows drew together. "Then who was she looking at?"

"Ailsa."

"That child has done nothing to her. Why would Effie abhor her?"

Glenna shrugged. "You would know more than me."

"Effie didn't even know I had a child. There's no reason for her to harbor hate for Ailsa. Angus and I've been looking into who could've shot the arrow."

She thought of the cloaked man Ailsa told her about and of Effie. "Did you find out anything?"

"Nothing. I can't believe someone in my clan would want to hurt my daughter. She's innocent of anything."

"What about Effie?" Something told her the cloaked man didn't fire the arrow.

He chuckled. "Effie wouldn't have done it. It was a man. Ailsa told me of a cloaked man who sent her to me."

"I know. She also told me. I still believe Effie had something to do with it. I don't like the idea of a traitor in your castle."

"Neither do I," he stated. "Women don't get involved in these things. It was the cloaked man, and I'll find him."

But she wasn't so sure, and she had to make Conall realize that.

"Angus is already questioning the clan," he continued. "We'll have the culprit soon."

She lingered until he walked away before she straightened from the wall. She turned to find two women waiting for her, their faces anxious as their eyes darted around them.

"Hello," she said, not expecting them to do anything other than their usual and throw their verbal barbs.

"Hello," said the one with light brown hair braided down the middle of her back. "My name's Grizel and this is Jamesina," she said, indicating the dark-headed woman.

"It's nice to meet you," Glenna said.

"We…ah…heard that you really aren't a MacNeil," Grizel said, and shot Jamesina a look.

Jamesina stepped forward. "Is it true?"

So that was why they were suddenly nice to her. "Aye. I just found out MacNeil took me from my parents."

"Do you know who your parents are?" Grizel's hands were clasped together in anticipation.

"Sinclair. Duncan and Catriona Sinclair."

Both woman gasped and looked from each other to Glenna. "Every clan in the Highlands heard what happened at the Sinclair castle ten and eight years ago," Jamesina said.

Grizel nodded. "Have you found out anything of your sisters?"

Glenna's heart plummeted to her feet. "Sisters?"

"There were three Sinclair daughters. When the castle was raided, it was just days after the youngest was born. It was said the other two were killed."

"I knew nothing of sisters." Glenna's mind struggled to find some memory of sisters or a family but came away empty.

Jamesina touched her arm. "Then you must be the infant everyone thought also died."

Glenna's head began to pound. "Please, excuse me," she said, and turned to enter the castle.

* * * * *

The Shadow pulled the cloak tighter around him. Now was his time to get revenge on Glenna. She would die this time, he thought.

He looked around to make sure no one saw him as he followed her into the castle.

* * * * *

Glenna had wanted answers and she was definitely getting them but faster than she expected. Her feet took her to the stairs and climbed until there were no more. She followed the bare hallway until she came to one of the six towers.

It was a square tower and not in use by the darkness and emptiness. She spotted more stairs and hurriedly climbed them, wanting to see where it led. At the top she found a door, its hinges rusting, and opened it to find herself looking over the loch. The breeze blew the hair out of her eyes, and she raised her face toward it as she walked to the edge and put her hands on the wall.

Why hadn't Moira told her of her sisters? She had a family. Sisters. But it had all been taken from her.

Tears blurred her vision, and hatred for MacNeil swelled in her heart. Not only had he taken her from her parents but he had killed them and her sisters.

All her years she had wondered why MacNeil hadn't shown her compassion or any feeling at all when he claimed to be her father. Things began to make sense now, especially why she had been kept inside the castle walls.

He hadn't wanted her to learn the truth, and he had been right to fear she would learn everything outside his walls. What hurt worse was that Iona had also known. And hadn't told her.

If she was a Druid, did that mean her sisters were also? Obviously MacNeil had known what she was, which is why he had taken Iona. She had to know why MacNeil killed her family, and she knew who held that answer. Moira.

She needed to talk to Moira, and it couldn't wait until tonight. Her decision made, she turned to leave when rough hands grabbed her by the shoulders. Her hands clawed at anything she could find when she saw the edge of the tower coming toward her. A scream tore from her throat. The attacker intended to push her over, but she hadn't escaped MacNeil to be killed so easily.

She squirmed and elbowed him in the kidneys until she escaped her unseen attacker. She turned around to face him, only to find a cloaked figure. The cloak was about to come off his head, but before she got a look at his face a fist connected to her jaw.

The world tilted and spun as she landed with a jarring thud. Those manacle-type hands clamped around her throat. She resisted the blackness that threatened to overtake her to get a look at who was trying to kill her, but she could no longer breathe.

* * * * *

Conall's head jerked up as the scream echoed around the hills. "Glenna," he said, and ran into the castle, his sword still in his hands.

By the time he reached her chamber he shook with trepidation. He flung open the door to find it empty. Gregor and Angus ran into the chamber and looked to him.

"The towers," Angus said as he pivoted and raced to the stairs.

Conall's heart pounded loudly in his ears. That scream repeated again and again in his mind, her terror clear. They reached the top and each took a different tower.

"Here," Gregor called from the square tower.

Conall rushed to the tower door and stopped. Gregor stood looking down at Glenna, her body lying still and silent. "Nay," he murmured, and ran to Gregor's side the same time Angus hurried to them.

Her hair had come loose from her braid and covered her face, but already bruises marred her cheeks and neck. Conall's mind refused to believe she was dead, but he couldn't make his body move to check.

Thankfully Gregor knelt beside her and moved her hair. "She lives."

Conall's legs nearly collapsed at those words. Relief surged through him and made him dizzy. But his elation was short-lived when he realized someone had tried to kill her. First Ailsa now Glenna.

"Who did this to her?" Gregor asked.

Conall bit the inside of his mouth and looked over the edge of the tower to his clan below. People milled around, their faces raised to the tower, waiting to know what happened. "We'll know more once we get her safely to her chamber."

"Something isn't right, Conall." Angus scratched his chin, his face lined with worry. "I thought the clan was coming around after they found out MacNeil wasn't her father."

"What?" Gregor asked. "MacNeil isn't her father?"

Conall shook his head. "Duncan Sinclair was her father."

Gregor whistled through his teeth. "That explains a lot. And changes many things."

"You'll have to explain that later. Right now I don't want anyone else to know what happened. I especially don't want the clan to know Glenna is hurt."

They nodded in agreement. As gently as he could, Conall picked her up and carried her to her chamber. After he laid her on the bed, he looked up to find Moira standing beside him.

"I can heal her."

He looked at Glenna, her body bruised and scraped and couldn't stand the thought of her being in pain. He would suffer through a Druid helping her if it meant she would heal. He nodded and began to wash the blood from the scrapes along her arms and face.

Glenna had put up quite a fight, and he was going to make sure the bastard paid for hurting her. Moira caught his attention. He watched as she prepared her herbs. "How did you know?"

She stilled. "I heard the scream and knew it was Glenna." After a few moments she went back to her preparations. "I'm surprised you're allowing me to help."

"I'm only doing it for Glenna."

Moira looked at him over her shoulder. "You're doing the right thing."

But Conall didn't want to think on that. His mind centered on Glenna and her twitch of pain as Moira spread a cream on her cuts. He stopped her when she brought Glenna a cup of liquid to drink. There would be nothing that passed her lips that would alter who she was.

"What is it?"

"It's to help with the bruises. I've no need of enchantments. Druid blood flows in her veins and no amount of turning will sway her. More powerful beings than me have set Glenna on her course."

He waited for his ability to tell him she was lying, and it took great effort to learn that she wasn't. It frightened him a little to know his power didn't come as easily as it used to, but he didn't have time to think about that right now. He needed to concentrate on Glenna. "We'll see about that."

Moira shrugged and reached for Glenna's head. Together they got most of the liquid down her. After Moira wiped Glenna's face, she touched his hand. "Please let me stay beside her."

He looked into her green eyes and saw the pain reflected there. He nodded quickly before he changed his mind.

Chapter Fifteen

ಬ

Conall held Glenna's hand silently, begging her to wake. It had been almost two days since they had found her and neither he nor Moira had left her side. And during that time he had imagined every way possible to extract his revenge on the person who would dare hurt Glenna.

The fact it was someone in his clan didn't soften his resolve. He had told them he protected her. That should have been enough to keep everyone away from her. He looked up and studied Moira as she stared out the window. For just a moment she reminded him of someone, but he couldn't quite grasp who.

Then he knew. It was the subtle shift in her head that did it.

"When do you plan to tell Glenna you're her sister?"

Moira's blonde head jerked around to gawk at him. "How did you know?"

"Similarities between the two of you. There is supposed to be three sisters. What of the other?"

She looked away. "So you remember the prophecy."

"Aye."

"All of it?" She lifted her eyes, staring hard into his.

"Aye."

She laughed, but it didn't reach her eyes. "Nay, you don't. You must remember all of it, Conall. Your future depends upon it."

"Tell me."

She sighed and took the chair on the opposite side of Glenna. "I cannot."

"You still haven't answered me about your other sister. Since Glenna was taken as an infant I know she's the youngest."

"And I'm the eldest."

He waited for her continue. "You know where the other is?"

"Aye. She's safe for the time being."

"Where?" Something goaded him to ask, though he wasn't sure what.

"Safe. Where Glenna should've been as well. Nothing turned out as it should have that night."

"It's not your fault." Her pinched lips told him she blamed herself.

"I'm the eldest. It's my job to keep my sisters safe. I failed that night. I won't fail again," she said, and turned her gaze to him.

They sat in silence until Glenna murmured. Both jumped to their feet. "Glenna," he called out to her. "Wake up."

"Aye," Moira said. "You've slept long enough."

To their relief her eyes fluttered open. She looked from Moira to Conall and gave him a smile. She groaned and put a hand to her head. "What happened? I feel awful."

"I was hoping you'd tell me," he said, and sat. "You don't remember anything?"

She thought for a moment. She tried to nod, but stopped after a grimace, and said, "Aye, I remember. Someone tried to push me from the tower."

Conall's gut twisted. "Who was it?"

"I never saw a face. All I remember is the hands around my throat. A man's hands, big and very strong. And he was cloaked."

He sighed and gave her a smile when he saw her eyes closing. "Rest. We'll talk later."

"Wait," she said, her brows furrowing. "He had a mark on his hand."

Conall froze. "A mark?"

"I didn't see it clearly, but it was like the tattoos I've seen on some of the Druids. Except this one wasn't black as the others were. It was a vivid blue."

"Sleep," Moira urged, and ran her hands over Glenna's eyes. She raised her gaze to Conall. "Find who did this."

"Only Druids hold those marks."

She straightened and clasped her hands in front of her. "Not only Druids."

"The warriors," he said.

"Find him. He's upsetting the balance."

"Oh I will," he promised.

*****

Two days later he still hadn't come any closer to discovering who had tried to kill Glenna. Frang and the Druids had aided him in his search, but it proved futile. Even the warriors had shown him their hands though it was evident they only did it by Frang's request. Every Druid and warrior in the glen had markings on their hands but there wasn't anyone who had the color mark Glenna saw.

Conall stopped next to Frang. "This changes everything. My ancestors vowed to keep the Druids safe, but I'll not honor that vow with a rogue Druid out to murder my family."

"It wasn't a Druid who attempted to kill Ailsa."

"How do you know?" Conall asked, not masking the anger. "Does your infinite wisdom point to the attacker? My family isn't safe."

"Because he's the high priest."

Conall looked beyond Frang to find a warrior. This man was different. Not quite human. "I don't remember asking you," Conall said, and stepped to the side of Frang. "Who are you?"

The warrior lifted one side of his mouth in a mocking grin. "Dartayous. And if you question Frang, you question all Druids."

Conall sized up the warrior. By the many daggers placed strategically on his body, the giant sword hanging on his hip and a bow of the like he had never seen before, he was every inch the warrior. And one the others looked to.

Dartayous' smile grew when Conall placed his hand on the hilt of his sword. "Finally," Dartayous said, and took a step toward Conall.

"Stop," Frang said to Dartayous. For the first time in his life, Conall watched as Frang allowed his weariness to show. "We'll keep your family safe, Conall."

"I think not. You didn't keep Iona safe, nor my father, for that matter. I'll take care of them myself," he said, and strode back toward the castle.

Conall waited for a parting remark from Frang and was relieved when none came. His vow hung over his head like a dark thundercloud ready to unleash its power. He wanted peace. He wanted a family. He wanted happiness. Was it too much to ask for? He didn't ask for riches or power. His wishes were simple but beyond his reach it seemed.

He had slept little after the attempt on Ailsa's and Glenna's lives. Someone, somewhere wanted them dead. Whether it was the same man or not, Conall was determined to find him. He would tell Angus to increase the questioning of his clan.

Most of his clan, once they heard Glenna wasn't a MacNeil, had readily accepted her. Despite his order to Angus and Gregor, the clan quickly learned what had happened to Glenna. Their outrage warmed his heart.

Conall stepped into the hall and took the chair at the head of the table where Angus and Gregor sat.

"I thought we'd have found the man by now," Angus grumbled, and bit into a fresh tart.

Gregor nodded.

Conall looked around the hall and his men that mingled about. "Our clan numbers near two hundred, Angus. You didn't expect to talk to everyone in two days, did you?"

"Aye," came the surly answer. "It has to be a man."

Gregor nodded again, but Conall recalled something Glenna said. "What if it wasn't?"

Angus and Gregor looked at him as if he had sprouted horns. "A woman wouldn't have that kind of strength," Gregor reasoned.

"Wouldn't she?" Conall asked. "We know a man attacked Glenna, but what if it was a woman who shot the arrow?"

"The two could be related somehow," Angus said slowly.

They all looked at each other.

"Guess we better start questioning the women," Gregor said, and leaned back in his chair.

Conall rose to his feet. "And I know who to start with."

* * * * *

"I already told you I was here in the kitchens when Glenna was attacked."

Conall narrowed his eyes at Effie while she kneaded the dough for bread. As soon as she had seen him, she attempted to run. After a great amount of effort, his power told him she told the truth. Still, he couldn't understand why she was so defensive. "Why do you hate Glenna?"

"She's a MacNeil," Effie said, and continued to roll the dough.

"You know she's not. I know how fast word spreads in a clan."

She shrugged. "She may not be blood to the MacNeils, but she was reared as one of them. It's all the same to me."

He watched as she ripped apart the dough, showing her agitation. Once again he reached out with his power to see if she spoke true, and for a moment there was nothing. Immediately he stopped. "Then tell me why you don't like my daughter?"

Her head jerked up, her eyes round from her surprise. "I...I don't know what you mean."

"Aye, lass, you do." He didn't need his power to know she was lying. "What has that child ever done to you?"

Again she shrugged and continued to beat the dough. "She's just a child. She means nothing to me."

He clenched his jaw and crossed his arms over his chest. "If you keep beating that dough to death it'll never rise." He waited for her to look at him, and when she didn't, he placed his hands atop hers to gain her attention. "Tell me who harmed Glenna."

"I wouldn't know."

Without even trying his power told him the truth. *Liar.* He wanted to throttle her. "Did you shoot the arrow at Ailsa?"

Her blue eyes glared up at him. "You were never supposed to know you had a daughter."

"And I suppose you were responsible for that," he spat. How could he have ever thought her remotely pretty?

She threw the dough across the room, her eyes shooting daggers. "I was supposed to be the one who gave you children."

"I can safely say that will never happen. Now. Answer me. Did you try to kill Ailsa?"

She laughed hysterically. "Nay."

He struggled with his powers but couldn't determine if she lied or not. "I will find out, and if you had anything to do with the attempts on either Ailsa's or Glenna's lives, I'll banish you."

He almost smiled when she went white at his threat. He turned on his heel and walked from the kitchen.

"Well?" Angus and Gregor asked him when he slid into his chair at the table.

"She knows who did it."

"And you didn't make her tell you?" Gregor sighed. "In my clan…"

Conall waited for him to finish. "I thought you said you didn't have a clan."

"I don't. Not anymore."

"Just what clan did ye belong to?" Angus wanted to know.

Gregor quickly changed the subject. "How long are you going to give her to tell you?"

"A day. She's afraid she'll be banished. She'll tell me," Conall said, assured of his victory.

* * * * *

Gregor waited until Angus and Conall left the hall before he made his way to the kitchen. Effie sat on the floor, rocking back and forth. He was about to go to her to seek out information when the hiss of a whisper reached his ears.

Effie jerked her head around and scrambled near the shadows by the back door. Gregor's instinct told him it was the cloaked man they searched for. He could attack now and take him down, but if he did they would never find all the answers.

His conscience warred within him. What he wanted to be and what he was fought a battle that soon had his head pounding.

I'll follow her and see what I find. I'm not taking any side in doing this small thing.

Why can't I chose what's right? he thought to himself. Was he as wicked as his father claimed him to be?

The scurrying of feet signaled Gregor he could no longer debate himself. He quickly followed Effie and the stranger as they made their way toward Effie's hut. Before they reached the hut, the man stopped and bent next to her.

Gregor strained his eyes but could make out nothing of the man other than he didn't wear a kilt. The man moved swiftly in the shadows, and Gregor was awed at his fleetness that rivaled that of a deer.

With his attention centered on Effie, Gregor watched as she ran to her hut. He didn't knock as he strode through her door.

She jerked around, her eyes wide. "Oh. It's you," she said with a smile. "If what you said is true, that you want to hurt Conall, then you can help me."

Gregor didn't respond to her words, but she took his silence as agreement and flung herself into his arms. "I knew you were like me."

Never.

"We'll make a grand pair, you and I, and we'll rule this castle like a king and queen."

He pulled her out of his arms and plastered a smile on his face. Apparently it was good enough for her because she ran to finish packing.

"We must hurry," she said while wrapping some bread. "We can ride through the night and reach MacNeil's by tomorrow."

Gregor's gut twisted. He was getting deeper in this than he wanted, but he didn't have a choice. MacNeil expected him to dupe Conall, and Conall expected him to be a friend.

Conall expected too much. Gregor was friend to no one but himself. *I could change*, he thought inwardly.

Who would ever trust the likes of you? You've proven only coin matters to you.

"Are you ready?" Effie asked. She walked to the door and held out her hand.

Gregor stared at it for the longest time. He could throw her over his shoulder and take her to Conall. They might be able to gain some information out of her.

Might.

But he had given his word to MacNeil, not Conall. Nay, Conall had never asked for his word because Conall knew what he was.

A mercenary.

And who was he to think he could change himself. A plan formed in his head.

* * * * *

Conall just thought Effie would tell him everything. The next morning when he went to Effie's cottage, he found her gone.

"St. Thomas," he bellowed. He turned to the startled woman beside him. "Liza, are you sure it was Effie?"

"Aye, laird," The woman bobbed her white head. "Me eyesight's not that good anymore, but there be no mistaking that red hair of hers."

"Do you often spy on your neighbors?" Gregor asked.

Liza cackled and smiled a toothless grin. "I admit to wantin' to see just who she's meeting from week to week."

"Meeting?" Conall repeated. "She often left her cottage after dark?"

"Every night."

"Did you see anyone with her last night?"

Liza thought a moment. "Can't says as I did, laird."

"Who's she been seen with lately?" Angus asked.

Liza shrugged. "That's why I was lookin' so hard. She's been keepin' him a secret. For a while I thought it was you, laird." She looked at Conall.

Conall squeezed his eyes shut. "Angus, go talk to the castle servants to see if someone saw her this morning. Gregor, talk to the guards at the gatehouse. They wouldn't have let her out in the middle of the night."

He needed to talk to Glenna and Moira. If anyone knew anything it was one of those women. He walked into Glenna's chamber and found her sitting up in the bed. The bruises had taken on a purplish-yellow tinge but were healing faster with Moira's help.

"How are you feeling?"

She smiled. "My head still aches but I'm alive."

He turned to Moira. "I need your help."

"With what?" she asked as she mixed rose petals in water. She then dipped a cloth in the water. After wringing the cloth, she placed it on Glenna's forehead. "This should help the ache in your head."

Conall ground his teeth. He hated asking for Moira's help because he knew she was going to lecture him before she told him anything. "Moira, I'm trying to find the man responsible for trying to kill Glenna. I searched the Druids and warriors at the circle, but none had the blue mark on their hands."

"I know."

"What happened?" Glenna asked, the rose-water cloth forgotten. Her eyes were wide with anticipation as she stared at him. "Do you know who did it?"

He shook his head. "But I was close. I should've pushed her to tell me last night, but I thought she'd come around on her own."

"Effie," Glenna said. "She had something to do with it?"

"Aye. She didn't do it, but she knows who did. I told her if she didn't tell me I'd banish her. I also think she was involved in the attempt on Ailsa."

Moira raised her green eyes. "Effie left."

"Last night," he said. "She's been seeing a man, but no one knows who he is."

"Did she say why I was to be killed?" Glenna asked.

He shook his head. "I was hoping to get that answered today."

"You have bigger worries," Moira said, her face turned toward the window.

"MacNeil will be here soon."

After one look at Glenna, he turned and strode for the door. Effie would have to wait for the moment. The lives of his clan were more important.

* * * * *

Glenna waited until Conall left before she turned to Moira. "My training isn't finished."

"I can train you here. We haven't much time, and you must be ready for MacNeil."

She nodded and replaced the rose-water cloth. It had lessened the ache in her head. If only there was something to lessen the ache in her heart.

"Don't ever give up hope," Moira said.

"Hope," Glenna repeated. "Is there such a thing?"

"Many things can be accomplished with hope."

Glenna sighed and looked at her door, wishing Conall were beside her.

"You and Conall have many obstacles to overcome, but they can be conquered."

"What aren't you telling me?"

Moira lowered her green eyes and pointed to the hearth. "We'll talk later. You must be ready for MacNeil."

* * * * *

"I want every man from the clan questioned. Liza told me the names of the men Effie has seen, so we'll start with them," Conall told Angus.

"This is going to take days."

"Weeks," Conall added. "Take a man with you. You'll need some help."

Angus gave him a curt nod. "We'll find him."

We better, thought Conall. He was chancing a lot by sending his commander away when their greatest enemy would arrive any day, but he didn't have a choice. The attempts on Ailsa's and Glenna's lives left him vulnerable. Ailsa had just been given to him, he couldn't have her taken away, and he couldn't face his feelings toward Glenna.

He kept telling himself he wanted her alive to be able to trade with MacNeil for Iona, but it was more than that if he was honest with himself. Of all the times in his life to find someone as alluring as Glenna, now was the worst.

His mind should be focused on MacNeil not when he would be able to bed Glenna. He had a maniac riding toward him, an unknown attacker hiding in his clan and the powers he had never wanted were failing him.

Yet his mind stayed on Glenna.

* * * * *

Gregor nodded to a guard as he neared the gatehouse. He slipped into the shadows and past the guards like a wisp of wind. A group of men traveled to the forest, and he quickly joined their group.

Once they reached the forest, Gregor slowed his pace until he was able to slip into the thick trees without being seen. He whistled and his horse trotted to him.

"Good, lass," he said, and rubbed the soft nose. The sound of horse hooves reached his ears a second before it came into view.

"You can pet the beast later. We've wasted enough time. We must go now," Effie demanded.

Gregor ground his teeth together in an effort to keep what he wanted to say quiet and swung atop his horse and cast one last glance at MacInnes Castle before he urged the horse into a run.

* * * * *

Glenna leaned her head against the back of the chair, feeling better just being out of bed. She was much improved, but her body and throat still ached from the attack. A glance out the window showed her the sun had set and the moon made its ascent.

"You're looking better by the hour."

She glanced up to find Conall standing in the doorway. "I feel much better thanks to Moira's skill."

Nothing had been said of their night together, Beltaine or the Otherworld beings. Glenna longed to speak to him about it, to make sure it wasn't all a dream.

"Did you and Moira…talk?"

"Of course we did." Something in the way he asked the question got her attention. It was as if he expected something.

He rocked back on his heels, his hands clasped behind his back. "Did she tell you the prophecy?"

Suspicion began to grow in her heart. He was trying to tell her something.

"Why?"

"I'm just curious."

"You're never curious, Conall. You make a decision and never waver from it. You hate all things Druid."

"Not all," he said, and moved to take the chair opposite her. "I don't hate you."

"Only because I saved Ailsa's life."

He took hold of her hand. "You've done a lot more than that."

"Eventually you'd come to hate what I am." She looked away from him, not wanting to see the distaste for what she was shining in his beautiful silver eyes.

"You don't have to be a Druid."

She jerked her eyes to him. "What?"

"My family for generations have married Druids and have had the calling. I didn't follow it."

"Only because you became laird."

A flash of pain flickered in his silver depths. "The point is you don't have to follow the call."

"It's what I am."

In a heartbeat he was out of his chair and kneeling in front of her. "I can't tell you the pain it caused me when I thought you'd died."

"Conall..."

"Shh," he said, and put a finger on her mouth before tracing her bottom lip with his thumb. "We do things differently in the Highlands. You wouldn't know because MacNeil locked you away."

She searched his eyes but couldn't figure out what he was trying to tell her. She opened her mouth to ask but found her breath stolen by a fiery kiss.

He plundered her mouth and sapped her willpower to think. Then his lips softened, nibbling and sucking her mouth. When he raised his head, she could barely string two thoughts together. She raised her eyes to find him walking toward the door.

"Aren't you going to finish what you were telling me?"

He stopped and looked at her over his shoulder, a satisfied smile on his face. "I did."

Chapter Sixteen

ಬ

Glenna rubbed her eyes. "Men."

"What are you grumbling about?" Moira asked as she walked in the chamber.

"Men."

Moira laughed. "Since I saw Conall leaving, I gather you're referring to him."

"He was trying to tell me something. Kept saying I didn't have to follow the Druids' call."

Moira dropped the wooden bowl and whirled around to face Glenna, her face ashen as she clutched her hands to her chest. "He doesn't know what he's saying."

"Then I think it's time you told me," Glenna said, and folded her arms over her chest.

Several heartbeats later Moira sighed and pulled the chair out. "Conall refuses to acknowledge his Druid blood and in doing so is causing great friction within himself."

"He blames the Druids for Iona's disappearance."

"What you don't know is that he wanted to be a Druid priest. His father told him he needed to be laird of their clan. When he made the decision to be laird, Conall closed off all memories of Druids."

"How does that affect me?"

Moira twirled a blonde lock around her finger. "The prophecy that I told you about involves him. It began when he took you from the MacNeil."

Glenna's stomach fell to her feet with a thud. "There's more."

"Aye. He'll be a part of the three Druids who bring down the MacNeil."

"Who are the other two?"

"Your sisters," she answered after a lengthy pause.

The room spun around her at Moira's words. "So. It's true."

"You know?" Moira asked, the doubt shining in her eyes.

"A couple of days ago two women welcomed me after they learned I wasn't a MacNeil. When they asked who my real parents were, they told me that the Sinclairs had three girls. Where are my sisters?" she demanded.

Moira visibly swallowed. "One has been raised in another household just as you were."

"And you haven't brought her here yet?" She was furious. Just thinking her sister had to suffer what she did was like a knife in her heart.

"She has no idea the people aren't her real parents and they've treated her wonderfully. We didn't want to send for her until the time of the prophecy was near."

"Has she been trained as a Druid?"

Moira nodded her head.

"When is the prophecy to begin?"

"Soon," Moira answered, and bent her head.

"Soon," Glenna repeated. "Don't you think you ought to get her?"

"It isn't time. There are other things that must be taken care of first."

Glenna stared hard at Moira, waiting to hear more. Finally she said, "And my other sister?"

"She was raised by the Druids," Moira said, and slowly raised her face.

Glenna blinked and rose to her feet on shaky legs. "You? You're my sister?" Anger and jubilation at finding her family mingled together. "Why didn't you tell me?"

"You needed time," Moira began. "You didn't take finding out MacNeil wasn't your father very well, and I didn't want to push too much on you at one time."

"What else are you keeping from me?" Glenna knew she was screaming but anger had taken hold. Out the corner of her eye she saw the fire roar to life but she couldn't stop it.

Moira stood and held out a hand to her. "Nothing. I wanted to give you time to adjust."

"You're lying." She knew it just as she felt the air in her lungs. There was much more Moira kept secret, and Glenna simply couldn't stand to be kept in the dark any longer. It would stop.

Now.

Rage blinded her. She heard Moira screaming, but couldn't see what was wrong. It wasn't until a heavy weight hit her and brought her to the floor that the rage departed.

She turned and saw men stamping out fire that had spread from the hearth. Moira's gown was scorched, her face black from the smoke.

"What happened?" Conall asked.

Glenna turned her head and found him lying atop her. She needed to get away, to find some peace. "Get me out of here."

Without a word he stood and gathered her in his arms. He walked her outside to the battlements and gently set her on her feet. He stood beside her, his arms crossed over his bulging chest, as she stared at the stars.

She needed to talk, needed to explain what happened. "Moira told me of my sisters."

"Ah."

She smiled despite herself. Ever the laird, he would give nothing away. "You knew."

"Aye, but she asked for me not to tell you. Is that why you became so angry?"

"She's keeping something else from me. I was very angry at finding out she kept her identity from me, but when I asked her if there was anything else and she said nay..."

She turned toward him. "I've never felt such rage. I couldn't control it."

"Like how MacNeil used you?"

"Much worse."

"You were an innocent."

She raised her eyes. "Not so innocent."

"Tell me," he urged, and brushed her hair back.

She licked her lips. "I got angry at MacNeil because he wouldn't let me go out with the other young girls. He wouldn't explain why, just refused. The next thing I knew the barn caught on fire and a young lad was burned very badly. He almost died."

"But he didn't," Conall said.

She didn't protest when he enveloped her in his arms. She needed his strength and much more if she let herself dream. To have a family of her own and a man that would stand beside her was a dream she had had for a long time. He had even listened as she told him her deepest, darkest secret and he was still beside her. He would make a great husband.

"Why haven't you taken a wife?"

He started at the question. "I hadn't found her yet."

"What happened in my chamber reinforces my need to be with the Druids." She pulled out of his arms and missed his warmth. "I'm a danger to everyone. I must learn to control it."

"You'll learn to control it."

"I need the Druids for that. They call to me. Beltaine proved that."

"Beltaine calls everyone," he argued.

"Those Otherworldly beings gave me my powers for a reason. To deny it would be to deny my heart."

Conall had known this was coming from the moment he walked into her chamber and saw it nearly ablaze. Moira had been correct in saying Glenna's powers were great. But he couldn't let her go. The thought of going a day without seeing her beautiful smile, without touching her dark tresses, without hearing her musical voice saying his name wasn't something he could do.

"Don't fash yourself about it now. You gained a sister this night. Rejoice in that."

"I did, didn't I?"

He was rewarded with a smile that could have breathed life into the dead it was so beautiful. And she was his.

Mine.

She didn't know it yet, but the time was drawing near when she would.

* * * * *

The Shadow threw his goblet across the room. Not only had he been unable to kill Glenna, now he must reevaluate his plans. His mind simply refused to believe Moira was her sister.

How had he missed that? It had been well hidden among the Druids. He had to keep Glenna and Moira apart. They had strength in numbers, and his time was growing short.

The Fae had suddenly developed an intense interest in the goings-on of MacInnes Castle. He must kill Glenna as soon as possible since his plan to toss her over the battlements was interrupted by the arrival of Conall. Without Glenna he could convince Moira to come to his side.

* * * * *

MacNeil raised his face to the moon and sighed contentedly. Soon. Soon everything he had always wanted would be his. It would show the MacInnes that a feud with the MacNeils meant only death. He would have MacInnes Castle as his new fortress, and he would rid Scotland of every last Druid.

A thought in the back of his mind kept nagging at him that things might not go to plan, but he pushed it away. He had killed Glenna's sisters. The prophecy could no longer come to pass.

He had done it because his father had been a coward. He had looked up to his father until he had refused to kill the Sinclair girls just because they were the daughters of the woman he loved. MacNeil hadn't hesitated in murdering his father to ensure his life would continue. It had been humiliating to have his father in love with a woman half his age.

A rustle behind him drew his attention. He turned slowly and saw the woman stretching beneath the covers. A bare leg crept out of the covers and the tip of her breast peaked out as she raised her arms above her head. She would be the one to give him an heir. The others had lacked the resilience. Only a strong woman would give him the sons he needed.

"Come to bed," she purred, and held out her slim hand.

Aye, he thought. Between this minx and Effie he was sure to conceive a male child who would eagerly accept his place.

* * * * *

Glenna stood outside the stone circle, the morning mist hanging on to the tree branches as the sun rose higher through the impenetrable gray clouds. She had gotten little sleep the night before as she wondered about her sister and the life they could have lead had MacNeil not interfered. She bit her lip.

After what she had done to Moira, she doubted she would be allowed in this morn, but she had to try.

In her mind she called to Moira's. In a blink the stones yielded and parted. Glenna walked into the circle and spotted Frang, who stood waiting for her.

"Where's Moira?" A quick glance around showed her things had changed within the circle.

The animals still milled about, the songs of the birds filled the air, plants still bloomed their vibrant color and the water still sparkled crystal clear. But it was the occupants who showed the real change. The Druids weren't as active as usual, and she noticed several men she hadn't seen before.

Most wore kilts while a few dressed in breeches, and one in particular drew her attention. He was clad in a leather jerkin and breeches with black boots that reached his knees. He was armed with a sword, bow and arrow as well as several daggers she saw protruding from his belt and boots. And only God knew what else was hidden in his clothing.

But it was his eyes that stood out. There were the clearest, brightest blue she had ever seen, almost the same type of blue of the Fae. When she realized he was staring at her as boldly as she was him, she dropped her gaze, but not before she spotted a Fae next to him.

"They are protectors of Druids. We call them warriors," Frang said as he guided her deeper into the circle.

"But Druids have special powers."

"Not all. You are special, blessed by the Fae. Most are like Conall and can easily be killed. So the protectors watch over the others."

She nodded. "I need to speak to Moira."

Frang stopped and turned toward her. "Don't be angry with her. She did what she thought was best."

"I'm no longer angry. I want to apologize."

He gave her a smile and gestured with his hand toward a cluster of boulders where Moira sat with her back to them.

Fear encased her as she walked toward Moira. She was scared of losing her sister after just finding her. Scared Moira wouldn't want to be her sister now. But most of all she was scared of being alone again.

She stood behind Moira and watched as she scribbled on a parchment, deep in thought. Moira was everything she wasn't. Self-assured, in control of her destiny, poised, tall, beautiful and loved. Tears sprung and rolled down her face, but she didn't wipe them away. She loathed herself for what she had done and prayed it wasn't in her nature to lash out like that at others.

I don't think I can ever apologize enough for what I did.

Moira turned and stood. "There's nothing for you to apologize for. I shouldn't have waited to tell you."

"You *heard* me?"

"I did," she smiled, her green eyes sad. "We've a connection being sisters. I didn't know about it until recently though, or I would've done anything in my power to get you from MacNeil years ago."

The tears flowed freely now. She shook her head to try to stop Moira's words. "Don't. We can't change the past."

"We can only make the future," Moira finished with a smile, and held out her arms.

Glenna rushed into her sister's arms and reveled in the love and safety. After a few moments, she lifted her head. "Did the fire hurt you?"

"I'm fine," Moira said, and brushed at her own tears. "My healing abilities have grown over the years."

"We're strangers really, with so many years to catch up on."

"And we've got the rest of our lives to do it."

"After we fulfill the prophecy, that is."

Moira's face lit into a smile. "Then let's not waste any more time."

* * * * *

"When are ye going to tell her?"

Conall looked up to find Angus standing before the table. He lifted his goblet and drained the rest of his ale before he glanced around the hall to see who might be listening. "What are you talking about?"

Angus sighed and sat in the chair beside him. "When are ye going to tell Glenna she's to be yer wife?"

"How did you know?" He hadn't told a soul so there was no way Angus could know for sure.

"I see the way you look at her. If I'd find a lass like her I'd make her me wife quick."

Conall shook his head but couldn't stop the grin. "She wants to live with the Druids."

"After the display in her chamber, I think she's making the right decision."

He didn't tell Angus the real reason. That Glenna had made this castle a home, and for the first time since his mother's death he had some hope. Now that hope was fading once again. "I can't let her go."

"Well, that only affirms she's yer mate."

"If only it was that easy."

"She's one powerful Druid, and she doesn't even know it."

Conall groaned. "Aye."

"What are ye going to do?"

"Convince her we're meant to be together and then convince her to forget about the Druids."

Angus slowly gained his feet. "Ye ask the impossible of her. Maybe ye should reconsider how ye view the Druids. If ye want her, ye'll have to accept what she is."

"That I can't do, my friend."

"Then ye don't deserve her," Angus said.

"I have oaths I must consider."

"Ye aren't going to be able to carry through with both oaths. Even if ye marry her it doesn't solve yer problem."

"I know," Conall sighed. "My oaths are my bond, my honor. If I don't honor them I'm not fit to be laird."

"Ye're consumed by those oaths and aren't using yer head," he said, and walked away.

Conall stared after his long-time friend lost in thought until he recalled Angus might have news for him. He gained his feet and strode after him. "Hold, Angus," he called.

Angus stopped and waited. "Change yer mind already?"

Conall looked pointedly at him. "What did you find from the men? Any of them know of a man who's been with Effie, or who might have shot that arrow at Ailsa?"

"Nothing. Everyone I've talked with so far said Effie refused to see any of them. She told them she'd found someone else."

"Did they know who the other man was?"

"Nay. I'm still working on that. There's a lot of men in our clan."

"Ailsa?"

"Nothing there either. I never thought it'd be this hard to get information from our clan. I do not like this, Conall. Not one bit. I never thought I'd see the day that we had a traitor among us."

"We must hurry. I've a bad feeling about all of this."

"Me as well."

Conall set out to find Gregor, hoping he had found something from the gatehouse guards. But Gregor was nowhere to be found.

He decided to try the gatehouse. After grilling the guards, he was surprised to find Gregor hadn't questioned them. Suspicion began to gnaw in his gut like a hungry rat. Gregor had told him MacNeil's plan, but he had also protected him and the people in the castle. Was Gregor Glenna's attacker? Could he have been so wrong about someone that he let a potential threat into his clan without even knowing it?

* * * * *

Gregor looked straight ahead and ignored the plaintive looks from Ailsa. For the first time in his life he had considered murdering a woman. Effie hadn't bothered to tell him they would be taking Ailsa, but then again, Gregor really didn't have an option. He had chosen his lot in life, and he would see it through.

He was good at what he did. One of the best and that is why he made as much coin as he did. But a child?

After that first look into Ailsa's silver gaze that was identical to Conall's, Gregor had refused to glance at her again. If MacNeil wanted Conall's ire, he would definitely have it now. Only a maniac would kidnap a child.

"Please," Ailsa whispered.

Gregor clenched his teeth together at her scared voice.

"Shut up," Effie screeched, and slapped Ailsa on the side of the head.

Without hesitation Gregor reached over and plucked Ailsa from Effie's horse and sat her in front of him. "Hit her again and you'll feel my hand," he warned Effie.

"Just whose side are you on?"

"You know who's paying me. Just don't hit the child again."

Effie stared at him a moment before nodding and falling behind him as the lane became more narrow.

Gregor could feel Ailsa trembling. "Whatever happens, keep your mouth shut, Ailsa." He wrapped his arm around her and memories of his sister surfaced like a flood.

She would never have let him take this course, but then again, if he hadn't killed her he would never have left the clan. He should have listened to his instincts when they told him to run from Conall.

Being at MacInnes Castle had done something to him. Something he didn't want to think about. Changed him somehow and he didn't like it. Not one whit. He would have to be sure to push aside these emotions being around Conall brought out. But first he would have to make sure Ailsa returned home safe and sound.

His conscience couldn't afford another death on it. His sister's had done enough damage for one lifetime.

Chapter Seventeen
෮

The late afternoon sun sank behind the mountains. Glenna quickened her pace back to the castle. She decided against venturing into the caves despite her recent victory over them. Besides, nature gave her solace.

She stopped to admire one of the giant oaks and stroked its gnarled trunk. It beckoned to her. She placed both hands on the tree and could have sworn it heated beneath her. Memories of the clearing and the mound filled her.

Her feet moved of their own accord, taking her to the clearing. She had thought it was beautiful with the moon shining down upon it, but it was just as lovely in the sunlight. Butterflies abound here. All different colors and sizes twittered over the mound as if waiting to be let in.

The mound itself was a brighter green than the surrounding grass, and Glenna could almost swear she could feel its magic. The power within her pulsed as she neared the mound. Hesitantly, she fell to her knees and gently laid her hand on the raised ground. Had she dreamed Beltaine and the Fae?

Surely not.

A songbird perched on an oak near the mound called to her. Glenna rose and walked to the oak. She smiled to the little bird before it flew off. She had been gone a long time, and she didn't want Conall worried.

With one last look at the oak she turned and found Conall lounging against a large boulder, twirling a blade a grass in his fingers. His raven locks hung loose about his bare chest and blew in the soft breeze that trickled through the branches.

But it was the half smile that stole her heart. "I didn't expect to find you here."

"I missed you," he said, and winked.

She tripped over her own feet, surprised at his playfulness. But she couldn't hide the excitement in her voice. "Really?"

His smile broadened. "Aye. How was your day?"

"Wonderful. I'm getting to know my sister, and I can tell you it's quite fantastic to have a family." It wasn't until after the words left her mouth that she realized her mistake.

He tried to hide the flicker of sadness from her, but she saw it nonetheless. "How much longer on your training?"

No matter how hard he tried, he couldn't hide the fact he hated her coming here, and the exhilaration at finding him waiting for her waned. "Why are you doing this?"

His smile dropped and his forehead wrinkled in confusion. "Doing what, lass?"

"You don't like me coming here."

"Here?" he asked, and looked around. "This is a nemeton. It's sacred to the Druids, which is why Beltaine and the other feasts are held here."

"Sacred?"

His eyes twinkled. "I can't believe Moira didn't tell you."

"She doesn't know I was here during Beltaine."

"The raised ground is what some call a Faerie mound."

She gasped. "That's where the beings came out. How can I reach them? I want to speak with them."

"Only on a Druid festival does the veil between the worlds thin."

"Oh," she said, and turned away only to feel Conall's hands close around her shoulders.

"An old wives' tale says if you circle the mound nine times to the right you call a Faerie to your side," he said into her ear.

She whirled around to face him. "You know so much. Why don't you put aside your hatred and join the Druids?"

He sighed loudly. "I cannot help how I feel, Glenna. I am who I am."

"As am I," she countered. "You can't stand the sight of Moira."

"Not true," he interrupted. "I don't like what she is."

"You'll come to feel the same about me despite your vow."

He shook his head. She held her breath when his hand rose to caress her jaw. "Never," he vowed before he lowered his head.

The kiss seared her. Her body came to life under his hands as they roamed over her. She moaned and wrapped her arms around his neck for fear he would end the kiss. He crushed her to him. His cock pressed hungrily into her stomach. With a boldness she didn't know she had she reached between their bodies and wrapped her fingers around him.

He groaned and deepened the kiss until she had no thought other than to be one with him. With one flick of his wrist his plaid fell away. She let her eyes roam freely over his body.

There wasn't anywhere on his body where muscles didn't bulge she realized as her eyes traveled from his head to the tips of his toes. A glance near the boulder showed her his boots. She wanted to ask how longed he had waited for her but didn't want to ruin the moment.

He stood silently, waiting for her to finish her inspection, but she would have been content to gaze at his wonderful body all day, inspecting every inch of him with her eyes, hands, mouth and tongue.

She raised her eyes and found his gaze intense and searching. She knew what he wanted, and she wanted it nearly as badly as he. He smiled seductively when she began to divest herself of her clothes.

When she stood as naked as he, she found he had spread his plaid on the ground. He held out his hand and she didn't hesitate to accept it. It seemed right for their joining to be outside amongst the trees and nature in this nemeton where magic rained around them.

As soon as she stepped onto the plaid, he had her flattened against him, his mouth hot, slick and demanding. The contact of skin on skin was just what her body needed, craved. Neither could get close enough to the other.

She groaned when he broke the kiss. He lowered her to the ground and lay beside her. She looked into his silver eyes, amazed at the desire burning fiercely for her. His fingers skimmed her skin as he traced patterns across her stomach then around her breasts to her neck. She closed her eyes and basked in the feel of his hands bringing her to life.

Conall stared down in wonder at the woman beside him. Even knowing how he felt about the Druids and his oath she was giving herself to him. "You're mine."

"Oh aye," she agreed, and ran her hand down his chest.

Her touch, so soft, so gentle, set him afire. She was his mate. She was *his*. And after tonight she couldn't run from him anymore. He had to make her see the Druid way would take her nowhere but away from him.

He bent his head and took a nipple in his mouth. It hardened as she gasped and raked her nails across his shoulders. He ran his hand up and down her legs, learning the feel of her, and when he lightly pushed them apart, she opened for him.

She whispered his name as she wound her fingers in his hair. He gloried in her skin, the color of cream, flawless except for a mole on her left hip. With his tongue he traced a path from her breast to the mole and kissed it.

He settled himself between her legs to give himself better access. She smoothed the hair from his face and gave him a heart-stopping smile. He kept eye contact with her as he bent his head and licked her navel.

Her eyes crinkled at the corners at his playfulness, but when his tongue swirled around a nipple, her eyes rolled back in her head, her breath coming in gulps. He focused his full attention on her breasts, sucking, squeezing and licking until she rubbed her hips against his abdomen. With his hand between their bodies he found her moist and ready. He couldn't stand to wait another moment. He had to be inside her, to make them one.

Now and forever.

He guided the tip of himself inside and her eyes flew open.

"Aye," she whispered, and brought his head down for a kiss.

His heart nearly burst. He slowly entered her, and to his surprise she wrapped her legs around him. "The stretching may hurt a wee bit."

"I trust you," she said, and lightly nipped his shoulder.

He lifted himself onto his elbows and stared into her golden-brown depths. "Look at me," he told her as he pulled out then sank into her.

She gasped and clung to him. He held her tightly, wishing he could take away any discomfort.

"Is it over?"

He nearly choked. "Not even close."

He moved within her. She gasped and matched his tempo, and she sent him to new heights, heights he had never come close to with other women. He rolled onto his back and pulled her on top of him.

"Do what you will, lass," he told her, and saw the fire light in her eyes.

Glenna stared down at the man who was giving her the first taste of heaven. She ran her hands down his sculpted chest, marveling at the many scars that crisscrossed his abdomen.

She leaned forward to kiss him and got her first taste of him inside her while in control. She sat straight and rotated her hips, glorying in the feel of him inside her, so hot and hard. His hands cupped her breasts. She sucked in a breath at the exquisite pleasure he gave her.

With her hands upon his chest for support, she began to move back and forth and soon their bodies glistened with sweat. Just as she was about to find her release, he sat up.

"Not yet," he murmured in her ear, his hot breath causing chills to run up and down her body.

He moved behind her and spread her legs. With one thrust he entered her, and she nearly came undone. He placed on hand on her hip and with the other found her sex. His thumb swirled around her pearl while he continued to pump in and out of her.

Before she knew it the climax claimed her. She shattered into a million pieces, but he didn't stop. He thrusts became harder and deeper, and when she thought she couldn't take any more, she climaxed again just as she heard him shout his release.

They collapsed together, their bodies entwined, and she knew she would never experience anything like this with another man.

"You're mine," he whispered.

She smiled and snuggled closer. "Aye."

"Forever."

When she didn't answer, he pulled her away from him. "You are mine."

She licked her lips, her stomach fluttering at the possessiveness in his gaze. If it wasn't for their doomed future she would be celebrating what was between them. Such sweet sorrow, she thought. "Aye."

"Then why are there tears in your eyes?"

"Because it can never be."

"I won't let you go. We Highlanders take what we want, and I want you. You will be mine, Glenna."

She let him squeeze the breath out of her. It was no use arguing. He would soon realize theirs was a hopeless situation. Until then she would take these moments and keep them locked in her heart forever.

* * * * *

Aimery celebrated a toast with his fellow Fae. Conall had finally taken Glenna. Their souls had taken the other in. There was no way for either of them to turn from the other.

The merriment soon died as word spread of Ailsa's kidnapping.

"MacNeil," Aimery hissed. They needed to know what was going on at MacNeil's castle. "Send the scouts."

* * * * *

"I'm not sure why you came today. Your mind sure isn't here."

Glenna ducked her head. Moira was right. Her mind was elsewhere, and that was in the forest making love to Conall with the sun's rays falling around them. "I'm sorry."

She had snuck away again that morning or had thought so until she spotted Angus watching her from the battlements. They had started her training as soon as she had arrived in the circle.

Moira wrapped an arm around Glenna's shoulders. "Don't fash yourself. All will work out."

"What do you know that I don't?"

Moira shrugged. "Just keep the hope in your heart. Conall is right. You are his and he is yours."

Glenna was mortified. Somehow Moira knew what had transpired in the woods last eve. "Please don't think less of me."

"Nay," Moira said, and held up a hand. "There's no need for you to say anything. I'm not your judge. You let your heart guide you, and it guided you to your mate."

They shared a smile, and Moira cleared her throat. "Now let me tell you the prophecy. Most only remember a part of it but there's much more."

"Why don't people know all of it?"

Moira shrugged. "For whatever reason they might have thought it wasn't important. MacNeil is one of those. He only knows the beginning."

> *In a time of conquering*
> *There will be three*
> *Who will end the MacNeil line.*
> *Three born of the*
> *Imbolc, Beltaine and Lughnasad Feasts*
> *Who will destroy all at the*
> *Samhain, the Feast of the Dead.*

"The rest says:

> *One who refuses the Druid way*
> *Inherits the winter and in doing so*
> *Marks the beginning of the end.*
> *For the worthy to prevail fire will*
> *Stand alone to vanquish the Inheritor,*
> *Water will soothe the savage beast, and*
> *Wind will bow before the tree.*"

Glenna blinked. "I don't understand. What does it mean?"

"We have our theories."

"But you won't tell me," Glenna surmised. "If it's about us, then I must be fire and Conall the inheritor."

Moira merely stared at her.

"You must be wind," Glenna continued. "But how will you bow before a tree?"

Moira shrugged. "I don't know."

"You don't know? Have you asked Frang?"

"Aye."

When Moira didn't say more, Glenna sighed. "He refused, didn't he?" At Moira's smile, she laughed. "We have to figure it out on our own?"

"Aye. If we know ahead of time things might not work out like they're supposed to."

"But if we don't know, then how can we make the correct decisions?"

Again Moira shrugged. "We must do our best."

Glenna thought for a moment. "If I'm fire and you're wind, then our sister is water. What's her name?"

"Fiona."

"I can't wait to meet her. How long until she comes?"

"Not long now," Moira said prophetically.

Suddenly she remembered Moira urging Conall to recall the prophecy. "Does Conall know the prophecy?"

"Aye. He and Iona were told as children. He just doesn't recall all of it."

"What if he doesn't remember in time?"

Moira raised sad, green eyes. "Then all will be for naught."

"Then I'll help him remember," Glenna vowed.

But she found it more difficult than she thought. Conall didn't wish to discuss anything Druid and in fact refused.

"What are you afraid of?" she asked him that evening after their meal as they sat before the hearth.

He jerked his head around to face her, his eyes leveled and in control. A warrior's stare. "I'm not afraid of anything."

"Then talk to me."

His nostrils flared, showing his anger. He rose and strode to her chair until he was standing over her. "Just because we shared our bodies doesn't mean I'll spill my secrets."

A knife plunged into her heart at his cruel words. She watched silently as he strode away. She had been a fool to think she could reach him, a fool to think she mattered at all to him.

After all she was the very thing he hated.

Chapter Eighteen

Conall tossed and turned, the bed much harder and smaller than before. He couldn't get the image of Glenna's soft brown eyes full of hurt out of his mind. It hadn't been his intention to lash out at her like that, but he had become angry when she had continued to ask questions about his past and the Druids.

She wanted something from him, but he couldn't give it to her, whatever it was. The part of his past that involved the Druids was closed off and would never to be opened again.

Never. She had to understand that if there was to be anything between them.

The wind howled viciously outside and soon swirled in his room. He tried to rise but found he couldn't move. His eyes grew heavy and the urge to sleep was strong. He couldn't resist whatever pulled him under.

He was falling. Blackness surrounded him when he chanced a glimpse. The world tilted and swayed until he couldn't tell if he was sitting or standing. Then everything came to a halt.

He opened his eyes to find his mother sitting beside two small children. The scene brought back a flood of memories on that sun filled day. He walked closer, wanting, nay, needing to hear what she said to him and Iona for he recalled the day but not her words.

And somehow he knew those words were very important.

"Now listen very carefully," his mother said, and looked around to make sure others weren't listening.

He strained to hear what she said, but she had bent her head next to the children. He walked until he stood next to her, but by that time she was finished telling her secret.

"That prophecy will come to pass during your lifetime. You, my children, will be a part of it. It's important that you never forget what I've told you."

Suddenly his mother's image dimmed. He reached out for her. "Nay," he yelled, but it was too late. She was gone, and when he opened his eyes, he was back in his chamber.

He leapt from the bed, his breath coming in gulps as he struggled to understand what had just happened. He searched his mind for that memory but still couldn't recall her words.

Many times his mother had sat them down and told them great stories of Druids and what they had done for the good of people. Oh, he knew the prophecy that Moira spoke of, the one that frightened MacNeil, but there was more. Moira had said as much. But no matter how hard he tried he couldn't grasp the threads of that memory.

His head began to ache at the base of his neck. He ignored the pain, the need to find that memory overcoming everything else.

* * * * *

Moira collapsed against Frang, her body limp from using her powers. "I showed him the memory, but I don't think it helped."

"You did all we can do," Frang said, and helped her to sit up as he wiped the sweat from her brow.

"This may all come to naught if he turns Glenna from us."

"Your sister is strong." He handed her some wine. "Drink. You'll need your strength."

She took a sip and set the wineskin down. "It's not enough. I need to see what's going to happen. If only I could've foreseen Effie leaving."

Frang sighed deeply. "We all want that, but that isn't something we have power over. We see what is shown to us, and the rest we're left to wonder about like other people."

"I have a very bad feeling Effie is involved deeper than we'd like her to be."

"Aye, lass," he said, and nodded sadly. "I'm afraid that's the truth of it."

She sat up, ignoring her weakened body, at hearing his words. "You've seen something. What is it?"

He looked at the ground for several moments before he spoke. "I'm not sure exactly. It's all very unclear."

Her stomach constricted. If Frang couldn't determine his visions, then they were worse off than she imagined. With so many enemies lurking around Glenna and Conall, it was hard to know where to start.

* * * * *

Glenna looked at the sky from her window to see dark clouds gathered overhead, ominous in their numbers. Thunder rumbled in the distance and lightning streaked across the gray morning sky. The fog was so heavy and damp it nearly choked her. She stuck her hand out the window and a fat raindrop landed on her open palm.

She had lain awake for most of the night as images so fleeting she couldn't name whether it was night or day, haunted her. A storm was coming for sure, and it wasn't the clouds gathered in the sky.

"MacNeil," she said.

Fear grew in her belly. A prickling sensation settled along the back of her spine. Something had happened. She whirled around and ran from her chamber to Conall's.

She pounded her fists on the door. "Conall."

The door flew open with him glaring down at her in his naked glory. She forgot to breathe. The prickling along her spine reminded her why she was here. She jerked her eyes from his body to his face. "Something's happened."

"Let me get dressed," he said.

But she couldn't wait. The fear continued to grow until she thought her heart would burst. She ran, letting her instincts guide her. To her astonishment it led her to Ailsa's chamber. She took a deep breath and flung open the door.

"Saints help us."

The bed was empty. The small chest at the foot of the bed had been opened and its contests thrown around the chamber. Chairs were overturned and the tapestry hanging on the wall was now in two pieces.

Conall ran up behind her.

"Nay," he roared, and strode to the bed. He kneeled beside it and laid his head on his arms.

Footsteps fast approached. Angus was the first to reach them. "Not wee Ailsa," he said as he surveyed the chamber.

Conall didn't move as more of his men filled the chamber. "I thought she was with her grandmother all day," Conall said. "I never thought..."

His grief and the look of utter helplessness sparked something within Glenna. She knew she could help, to find out anything so Conall would stop blaming himself.

She fled down the stairs and out the castle. Rain drenched her and nearly blinded her it came down so heavily, but she forged on until she came to the cave entrance. This time fear of the darkness and spiders didn't slow her. She didn't stop running until she came to the stone circle and found Frang and Moira waiting for her.

Moira wrapped a blanket around her and brought her inside the circle where, amazingly, it wasn't raining. "I was hoping you'd come."

"You know what's happened?" Glenna asked.

Frang shook his head. "We know *something* has happened, but we're not sure what."

"What good are the visions if they can't help?" Glenna asked, anger making her voice shake.

"Even I can't call a vision forth," Frang said. "As much as I'd like to control them, I can't."

Glenna let the tears fall unheeded. "Someone's taken Ailsa."

Moira wiped at her tears. "We'll do what we can to find her. Won't we," she said, looking pointedly at the high priest.

"Aye, we will," he agreed.

They watched as Frang walked a few paces away. He closed his eyes and held his arms wide.

"What's he doing?" Glenna asked.

"He's trying to find Ailsa. It doesn't always work though," she warned.

They sat quietly for what seemed like ages before he fell to his knees, and they rushed to him.

He looked at Glenna, his blue eyes shining bright. "MacNeil has her."

Glenna turned to Moira as determination filled her. "And I know what must be done."

"MacNeil will come here for you," Moira said after a moment. "There's no need for you to go to him."

Glenna no longer wondered how her sister knew her inner thoughts. "I must warn Conall."

Frang put his hand out to stop her. "Whatever you do, don't tell him you plan on trading yourself for Ailsa."

"Why?"

"He won't let you go, Glenna. You're his now."

She mulled over his words before she gave a nod of acceptance. She looked at her sister. "You've taught me well. I'll be ready."

* * * * *

Glenna found Conall with his head in his hands in the great hall, a goblet of mead in front of him. She sat in the chair next to him and touched his arm. His head jerked up and the emptiness in his eyes tore at her heart.

"You're wet," he said, looking at her gown and hair.

"I went to talk with Moira and Frang."

"I talked with Frances MacBeth. She said Ailsa never came this morning. She thought I had changed my mind about allowing Ailsa to see her."

"MacNeil has Ailsa," she said, hating to bring him such news.

He closed his eyes. "Why did they take her? She's just a child."

"You know why."

Slowly his eyes opened. "I promise you, MacNeil will never get near you."

She smiled at his disregard to the vow he made to his mother. Frang had been right. She would have to devise a plan herself if Ailsa was to come home alive. "I know."

His face twisted with anger and grief. "I'll kill him this time," he bellowed, and slammed his hand on the table, causing the goblet to overturn.

Red liquid poured over the table, and Glenna stared at it, transfixed as he barked orders to his men. It was then she noticed the absence of someone.

"Where's Gregor?"

Conall rubbed the back of his neck. "No one has seen him."

She knew what he was thinking, couldn't help thinking it herself. "I can't believe he was involved in Ailsa's kidnapping."

"There's no other explanation," he hissed. "I've tried to think of anything that would put Gregor in a good light, but there just isn't one. When I saw Ailsa gone, I knew he did it."

The rest of the day Glenna spent in her chamber, devising her plan. She would have to deceive Conall, but if Ailsa and Iona would be returned to him it would be worth it.

Everyone mourned the loss of another clan member and stayed in their homes. She was surprised when a knock sounded on her door. "Enter," she called, and turned to find Conall leaning against the doorframe.

He hadn't shaved and two days' growth of beard covered his face, shadowing his jaw. He strode to her, stood her up and wrapped his arms around her, squeezing her until she could barely breathe.

His pain seeped into her, and she knew of one way to ease the ache. She rose up on tiptoes and brought his mouth to hers. She nipped his lips and ran her tongue along his mouth until he moaned and slanted his mouth over hers.

The kiss was ferocious in its intensity and it scared her a little. His hands found her nipples through the gown and tweaked them until they hardened and her breasts swelled.

Hunger, hot and demanding enveloped her. She needed to have him fill her again, to have them become one. His hard body against her was gentle and insistent as he touched her.

He was her savior, her champion...her mate. Aye, and for the love in her heart she would give up her life for him.

She became mindless with desire as his mouth pillaged her lips. His hands ran down her back to cup her buttocks before he picked her up and wrapped her legs around his waist.

Her hands helped him shove her gown out of the way before his fingers found her. She cried out when he slipped a finger inside her. Her body surged around him and she moved her hips, desperately seeking the release he promised.

"By the saints, you're ready for me," he said into her ear, his warm breath on her skin doing crazy things to her.

She hung on while he shifted their clothing, her mouth licking and kissing his neck and face, his spicy scent sending her senses into a riot.

"I must have you now," he said, and pressed her against the wall.

With one shift of his hips he filled her. She threw back her head as rapture surrounded her. Her heart and body soared, welcoming his strength, his passion.

Conall buried his face in her neck as he pumped in and out of her. Her soft body pressed against him heightened his awareness of her, and her heavenly mouth drove him to distraction.

But it was her hands that had the most power. They skimmed across his heated skin, her touch light and urgent, and left a trail of need in their wake. She touched every part of him, even his soul.

He couldn't get enough of her touch, indeed he longed for more while he still had her in his arms. Her nails dug into his back as she climaxed and raked across his shoulders. He lost what little control he had when she spasmed around him.

With one thrust he buried himself to the hilt. He threw back his head and let her drain him. He stumbled to the bed and fell back on it while still inside her. She lay atop him and lightly ran her fingernails down his arm. She had managed to soothe the beast within him, and she didn't even know it.

"What are you thinking?" she asked, and moved her head to look at him.

He smoothed her unbound hair from her face. "You. I love your dark hair."

She laughed. "You're brooding."

"Aye," he agreed, and rolled until he faced her. "There's something I need to talk with you about."

Her smile died at the seriousness of his tone. "What is it?"

"I...we..." He never knew it would be so hard to tell her he wanted her for his wife. "You're mine."

Her golden-brown eyes twinkled in the candlelight. "You keep saying that. Just what does that mean?"

"It means I want you for my own. I want you for my wife."

Her eyes grew large and her mouth opened and closed several times before she leapt off the bed. "You don't know what you're saying."

"I do, lass." He slowly rose and watched as she struggled to lower her gown that had gotten tangled around her waist. "Let me help you."

"Nay." She held a hand up to keep him away. She finally gave up and sunk into a chair, her hand on her forehead. "I cannot be your wife."

"Why?"

Her look told him just what a lack wit she found him. "Because I'm a Druid. Or have you forgotten?"

"But you don't have to be." He knelt before her. "We are meant for each other. Do you deny that?"

She shook her head, the firelight causing her hair to look almost red. "But what of the prophecy."

"It won't matter. I'm going to kill MacNeil." Something in the way her eyes flickered alerted him that she was up to something.

"What of your oaths? Aye, Angus told me. You swore to protect the Druids with your life, and you swore to your mother you'd find Iona. I'm your only hope of getting Iona back."

"I don't need you to remind me of my oaths. I've laid awake every night thinking about them."

She gently touched his face with her fingertips. "I'm the one who can make MacNeil return Ailsa and Iona to you."

"There's nothing you could say or do that would convince me to let you go to MacNeil. I can get Ailsa and Iona back without you taking their place."

She smiled ruefully. "I know."

"Then you agree to be my wife?"

Silence. Then, "Let me think on it."

He pulled her up and took off her gown. "You can think on it while in bed."

* * * * *

The Shadow watched Frang and Moira talking together. His time had run out. The Fae were now among them and who knew where else. It had been hard to plaster a smile on his face when the Druids had been informed that Conall and Glenna had mated, that their souls were now bound together.

To everyone else it meant the prophecy was leaning in their favor, but he didn't need to destroy MacNeil to have all the power. He just needed Moira beside him.

His hands yearned to roam over her milky-white skin and see if the curls betwixt her legs were the same golden hue as on her head. Never before had a woman called to him like Moira, and she didn't even know what she did to him.

But she would soon.

Once her sister was out of the way. It would be easy. Soon Glenna would make her sacrifice and exchange herself for Ailsa and Iona. He chuckled and it earned him a disapproving look from the priestess beside him.

He ignored her and thought of Iona. Conall had much to learn of his sister, and it was doubtful he would like what he found out.

A prickling on his neck indicated a Fae was behind him. He turned and found not a Fae, but the Druid warrior Dartayous, staring at him with a suspicious glint in his feral blue eyes.

He nodded to the warrior and turned back as Frang began to speak to them.

Chapter Nineteen

∞

"Ah Gregor," MacNeil said, and rubbed his hands together. "I wondered when you'd return. Although, I must say I don't appreciate you killing one of my soldiers."

Gregor ground his teeth together at the mention of the soldier. What had MacNeil expected him to do when the soldier had attempted to take Ailsa from him? But he was determined to get through this without showing MacNeil his temper.

Instead of letting his mouth get away from him he shrugged.

MacNeil cackled. "You even succeeded in gaining Conall's trust. But there seems to be a wee problem."

Gregor crossed his arms over his chest and let his eyes roam the sparse hall. MacNeil Castle was a dismal comparison to Conall's, and it irked him that Conall intruded on his thoughts at all. "What problem would that be?"

"Effie tells me you've turned."

"Really?" Gregor sighed and leaned against the wall. He had known showing Ailsa compassion would make Effie suspicious. "Since when did you start believing women?"

"You're a mercenary, Gregor. You have no feelings. That's what I told her. Just make sure you don't cross me. You wouldn't want to be on my bad side."

Gregor bit his tongue. It wouldn't do to kill MacNeil because then he would never get paid and he needed that coin. He had waited long enough for it.

MacNeil stood, his hair grayer than Gregor remembered. He also noticed MacNeil's nose hadn't been set straight. At a wave from him, Gregor followed him into a private chamber. MacNeil reached into a chest. He turned and jingled the weighty purse.

Gregor clenched his hands in anticipation. His money. He reached for it, but MacNeil pulled it away.

"Ah, ah, ah," MacNeil said, and shook a finger at him. "Your job isn't quite finished."

It was all Gregor could do not to growl his frustration. "What do you want now?"

MacNeil's smile vanished, his eyes deadly. "You'll return to Conall."

"By now he knows I took Ailsa. There's no way he'll trust me again."

MacNeil shrugged. "You'll think of something. Once I arrive for Glenna, you'll attack inside. I want Conall to see that I've done what others couldn't."

Gregor held out his hand, his other ready to clasp the hidden dirk in his belt. "I want my coin. Now."

"I knew I liked you," MacNeil said, and threw the purse at him.

Without delay, Gregor walked from the castle and mounted his horse. "I know you're tired," he said to his mare. "I am too, but it looks as if we won't get any rest."

He gathered the reins and turned the horse. As he did he spotted Effie, a gloating smile on her face. For she knew, like him, that Conall would never allow him back into his trust and would most likely kill him.

Gregor sighed. He pulled back on the reins and sat for a minute. A commotion behind him told him MacNeil had come into the bailey. There was a need in him to reassure Ailsa that she would be returned to her father, but Gregor couldn't do it. He had made a similar promise to his sister.

He wasn't meant to guard such precious things as lasses. Fate had proven that to him with his sister's death. It was showing him again that he didn't have what it took to keep them safe.

"Gregor," Ailsa cried.

Out of the corner of his eye he saw Effie holding her back as she struggled to break free. Tears coursed down her dirty face, reminding him of his sister. He squeezed his eyes shut and for the first time in years begged whatever god might listen to help him. He had a job to do, and he had no other choice but to do it.

With a slight nudge of his heel he set his horse into a gallop and shut his ears to Ailsa's cries for his help.

MacNeil had waited patiently while Gregor sat atop his horse. He had half expected the mercenary to grab Ailsa, but, alas, he had ridden on.

"I thought he might hurt me," Effie purred next to him.

"I was hoping he'd try. It's been a while since I've seen some action."

Effie's eyes widened in alarm. "You'd have let him hurt me?"

MacNeil laughed and patted her cheek. "Of course not, my dear," he lied. "Gregor would've taken down many of my men, but I'd have stopped him from getting to you."

"I love your power." Effie rubbed herself along his side.

"Did Gregor not satisfy your appetites?"

She jerked straight. "How... Nay, he didn't."

MacNeil lifted a brow. So she wasn't going to deny it. She wanted power and he wanted sons. They would make a good pair, the two of them. "Come."

"What of the brat?"

He looked down at Ailsa who still stared after Gregor's retreating back. With a motion of his hand he called a guard to him. "Take her to the east tower and lock her in."

"Aye, my laird." The guard reached down and tossed Ailsa over his shoulder.

MacNeil raised his head and found Ailsa's gaze directed at him. It caused a chill to run down his spine. Children shouldn't know such hatred, he thought, but ignored the warning of her look.

* * * * *

The Fae hiding among the humans split into two groups. One group followed Ailsa to ensure her safety and the other followed Gregor.

Time was of the essence to the group who trailed Gregor as they sped across the country. They each knew their duty, and in order to keep the prophecy safe they would do whatever was necessary to ensure that the people involved stayed out of harm's way.

* * * * *

Conall couldn't believe his eyes. He leaned over the battlements and blinked. Below, Gregor sat atop his horse and asked for entrance. It had been almost five days since Ailsa had been taken, and in that time Conall had been busy readying his men.

"Your audacity amazes me," Conall yelled down. "Do you wish to die, then?" He itched to challenge Gregor.

Gregor raised his blond head. "It's not like you to act rashly. Don't you want to know who took Ailsa?"

"You took her."

"Nay. I followed the ones who did."

He reached out with his powers but couldn't tell from this great distance if Gregor was deceiving him or not. Damn. He liked Gregor, but could he take the chance if he was wrong and Gregor had taken Ailsa?

"He did help you when MacNeil arrived," Glenna said as she came to stand beside him. "If he did follow whoever took

Ailsa, he wouldn't have had time to tell you where he was going."

Conall stared into her golden-brown eyes. "That's what I'd like to believe."

"If you're not sure have Angus keep watch on him. As much as you hate to use your power, I think now would be a good time."

He shook his head and let her think it was his dislike of his power that kept him from using it. With a wave of his hand he motioned for his men to allow Gregor entrance.

"Come," he said, and took her hand. "Let's find out if it was Effie who's caused us so much grief."

They reached the bailey as Gregor dismounted and handed his horse to a stableboy. Conall expected him to say something, but Gregor stood there, arms over his chest, and waited.

"I don't think this should be done in front of the entire clan," Angus said, and brushed past Gregor, knocking his shoulder.

Conall grinned at Glenna when he noticed Gregor's jaw flex in agitation.

Once they were seated in the great hall and drinks brought, Angus leaned forward. "Well? Don't just sit there, man, tell us what happened before I slit yer throat."

Gregor sat with his legs stretched out in front of him, his hands clasped together. He shrugged. "You'd be sorry if you tried, Angus." He turned his black eyes to Conall. "Where would you like me to begin? When I first arrived and started bedding Effie, or when I saw her take Ailsa and followed?"

Conall stood and paced. "I knew it. So you were the man she was bedding but no one could put a face to."

"Aye. She offered, and I'm not a man to pass up such an offering. It wasn't until later that she let it be known just how much she hated Glenna."

Conall turned and looked at Glenna. She put her hands on the table and licked her lips. "Is she the one who tried to kill me?"

Gregor shook his head. "She laughed about it but admitted it wasn't her. She does know who did it though. I tried to get the information but couldn't."

"You never found out all she knew?" Conall demanded.

"I was getting there. It would've looked strange had I shown such interest in Glenna. Effie is very jealous of her."

Conall sat down and raked a hand through his hair. He had been probing Gregor to see if he was lying or not, but so far he hadn't been able to tell. Gregor had always been hard to read, but now he was completely closed off. "Tell me about Ailsa," he said, needing to know she was safe.

"She wasn't harmed. I made sure of that. Effie took her to MacNeil. He intends to use her in exchange for Glenna. She'll be safe."

"How did you find this out?" Glenna asked.

"I knew Effie had been acting strangely, and when Conall asked me to question the guards, I went to find Effie first."

"You should've sent someone for me," Conall said, anger growing at Gregor for taking matters into his own hands. After all, this wasn't Gregor's family, but his.

"It was my plan until I saw her taking food from the kitchens. I followed her the rest of the day as she gathered her things. I assumed she planned to leave the clan."

Angus slammed his hands on the table. "Ye're lying." He turned his bushy red head to Conall. "Isn't he?"

Conall read the urgency in Angus' expression. He shrugged and turned to Gregor, hoping Angus wouldn't push. "Finish."

Gregor stared at Angus for a moment before he continued. "That night I confronted Effie when I saw her sneak into the woods. She told me what she was about, and I knew in order for Ailsa to stay alive I had to act as though I were involved."

Conall's head began to ache as he listened. In all his years he had taken his power for granted. Now when he needed to know if Gregor was lying for the safety of his clan and he couldn't tell anything.

Nothing. And the harder he tried the more his head pounded.

"You went back to the MacNeil?" Glenna asked. "After what you did, I'd have thought you'd be dead."

Gregor's lips rose a little on the sides. "MacNeil thinks he's sent me back here to help him when he comes for you."

"Conall, why in the name of St. Peter haven't ye said anything?" Angus bellowed as he rose to his feet. "Ye've done nothing but sit there. Is Gregor lying or not?"

Conall couldn't meet Angus' gaze. Instead he kept his eyes on the floor. "I need to think."

Without another word he rose and mounted the stairs. He knew Glenna would follow. Once he entered his chamber, he walked to the window and gazed at the night sky.

Glenna licked her lips and shut the door behind her. "Conall? What is it?"

"I can't tell if Gregor is lying."

Now she understood why he hadn't said anything to contradict Gregor. His anxiety and fear hit her like a stone wall. She shrugged it off and walked to him. "What are you going to do?"

"What can I do?" he asked, and whirled around to face her. "I need his sword arm, but at the same time he could betray me. He is a paid mercenary after all."

She placed a hand on his shoulder. "Maybe you're trying too hard to read him. Ask me something."

His silver gaze rose to her eyes. "Will you give up the Druids?"

She swallowed, afraid he would ask something along those lines. "Aye," she lied.

For the longest time he stared at her then shook his head. "I cannot tell," he said, and placed his hands over his face. "Now, when I need it the most, it has abandoned me."

"You abandoned the Druid way a long time ago," she reminded him.

His head snapped up, and his eyes flashed angrily. "So what do you suggest I do?"

"Trust your instincts. You like Gregor. Do you think he's capable of doing MacNeil's bidding?"

He shrugged his big shoulders and slumped into a chair. "The truth is I don't know much about Gregor except what he's told me. I want to believe he's a good man, but not many mercenaries are."

She waited for Conall to say more, but he was lost in thought. Silently she exited the room and made her way to Moira. Mayhap they could help in this tangled web that had been woven around them.

Especially why Conall was no longer able to use his ability. Strange how her powers had grown while his had weakened then departed all together.

Chapter Twenty

Once Glenna stepped into the forest, it calmed her. But she couldn't take the time to sit down by the ancient oaks and quiet her restless soul. People's lives were at stake.

She moved into the stone circle, ever amazed at the serenity and quiet beauty within the stones. Her eyes drifted until she found Moira sitting with some young children. Moira raised her eyes and nodded. After a few words to another Druid, she stood and made her way toward Glenna.

"Something troubles you," Moira said, and reached for Glenna's hand.

Glenna closed her eyes as Moira's cool hand enclosed hers. "It's Conall."

"Rest your mind," Moira said.

At once the many worries that swirled through Glenna's head disappeared and peace reigned once again. Chaos was replaced with order.

She opened her eyes. "What did you do?"

"Helped you empty your mind. You can't help anyone if your mind isn't clear. That's a very important lesson to learn. If you can clear your mind, MacNeil, nor anyone for that matter, can have control over your emotions."

It was just another reminder that she had much left to learn. So much to learn, so little time. Would she be ready for MacNeil? Could she risk the lives of Conall's clan?

"I'll have to work on that."

"So," Moira said, and sat on a smooth rock. She patted the space beside her for Glenna to sit. "Conall has lost his power. I wondered when it would happen."

"How did you—"

"When I cleared your mind that was one of the strongest worries within you. I couldn't help but know."

Glenna sighed and fought back the sting of tears. "Is there anything he can do?"

Moira shook her head. "I'm surprised the power has stayed with him this long. Once a person turns from their Druid blood, their mind refuses to let them believe they have any special ability."

"In other words, it's only been recently that he's truly turned from the Druids, despite his words."

"Exactly."

"I don't understand why now."

"Don't you?" Moira asked, and gazed steadily at her.

Then it hit Glenna. Her mouth opened in denial. She licked her lips. "It's me?"

Moira nodded. "He wants you, but you are the one thing he despises above all."

"A Druid," Glenna said. Sadness encased her. She had known it was true, and despite his objections it was happening.

"And while you've learned and grown in your power you are a reminder of what he couldn't be."

She thought about that a moment before she asked, "Can his power be returned?"

"Only if he has a reason to believe in his Druid blood again."

"That will never happen," Glenna said. She had hoped to be able to bring Conall some good news.

"Don't ever say never. Can't you think of one person who could give him a reason to believe?"

Glenna stared into her sister's green eyes. An image of her and Conall laughing and holding a baby flashed before her.

She shook her head and looked to Moira. "It's the truth he wants me for a wife but only if I give up the Druid way."

"Don't give up hope," Moira cautioned. "Without hope there is nothing. Do you love him?"

"So much I would die for him."

"Let's hope it doesn't come to that."

* * * * *

Conall stood atop the round tower and watched as Glenna walked into the bailey from the caves. He didn't need the sight to know she had been to see Moira, and by the look of her downturned face he knew the news wasn't good.

With a sigh he looked out over the land that had been the MacInnes' for hundreds of years. Since the beginning his ancestors had accepted and hidden the Druids from harm, and the laird was expected to marry one.

Yet he could not.

He couldn't deny his soul yearned to have Glenna by his side for the rest of their lives, but his heart refused to disregard she was a Druid. It was just as well. The Druids had all but been driven out of Scotland, and the rest hid in fear of their lives. Nay, he wouldn't follow his ancestors. His wife wouldn't follow the Druids, of that he would make sure.

On their own, his eyes found Glenna, her slight form standing next to Angus. She was perfect for him. His mate. And his heart and soul knew it. She did as well if she would listen to her heart.

She would be his wife, and he would rule his clan without his power. He didn't need his power. His instinct would lead him.

* * * * *

Glenna looked around the bailey as Conall's clan readied themselves for an invasion. Emotions were strung tight at the prospect of MacNeil's arrival.

Many of the clan still didn't look upon her favorably, but they didn't harbor hatred in their hearts any longer. Of that she was most grateful.

"He's lost it, hasn't he?"

She looked up at Angus, his hazel eyes creased with worry. "Lost what?"

"He can't tell if Gregor is lying, can he?"

She didn't know whether to tell Angus the truth or not, but in the end she knew he would find out. "Aye, it's gone."

He stroked his red beard and followed Gregor with his eyes. "Then we'll have to make sure it's returned."

She couldn't stop the smile that spread across her face. "Exactly my thoughts."

"Go talk with him. He may say he doesn't need the power, but I know he's troubled more than he'd like to admit. He's brooding atop the east tower. I'll stay here and make sure Gregor doesn't run off."

"Gregor won't leave, Angus. Trust me on that."

"I wish I could, lass," he said sadly.

* * * * *

By the time Glenna reached the top of the east tower her breath came in great gulps. She leaned against a wall and struggled to even her breathing after the many winding steps she had made.

She looked up and found Conall staring at her. One shoulder was braced against the stone and his arms were crossed over his muscular chest. A gust of wind whipped around them, and she longed to see his hair unbound and blowing in the wind.

"Did Moira have anything to say?"

She ignored his question and pushed from the wall. "Angus was right. You are brooding."

"I'm not brooding," he said, and turned his back on her.

She came to stand beside him and looked over the land. "I've never been to this tower. The loch is my favorite to look over, but this view is magnificent."

He cast her a brief glance.

"The loch gives me a bit of solace but watching your clan is quite intriguing. I think I'll come up here next time to watch you train."

"You watch me train?"

Glenna could have bitten her tongue off. She had never meant for him to know she watched. "On occasion."

He laughed, the sound pleasing to her mind and spirit. "I don't need my powers to know you're lying."

"Oh all right. So I like to watch," she confessed. But she would never tell him how much seeing his muscles ripple caused her heart to pound and her body to sweat.

"Then I'll have to do something extra for you from now on."

She chanced a glance and found a genuine smile upon his handsome face. Her eyes found his lips and she forgot everything except how they felt on her body.

"Don't look at me like that," he warned softly.

She put what she hoped was an innocent look on her face, and asked, "Like what?"

"Like you want to devour me."

She flipped her hair over her shoulder as she had seen a woman do yesterday and looked back at the bailey. "It just so happens I do want to devour you."

Disappointment shot through her when he didn't say anything. Obviously her attempt at being coy didn't work. She would definitely have to work on her flirting skills, she thought sadly.

Suddenly his hard body pressed behind her and his mouth did delightful things to her neck while his hands grabbed her hips and pulled her against him.

"You can't say things like that to me and not expect me to do something," he whispered before his tongue traced her ear.

She shivered. Her body longed to be joined with him again. She was only half a person when she was parted from him. "Oh, I most certainly want you to do something."

"You'd tempt a saint." He turned her to face him. "All right. I admit. I was brooding, but I'm not anymore. I can never brood when you're near."

She smiled, her heart doing a little leap. "Then it's a good thing I came up here."

"You came because you saw Moira."

His silver eyes held hers and waited. She had wanted to put off telling him, but she could see he would probe until she confessed all. "Aye, I saw her. I wanted to know why you'd lost your ability."

"Because I've turned from the Druids."

"That's right."

"Then explain why it's stayed with me until now? I've turned from the Druids long ago," he said, and ran his hand through his hair.

She hated to see him hurting and debated on whether to tell him all of what Moira said. In the end, she knew she had to tell him everything. "Moira says it's because of me. I'm a reminder of what you wanted to be."

"Can I get it back?" he asked, ignoring her words.

"You want it back? I thought you hated it?" She wouldn't have been more surprised if he had have said he wanted to become a Druid.

"I never wanted it, but now that it's gone..."

She reached up and placed her hand on his cheek. "You're a great laird. You don't need any special ability to lead your clan, and they know it."

His face softened into a small smile. "I hope you're right."

"Of course I'm right. A Druid is always right."

His smile broadened before he claimed her lips.

* * * * *

That evening after supper Conall sat with Angus and went over their strategy against MacNeil.

"I know Glenna is going to try something."

Angus nodded and looked at her sitting by the hearth. "I think ye're right, but next to locking her in her chamber, I don't know what to do."

"I'll have to think of something. Are the men prepared?"

"Aye. The people have also been warned and are ready for any surprise attack."

Conall nodded. "We need to get as many inside these walls as we can."

"It's being seen to."

He looked close at his friend. Angus wanted to say something. "Just spit it out."

"We could use Frang and Moira's help on this."

"Nay."

"Ye aren't being reasonable, Conall," Angus hissed. "MacNeil will do everything to get what he wants. Yer father would've asked for their help."

"I'm not my father," Conall said.

"That's for sure. Ye've made a great laird, but don't be making mistakes now just because ye hold a grudge against the Druids."

Conall thought on Angus' words after he left. He was mixed up inside, and what had seemed right yesterday didn't today. His clan needed a laird who could make decisions based on their welfare. He didn't know if he was that man anymore.

Glenna grabbed his attention when she rose from her chair by the fire and walked toward him. Her smiled dropped the closer she came to him.

Her small hand came to rest on his shoulder. "Decisions will be hard to make without a clear mind."

"I suppose the Druids taught you that." As soon as the words were out his mouth he regretted them. "Glenna, I—"

"Shhh," she said, and put a finger on his lips. "It's true I learned this from Moira, but it's the truth regardless of who taught me. You're making this more difficult for yourself."

"How's that?"

"You can't see anything other than your hatred of the Druids. It's the truth I don't know how you can stand the sight of me."

He longed to push aside his past and think clearly, but he couldn't. He was a laird, a warrior. Not a Druid.

For long moments he stared into her brown depths. She had said she would give up the Druids, but had she really told him the truth? He ached to tell her of his feelings but the words tangled in his throat.

"I need you."

"And I need you. I always will. Please remember that."

He grabbed her hand as she started to leave. "I've lost everyone. I couldn't stand to lose you as well."

"I'll always be here. Besides, you will have Ailsa and Iona returned to you. Of this I promise."

He stood and turned her face up to his. "I need a promise from you. I want you to stay away from MacNeil. I will get Ailsa and Iona home, but I can't if I'm concerned about you."

"I can't give you that promise. You need my help. Even if you won't admit it."

*****

Aimery looked down at Moira and wished he could ease the pain within her. Despite the calm the stone brought the Druids there was restlessness in her that couldn't be calmed. Instead, he focused on the task at hand. He inhaled deeply and looked around the stone circle and the Druids.

"The traitor is very near. He's also powerful enough to cloak himself so even I cannot say who he is."

Frang's eyes widened. "A Druid?"

"Glenna said as much when she talked of the tattoo," Moira said.

"I know. I just didn't want to believe." Frang leaned against a stone. "Few Druids have the power to shield themselves from the Fae. Not even I can manage it for an extended period of time."

Aimery put his hand on Frang's shoulder. "Don't blame yourself. Besides, I'm not so sure it is a Druid. This man has done everything to cover his tracks. But he needs to be found soon. He's already attempted to kill Glenna once. I'm afraid he'll do so again."

"What about Moira?" Frang asked.

Moira shook her head. "I'm safe. The traitor has had plenty of opportunities to kill me while in the circle. He hasn't, which leads me to believe this has nothing to do with the prophecy."

"Oh, but it does," Aimery stated. "Either he doesn't know you are Glenna's sister, or he thinks Glenna is an easier target."

Frang sighed. "Either way isn't good."

"I have many of the Fae already among you, and they shall stay until this is over."

Aimery turned to Moira. "Make sure Glenna is prepared."

"She'll be prepared," Moira stated.

Aimery smiled and nodded. Moira held the bulk of her power back, but there would come a time when she would unleash its full force and he would be sure to be there to see it. "I have faith in you."

Moira's eyes jerked behind him.

Aimery didn't need to turn around to know Dartayous stood there. The warrior was the best among them, which was why Aimery kept him here. That and another reason, he thought with a smile as he looked at Moira. "Just in case the traitor does come after Moira I want Dartayous nearby."

Moira's eyes narrowed. "I can take care of myself."

Aimery hid a smile and turned his head to see Dartayous' brow raised in question. "True you can, but Dartayous knows what to look for. I need you to concentrate on Glenna. Let Dartayous look after you."

He knew Moira wanted to object, but Frang had put his arm around her. For now she would accept Dartayous, and that's all that mattered.

Chapter Twenty-One

The night had claimed the sun yet sleep would not claim Glenna. She had gone over every conversation she and Iona had had in their brief time together. In all the warnings Iona had said nothing about Glenna's heart being ripped in two. Her heart ached with the decision she had to make, and she didn't know how much longer she would have before Conall would demand an answer.

She almost laughed at the irony of falling in love with her kidnapper. From the very beginning she had trusted him with her life and just recently her heart.

But one question remained. Would he turn her over to MacNeil for his sister and daughter? He had said nay, but if it came down to it she wasn't so sure. After all, he had made a vow to his mother, and everyone knew how Conall thought of a vow made.

There was only one thing she was sure of, and that was Conall wouldn't kill MacNeil. Her heart knew it for fact, but she also knew it was folly to try to tell Conall. He was a laird, a warrior, and would never listen to a woman, much less a Druid.

And she was both.

Restlessness claimed her. She couldn't look at her bed without thinking of Conall. A walk would soothe her body as well as her mind. It wasn't until she stood on the cliff above the loch that she knew what had called her out of her chamber.

Conall.

He swam with strong, sure strokes, the water glistening off his body in the moonlight. He rose up and shook his head, sending water spraying everywhere.

She tried to swallow, but couldn't. He raised his arms and smoothed the hair back from his chiseled face. His creased forehead showed he was tormented just as she was.

Her feet brought her to the edge of the loch. Her hands had never moved so fast in shedding her clothes. His head swiveled to her when she stepped into the water.

No words were spoken as she walked to him. Their need for the other suffused the air. He took hold of her when she was close enough and dragged her against his chest. Their bodies came together frantically, searching for comfort only they could give each other.

Their mouths collided frantically in an attempt to calm their racing blood. She couldn't get enough of him, never did. His hands moved across her naked body as though he knew every inch of her.

She leaned back as his mouth trailed kisses down her stomach. The stars winked down at her in the cloudless sky, and the full moon surrounded them in its white light.

Conall gazed down at the woman in his arms, her dark hair spread across the water. Her eyes turned to him and he wondered at her thoughts. So much pain. Would there ever be a time when he could love her and not have to worry about MacNeil or the Druids?

"Don't think," she whispered. "Let us love each other and forget for a brief time the world around us."

Right now he didn't even care if she could read his mind. He wanted her with a need that only increased each time she was in his arms. The time would soon come when she would have to make a choice, but he already knew he couldn't let her go. And that was the trouble.

He had taken her so he could get Iona, and now Ailsa, returned. But that would mean losing the woman who had his heart. A woman who had shown him how to have hope for the first time in many months, a woman who had let him dream of a family and love. What would that woman think of him if he turned her over to MacNeil?

But he knew the answer. She would hate him. Regardless of his vows, she would hate him. Though he had to wonder if Moira would allow her to be returned to MacNeil. If what she said was true, then they would do everything in their power to make sure Glenna was safe. In which case maybe he could maintain his honor and adhere to both vows.

Glenna twirled the water around with her hands, sending it dancing on her breasts. He didn't let himself dwell anymore on dark thoughts as he leaned down and ran his tongue around a pert nipple.

He couldn't wait for her. He needed her now, desperately or he would explode. He lifted her in his arms and carried her to the water's edge. There, he gently sat her down.

"Ah, you must be a Druid," she said, and leaned over to kiss his neck.

"Why's that?"

"Because you read my mind."

With that, she wrapped her arms around his neck and lay back. He followed her and marveled at her soft body beneath his. The water lapped around them as he entered her.

It was over far too soon and, as they lay there, he thought he sensed Glenna pulling away from him. Though surely it was his imagination. He knew she felt strongly about him. Love hadn't been mentioned, but he didn't need the words to know stronger forces bound them.

But there were things that needed to be discussed. "The MacNeil will come soon."

She sighed and ran a hand down his chest. "Couldn't we pretend, just for a bit, that he didn't exist?"

"My thoughts are centered on making sure you and the clan are safe while I get Ailsa and Iona back alive before I kill him."

"I thought I was to be exchanged for them."

She had said the one thing he hadn't wanted to discuss. Now he didn't have a choice. "I'll kill him."

"What if you can't? What if the only way to see your daughter and sister alive again is to trade them for me?"

"There's no need to even think those thoughts, Glenna. I told you I'd kill him."

"It's not your time to kill him. That's what the prophecy is for."

He leaned up on an elbow worried now. "You've seen this?"

"I don't have to. I know until the prophecy is fulfilled the MacNeil will live."

"That's not acceptable." He sat up and put his arms on his knees. "I will seek my revenge for what he's done to my family."

She leaned up. "And what about what he's done to mine?"

"I will kill him. The prophecy means nothing to me."

She looked away and rose to her feet. She roughly yanked on her clothes then turned back to him. "The prophecy means everything to you. You are part of it, and if you'd open your mind you'd remember just why it's so important."

Conall didn't stop her as she strode away. His body ached with such sorrow as he had never experienced. Even now with his mate so near he was losing her.

Mayhap he had never had her, just thought he did.

* * * * *

Gregor watched Glenna and Conall from atop the north tower. If any two people were meant to be together it was them, but the MacNeil stood in the way.

For the first time since he had left his clan and become a mercenary, he thought about what he was doing. He had known when Conall saved his life that things were going to change. For the better or worse he knew not.

But change they had.

His thoughts turned to Iona. He had asked Effie repeatedly what she knew, but obtained nothing. Even when he had questioned a few guards at MacNeil's he had found out little.

Now he had a decision to make. One that could destroy everything around him. He had prayed Conall's power would detect him a liar and end everything right then, but it seemed as though Conall's power had deserted him. That left him to make the decision on his own.

He reached inside his shirt and withdrew the medallion that hung around his neck. He ran his finger across the cross and Celtic pattern, his memories turned to his family. An owl's screech broke into his thoughts. He couldn't shake the feeling someone watched him. It wasn't from any of Conall's soldiers, though he knew Angus had kept a wary eye on him since he returned.

Nay, it was something else.

Though he knew Conall didn't believe in the Druids, Gregor most certainly did. The very air around him seemed different here more than any place else. It was almost magical.

Magical? Now you really are turning into the man Father accused you of.

He started to turn away when a flash of white caught his attention. He *was* being watched. By Moira. In a blink she was gone. But it had him wondering. What could have the Druids watching him? Could they know what he was up to? It was a possibility, and one that he would have to plan for carefully.

* * * * *

Glenna's feet flew across the earth as she ran to the nemeton. Blinded by tears, she allowed the magic to pull her as she pushed past tree limbs. She fell to her knees, hiccupping and wiping away her tears.

The moon broke through the clouds and its silvery rays lit the mound in an ethereal glow. Without the roaring fires and Druids, the nemeton was completely different from Beltaine. It was also vastly different from when she had come during the day and lain with Conall.

Memories of Conall telling her how to call forth the Faeries flitted through her mind. She stood on shaky legs and walked closer to the mound. An owl hooted near her and about scared her out of her skin.

She found him perched on a hawthorn tree. She found it rather odd the owl would choose such a shrubby tree with wicked thorns and dense tangle of growth. With a shake of her head to the owl she began to walk around the mound. What she expected to happen, she didn't know, but by the time she had walked around nine times she would have been happy to have the owl hoot again.

But, alas, nothing happened. She slumped onto the ground and noticed a tree she hadn't seen before. Even in the dark of night she could see how red the berries were that grew on the tree.

"It's a rowan tree."

Glenna whirled around to find a man leaning against an oak. He had no weapons and didn't wear a plaid. His blonde hair was long and flowing, and the glowing blue of his eyes reminded her of the Fae on Beltaine. He was as finely made as Conall but with a different air about him.

She chided herself for being so stupid as to venture away from the castle at night, but she didn't fear this man, if he was a man.

"Who are you?" she asked, and slowly got to her feet in case she needed to run.

He chuckled. "The rowan is an old tree of magical repute. It repels evil forces."

"Who are you?" she repeated.

"You called me here."

Her stomach fell to her feet with a thud. "But…"

"What did you expect," he said, and pushed from the tree. "A grand an entrance as Beltaine? That only happens when many of us visit."

She nodded, her mind taking everything in.

"Are you going to tell me what you called me for?"

Her mind went blank. There were so many things she wanted, but what to ask him?

He pushed off the oak and walked toward the rowan. "Did you know the rowan is associated with positive Faerie influence? It is the wood you Druids burn for the magical fires."

"I didn't know."

He gave her a sad smile that said he knew. "You haven't much time left to learn."

"I'm afraid I won't learn in time."

"We gave you and your sisters your powers because you are worthy, because if the Druids are to survive MacNeil must be destroyed."

"You can see into the future?"

"You could call it that."

"Then why didn't you save my parents?" Her anger began to consume her.

He raised his hands and instantly her anger diminished. "You must learn to control that rage. That is what your enemies will use against you." He sighed and looked at the owl still perched on the hawthorn. "As to your parents. We didn't foresee that. It happened suddenly and we didn't have time to stop it."

"I don't understand."

"There was a traitor in the Sinclair clan."

Glenna sank to her knees. The more she learned, the more complex things became. "I don't think I can do this."

"You have the strength and fortitude, or you wouldn't have been chosen, Glenna."

She raised her eyes. His smile was devastatingly handsome, but it didn't melt her insides like Conall did with a mere grin. "What are you?"

"An Otherworld being as some people like to call us, a Fae by others. What we are matters not. You will learn more of us later. It was my suggestion to Moira that she hold off filling your head with too much at once."

"And your name?"

"You may call me Aimery."

"Aimery," she repeated. "Can you help me?"

"What is it you wish? Do you want Conall's love? Do you wish to have him erased from your memory?"

"You can do that?"

"I can do many things," he said ominously.

"I want... I want..."

Aimery laughed. "You should've thought about what you wanted before you called me."

"There are many things I want."

"I know." The sorrow in his tone spoke volumes. "Sadly, I cannot help you in any of them."

"What? I thought you had magic."

"I do. However, you have enough magic yourself to make all your wants happen."

Glenna put her head in her hands. She felt as if the weight of the world held her down.

"Just don't doubt yourself and you'll be fine."

"But I don't know enough yet."

"You will in time."

She looked up and Aimery was gone. "Figures," she said, and stood. With one last look at the mound, Glenna began to walk back to the castle with more questions than when she had come.

* * * * *

"Aye, you will."

Glenna tried in vain to control her rising temper and ignore the crowded great hall and the many people who listened to her. No matter how hard she strived she couldn't clear her mind. Ever since she entered the hall to break her fast and Conall had informed her he would trade her for Iona and Ailsa. The pain of it cut more deeply than she had thought possible.

"I'll not let you stay there though," he said as though it would make the hurt less harsh. "I'll come for you."

She had tried everything to change his mind. He wasn't budging though. "I can help you," she tried again.

"I'll be more worried about you than finding MacNeil. I can't have that."

"Nay. You just can't stand there and tell me the truth, that you don't want me."

"Glenna," he said slowly, his jaw clenched. "You know that's a lie."

"Really? If you truly wanted me for your wife you wouldn't be willing to turn me back over to the man who murdered my parents."

"Glenna." His tone lowered, he rose to his feet.

"I was a fool to stay here and trust you. Iona was wrong. You aren't the man who would set me free." She turned on her heel ready to flee, but an iron grip on her arm stopped her.

"What do you mean Iona said I would set you free?" he asked after turning her around to face him.

For a brief moment she thought to refuse to answer him, but the pain in his eyes changed her mind. She hated herself then, for she knew this man held her heart though she didn't hold his.

"Iona told me there would be a man who could come and set me free. When you came and took me from MacNeil, I foolishly thought you were that man."

He stared hard at her. "What else did she say?"

"That I must trust this man with my life."

He let go of her arm and turned his back on her. "Go."

"What?" she asked, afraid she had heard him wrong.

"You're right, Glenna. I'm a monster for thinking of turning you back to MacNeil for my family. Go. Leave."

"How will you get Iona and Ailsa back? What of your vow to your mother?"

He braced both hands on the table. "I'll think of something else. You deserve better than me, and I proved it this morning."

Glenna opened her mouth to tell him he was wrong. He was doing everything in his power to get his family back yet here she was being selfish. He had lost everything and she was only thinking of herself.

With her powers she could easily escape MacNeil, and he knew that. Yet, he hadn't said anything. He was letting her go. And she knew it was forever.

She took a step toward him when he sat heavily in his chair. "Conall—"

"She'll come with me."

Every head in the hall turned to find Moira standing in the doorway. She walked with a confidence Glenna envied. She hadn't expected Moira, indeed was surprised Conall hadn't thrown her out already.

Instead he shook his head. "How many times have I said you aren't welcome?"

"You ancestors made sure there was always a place for the Druids here. You don't have the right to change that."

He came to his feet so fast his chair tipped over backward. "I'm laird here, and if I want you gone, you will go."

"You'll have to kill me first."

Glenna jumped in front of Moira before Conall could speak. "Hold your tongue," she told him. "Don't say anything I couldn't forgive you for."

"I don't want her here," he said between clenched teeth.

"Why? What's the difference between her and me?"

He blinked, his brow furrowed. "A lot."

"Nothing," Glenna answered. Suddenly she knew Frang was right. Conall would never let her go on his own. That's why he had pushed her away. He would never admit he wouldn't give her to MacNeil, but he wouldn't let her go either.

There was only one way to get Ailsa and Iona back and she was the person to do it. As much as it pained her she had to leave.

"Moira is right. I will go with her. That way you can fight the MacNeil without having to worry over me."

Glenna turned and walked toward the door before she could change her mind. It wasn't until she had walked out the castle gates that she realized Conall didn't try to stop her.

"Remember what I told you," Moira said beside her. "Don't give up hope."

"He didn't even try..." She couldn't even finish the sentence.

"Pride stopped him. Had you done it when it was just the two of you things might have gone differently. Everything this morning would've gone differently."

"He did all of this in front of everyone so I'd only have one choice."

"Aye. He was counting on me coming for you."

Her cracked heart split in two as tears filled her eyes. "He could've talked to me. We could've worked this out so everyone would win."

"That's the part you don't ken, my sister. Not everyone can win. Conall knows this. You have yet to learn it."

She stopped and looked at her sister. "Do you know what I did?"

"You left him to come with me."

"Nay." She laughed sadly through her tears. "I stood up for myself. I made a decision and did it."

Moira smiled and put an arm around her shoulders. "If you're to be a Highlander's wife you need a strong backbone."

What euphoria her actions had brought her evaporated at Moira's words. "He'll never accept me as a Druid."

"Regardless, never is a very long time."

"He showed me back there just how much he thought of my opinion."

"He's a laird, Glenna, and used to making decisions on his own."

"This involved me."

"It's something you'll have to teach him. It doesn't come easy for men to confide in women. They think they can take care of everything."

"When in truth it's the women who take care of everything."

"Aye."

Glenna looked to her sister and saw such soul-wrenching misery in Moira's eyes that it startled her. All this time she had been concerned about herself when Moira hurt just as bad.

"Moira—" Glenna began when Moira stopped in her tacks.

"We must hurry. MacNeil comes."

* * * * *

The Shadow followed close behind Moira and Glenna. There was no way he could kill Glenna now that she was with his beloved, but he would make sure to keep an eye on her nonetheless. One never knew when an opportunity would present itself.

If only Moira would spare him another of her heavenly smiles. She was always kind to him, but then again she was kind to everyone. Why couldn't she give him a little more? Just a hint that she shared his love.

But the time would come when she would take his hand, and he couldn't wait to see the look of astonishment on Frang's and Aimery's faces. It would be worth everything he had suffered.

He had to hurry, Moira had quickened her pace. He hoped she hadn't realized she was being followed. Just then he spotted the warrior Dartayous. He growled low in his throat.

It was no secret among the Druids that Dartayous and Moira didn't get along, and the fact he followed her didn't set well. He would have to kill Dartayous as well. No need to have a warrior on their trail all the time, especially one Moira didn't like.

He crept closer, using his power to shield himself from prying eyes. He had managed to come with five paces of Dartayous and was about to strike when the warrior stopped. He watched as Dartayous looked first one way then the other.

The sound of metal leaving a scabbard reached his ears, and he dived quickly to the side. A long dagger had struck the ground were he had stood just moments before.

"I know you're there, traitor," Dartayous said as he retrieved his dagger. "You can cloak yourself all you like but you cannot hide from me. You stink of evil. I will find you and you'll pay for what you've done."

He waited until Dartayous disappeared before he stood and let his shield drop. He was hidden by the trees and no one would see him. He would have to be more careful now.

It had been a surprise to know Dartayous could sense him. None of the other Druids had been able to. Maybe Dartayous was more powerful than he realized. He threw off his cloak and hid it behind the stone before he began picking the herbs he had come for.

Chapter Twenty-Two

"She left." Conall had repeated the same thing over and over since Glenna had walked from the castle, yet he refused to accept it.

The hall was empty now except for him, Angus and Gregor. He still couldn't believe she had walked away without another word. Nothing. Not even goodbye. She hadn't even looked back.

"You wanted her somewhere safe, and I'd say that was the safest place for her," Gregor said.

Angus cleared his throat and leaned his elbows on the table. "He's right, Conall. It's where ye wanted her to begin with."

"She would've refused had you asked her to go," Gregor reminded him. "You did the only thing you could to keep her safe."

Conall shook his head. "She thinks I really was going to turn her over to MacNeil. She thinks I'm a monster now. I saw it in her eyes."

"She's safe. Ye know Moira will make sure nothing can hurt her. After this is over ye can tell her what happened," Angus said. "Ye need to turn yer attention on the MacNeil."

Conall knew they were right, he just wished his heart would listen. His plan had worked though he had nearly thrown it all aside when he had seen her distress at thinking he would be so callus as to turn her over to MacNeil.

Though she was where he wanted her, the price had been her hatred for him. He hoped it was a high enough price to keep her safe.

* * * * *

The MacNeil sat atop his best steed and surveyed his soldiers. His clan was known far and wide for their thievery and murdering. They were good men.

Mostly because they would die for him. Some were hired like Gregor, but most were his clan, willing to fight and die alongside their laird.

His eyes roamed until he found the MacInnes' brat. She sat in front of Effie and glared at him defiantly. For a child so young she had spirit. She reminded him of Glenna's mother. It was a shame he had had to kill Catriona, but she had been a pagan after all. Glenna had turned out all right.

Until Conall had come.

MacNeil wondered if she knew the truth about her parents. Regardless, he needed her by his side. The conquering went much smoother when she aided him, unwilling or not.

He nodded to his commander. It was time to take back what was his.

* * * * *

Summer would soon arrive, Conall thought as sweat ran down his chest and the sun beat upon his back. He had trained with his men all morning, but all he could concentrate on was Glenna. She had told him she liked to watch while he trained yet she wasn't there.

Her absence was felt throughout the castle, but mostly within his heart, and it had only been a day since she left. A day that seemed as though an eternity.

He slipped and narrowly avoided being clobbered by Angus' sword. With a quick step to the side he ducked the swing and rammed an elbow into Angus' stomach.

"St. Brigit," Angus cursed. "Must ye knock the breath from me every time?"

"Reflex."

Angus snorted. "My arse. Ye're mind was wandering to a certain dark-haired lass."

Conall's life had lost its luster without her, but it must be worse than he thought if Angus would comment on it. He had to ask himself how he planned to live the rest of his life without her. For that's exactly what would happen.

He had given her to the Druids, and in doing so had let go of any hope of a future with her. He no longer cared about his honor or his vows. Without Glenna he was nothing.

It had nearly killed him to watch her walk from the castle and not beg her to stay by his side. Just as it had turned his stomach to feed her the lies about returning her to MacNeil.

Yet all had been done with the best of intentions. Keeping her safe. He had lost his sister and now his daughter to MacNeil. That bastard would take nothing else from him.

Conall buried his sword in the earth. Aye, by his life he had sworn to kill the man who would dare to disrupt his world, who had dared to murder innocent children's parents because of a prophecy, who had dared to kill for the fun of it.

Angus clamped him on the shoulder. "Ye're lost without her. After this is over, go to her."

He shook his head. "I cannot. As much as I need her by my side, she'll never forgive me for what I did."

"It was a ruse. I'll tell her that myself."

"Nay," Conall nearly yelled. He lowered his tone, and said, "She's better off without me."

Angus snorted his disapproval. "Ye'll never be whole without yer mate. It's the blessing the Druids put upon yer family for hiding them."

"It's a curse, Angus, not a blessing, not when you can't have your mate." Conall turned his attention from his friend to the two soldiers who ran up. "What news?"

"The majority of the clan is safe within these walls, laird," said Thomas, a tall, thin boy who was going to make a fine soldier.

"Good work."

"We're ready for the MacNeil," he said. "I've heard some of the men saying the Druids would aid us."

Conall shrugged and dismissed them before he turned to Angus. "What do you know of that?"

Angus slid his sword into his scabbard. "Don't be forgetting that I grew up in this clan too. I know how the Druids have always helped us. What makes ye think they'd stop now?"

What indeed? Conall thought. "We can handle the MacNeil ourselves."

Angus stared at him then turned and walked away. His disappointed expression burned in Conall's memory. Never once had Angus not stood by a decision he made. Until now.

He must be losing the ability to lead the clan. Once MacNeil was dead and Iona and Ailsa safe, he would step aside for a new laird. One who could lead the clan properly.

* * * * *

The Shadow peered at Moira's sleeping form. He wanted to get closer, but Dartayous was near. Did the cursed warrior never sleep? His eyes found Glenna who slept next to Moira. It would be so easy to slit her throat, but then Moira would wake and see that he had done it. He couldn't allow that.

Besides, he would never get past Dartayous. There had to be another way.

* * * * *

Glenna awoke suddenly, the serenity of the stone circle not reaching her troubled mind. She struggled to recall the dream she just had, but it faded as fast as she strained to remember.

She had to see Conall. Her mind urged her to seek him out, but she wasn't sure for what. She rose from her bed and walked past Moira's sleeping form. It never crossed her mind to wonder where the Druid warrior Dartayous who had been watching over them was.

With the waning moon to light her way, she moved quickly to the hidden cave entrance. She stopped just inside. Her fear of the spiders made her hesitate, but her need to see Conall pushed aside any apprehension. Besides, if she tried hard enough she might be able to roast any she spotted, she thought with a chuckle.

There were no torches here and walking through without one wasn't an option. She bent and picked up a sturdy stick. With eyes closed, she concentrated all her powers on lighting the stick, and to her utter astonishment it went up in flames.

She threw the stick to the ground as flames engulfed it and hurriedly stamped out the fire. When there was nothing left of the stick, she turned back to the darkened cave.

Doubts assaulted her. How would she ever defeat MacNeil if she couldn't light a simple stick to use as a torch? Her powers couldn't be summoned properly and that could cause many deaths. Moira was more than patient with her, but Glenna knew she had precious little time to garner years of Druid knowledge.

But Ailsa, Iona and Conall broke through her misgivings. She loved Conall though he didn't want her, and for her love of him, Ailsa and Iona she would do anything to keep them safe. Even brave the spider-infested caves.

She took a deep breath, closed her eyes to steady her nerves, and then rushed into the caves. She didn't slow, not even when her side ached and her lungs could barely fill with air.

When the bailey came into view, she slowed to a walk. Just before she stepped out of the cave a spider ran across her path. She sucked in a breath and froze until all eight legs were out of view.

So much for roasting him. I was too scared to do anything but pray he wouldn't come my way.

She squared her shoulders and stepped from the cave. A look around the bailey and battlements showed her Conall was prepared for the MacNeil's arrival. The guards were doubled on the battlements and more protected the bailey.

After a nod to the soldier guarding the cave entrance, she made her way to the castle. She entered and found the hall full of sleeping soldiers. Grunts and snores filled the hall. She spotted Angus sitting by the fire and gave him a small smile.

He winked and motioned her over. "I thought ye'd be coming for a visit, lass."

"Why?" she asked, and took the goblet he offered.

"Why?" He laughed. "Because he needs ye."

She shook her head and took a drink of the mead. "Nay. Conall needs his family."

He wiped his mouth after taking a big gulp out of his goblet. "True enough. But ye don't give yourself enough credit. Ye got to him, lass, and that's more than any woman here has done."

"If only it were true."

"Lass," he said after a deep sigh, "yer as stubborn as Conall. What ye don't know is that the Druids gave Conall's family the ability to only marry their mates."

She blinked and licked her lips as Conall's words came to mind. *"You're mine."*

"The Druids wanted the MacInnes' lairds to be happy, and for their family to be happy. Conall knows he's found his mate."

She thought over his words as she gazed into the fire. Could Angus be right? Did Conall need her as much as she hoped? She set the goblet on the table and gave him a smile.

Angus chuckled and pointed to the stairs. "He's in his chamber."

She returned his wink before ascending the stairs. With every step her feet became heavier. Her heart fluttered erratically in her chest, and her body heated at the thought of seeing Conall again. She had missed his teasing smile and the way his eyes smoldered when he looked her way.

But would he turn her away?

That question plagued her mind as she stood in front of his chamber door. She placed her hands on the wood and closed her eyes. A vision flashed of Conall lying on the ground as MacNeil soldiers swarmed around him, his life's blood soaking the ground. And she knew that even if he did order her from his castle she had to warn him of her vision.

The thought of him dying twisted her gut. She was a Druid and therefore obligated to help the MacInnes clan, even if the laird had no wish for aid. She unlatched the door and quietly pushed it open. Her eyes hurriedly scanned the chamber until she found him. He sat before the fire in his favorite chair his sword between his legs as he sharpened and cleaned it.

But it was the shadows moving across his muscular back that made her blood pound. A gasp escaped her as she recalled the fell of those muscles beneath her hand as they made love.

With the quickness of the Fae he whirled around, the tip of his sword pointing at her neck while he crouched ready for battle. His gray eyes widened in astonishment before they narrowed in confusion.

"Glenna?"

She smiled and pushed his sword away. "Aye. It's me, laird."

"You've come back?" he asked, his expression guarded now.

"I had to see you."

He lowered his sword and cocked his head to the side. "Have you returned?"

"You don't want me here, Conall."

"You don't know what I want," he said, and raised himself to his full height.

"Because you won't talk to me." When he opened his mouth to argue she hurriedly went on. "But I'm not here to debate the issue."

"Then why are you here?" he asked, and resumed his seat before the fire.

She moved to his side and knelt beside him. With a deep breath and a quick prayer that it would work, she closed her eyes and touched his hand.

Her vision came clear and sharp. Conall and the MacNeil fought, their blades clanging loudly. Conall turned and cried out as a sword sank into his back. She jerked open her eyes. The vision faded when she looked at Conall.

He narrowed his silver gaze. "What did you see?"

"Your death by the MacNeil's hand."

He laughed and continued sharpening his sword. "He won't kill me."

"You aren't invincible. Why won't you listen to me?" Once she had seen the vision, she knew it was the dream she had had. She had to make him realize he was in danger.

"Not all of the Druids' visions are correct." He stopped and looked at her. "If it makes you feel better, I'll be more careful when I meet him."

"You're a fine laird, Conall. The finest I've ever met."

"You've only met two."

Oh, he infuriated her sometimes. "It wouldn't matter if I'd met hundreds. I know you're the best. But in order for you to continue to lead your clan you must remember the rest of the prophecy."

"Why don't you just tell me? It would save everyone a lot of time," he said, and rose to his feet. "Why are you here anyway?"

She stood and watched as he poured himself some wine. "I had to warn you of your death. We need you to fulfill the prophecy."

His laughed resonated around the room. "Maybe my death will fulfill your prophecy."

"I need you to live."

Slowly he turned to face her. "Have you returned to me?"

"Nay."

Silence filled the chamber as he stared at her. "I need you."

Warmth flooded her at his words, but their future hinged upon the prophecy. "I can't be here now. It's not time."

"Enough with the riddles," he said, and threw the goblet into the fire. "Speak plainly."

"I am. I'm telling you I can't be here now."

"Why?"

Surely there wasn't a more stubborn man in all of Scotland, she thought. First, he wanted her away from the castle and had gone to great lengths to get it, and now he wanted her here. She sighed wearily. "Because of the MacNeil."

"I will protect you from him."

"Aye, you would try." She walked to him and ran her fingers along his strong jaw. "I must go now."

He closed a hand around her wrist. "Stay. Stay with me tonight."

"I've never left you."

"I need you, Glenna," he said, his eyes molten with desire.

Her body flared to life at those simple words, but there was also an air of despair in his words. She gazed deep into his eyes and saw the self-doubt and fear buried deep within him. She could do nothing to ease his doubts now, only grant him his one wish—to have Iona and Ailsa safe beside him again. That she could, and would, do for him. Because she loved him.

She also knew if he was to live another day she had to leave. Staying would only make him lose focus and prolong his remembering the entire prophecy.

"I've always needed you." She withdrew her arm and walked to the door. "Don't give up hope," she called over her shoulder.

* * * * *

The Shadow rubbed his hands together. It had been easy to follow Glenna into the caves where he waited for her to return. He had to kill her this time. Even if she did yell they would be so deep in the caves that no one would ever hear her. It was perfect. Just perfect.

"She comes," he said as she appeared in the bailey.

He hid in the shadows and waited until she was deep in the caves before he crept closer to her. With his power he shrouded himself so she couldn't see him. He was almost upon her when she whirled around, swinging the torch in her hand.

"Who's there?" she asked, her voice pitched high from her fear.

There was no need for him to say anything. He smiled and pulled a dagger from inside his cloak. He had moved to her side and watched in amazement as her fear grew.

It was a good thing she hadn't learned all her powers or he would never be able to carry this out. He raised the dagger and was about to pounce on her when a roar filled the cave.

He raised his eyes in time to see Dartayous jumping from a crevice in the top of the cave. The warrior landed in between him and Glenna. With a curse he slid the dagger back into his cloak and melded with the shadows.

"Dartayous," Glenna said. "What are you doing here?"

"He was here," the warrior stated, his sword drawn and held in front of him as he looked around the cave.

"Who was here?"

"He was about to kill you, Glenna," he said, and turned to face her. "I followed you because I knew he would as well. He's very powerful to shroud himself so well from my eyes."

"I shouldn't have come," she said, and bowed her head.

"Come. We must return to the circle. He can't harm you there."

The Shadow didn't wait for them to leave. He ran as fast as he could through the caves so he could return to the circle before he was missed. He had made another mistake this night, and if he weren't more vigilant his carefully laid plans would be for naught.

Chapter Twenty-Three

The sun's rays sprang around the mountains and spilled its golden light upon the ground still damp with the morning dew. Conall stretched his sword high above his head and began his morning ritual.

He liked to be alone first thing in the morning. The dawn usually set his soul at ease with new hope, but nothing would ease his torment this day. He dropped his arms and shook his head to clear it. He practiced until sweat dripped from his body, but still he couldn't concentrate.

Glenna's words had haunted his sleep, and when he had risen at first light, he knew it would be the day the MacNeil came. His wits needed to be about him, and his morning exercise had always put everything into perspective before. But things were different now.

He had lost everything. Iona, his mother, Ailsa, his power and now...Glenna.

The sun blinded him as it crested the mountain. He closed his eyes and heard his mother's words. *"Open your mind, Conall. It's amazing the things life can give us if we but give it a chance."*

With a roar he swung his sword around and became one with it. This is what would avenge Glenna's parents. This sword would return Iona and Ailsa, and it would fulfill the vow he had given his mother.

Damn everything else, especially his vow to the Druids. He had found his mate, and he refused to live without her. After all it had been the Druids who gave his family the ability to marry their mates.

His mind was fixed now. Everything was clear. He would vanquish MacNeil and once again have Iona, Ailsa and Glenna out of harm's way beside him. Then every Highlander in Scotland would be safe from MacNeil's butchery.

Conall turned to find Angus and Gregor leaning against the wall. "Ready the soldiers. The MacNeil arrives this day."

Both men jerked from the wall. Angus ran off to do as he commanded, but Gregor didn't move.

"Are you sure?" Gregor asked.

"As sure as I know the sun will set on this day."

Gregor looked at his feet, his face lined with uneasiness. "I better get ready then."

"Hold," Conall said. When Gregor had turned to face him, he said, "I don't know whether you've lied to me or not."

"I ken. You've lost your ability."

Conall nodded. "I'm going on my instinct, but if you do betray me and this clan know that the Druids will hunt you down for it."

"I didn't think you accepted the Druid's help," Gregor said, his arms crossed over his chest.

"I haven't. Many centuries ago the Druids and the MacInnes clan made a pact. Nothing can destroy that pact, no matter how much I'd like to."

For long moments Gregor looked at him before giving him a curt nod and walking away. Conall sighed. He prayed he wasn't wrong about Gregor.

He had just emerged from dunking his head in a vat of water when he heard a sentry call that riders had been spotted. Conall wiped the water from his face and grabbed his sword and bow before running to the gatehouse tower.

Once he reached the top, he searched the land but saw nothing. He was about to ask the sentry if had indeed seen a rider when thunder rumbled in the distance. Except it wasn't thunder.

It was an army.

"The MacNeil has arrived." He turned to his soldiers. "Ready yourselves, men. The devil has come to MacInnes Castle."

* * * * *

Glenna bent next to the river outside the circle and washed her face and arms. Moira had accompanied her and they laughed at the antics of a baby bird learning to fly.

Suddenly she stood. "Moira."

"I know," her sister replied, and rose. "MacNeil has come."

Glenna ran to the cliff that overlooked the valley. She watched, horrified, as line after line of MacNeil soldiers came into view. "There's so many."

"We can handle them," Frang said as he came to stand beside her and Moira.

She couldn't hide her surprise. "You're going to help Conall?"

"Of course, child. The Druids and MacInnes made a pact long centuries ago."

Moira laughed. "So whether Conall wants our help or not, he's going to get it."

Relief filled Glenna until she thought of her vision of Conall's death. "I just hope it's enough."

"You've had a vision," Moira said, her eyes gazing intently at her.

"Of Conall's death."

Frang hung his head. "We need him to fulfill the prophecy, so we must make sure to keep him safe."

Glenna spotted Effie riding next to the MacNeil. "The traitor has returned."

"And she holds Ailsa," Moira said.

"Then it begins."

Moira grabbed hold of her arm before she could turn away. "Be careful. We need you yet."

"The MacNeil won't kill me. He has use of me, remember?"

"Please. Just be careful. We aren't immortal."

* * * * *

"St. Brigit," Angus whispered.

Conall quite agreed when he saw the amount of men the MacNeil had brought with him. Fury erupted when he spotted Ailsa sitting in front of Effie with her hands tied together.

The MacNeil broke away and walked his horse closer to the gate. Two burly men flanked him on either side. "Well, Conall, I told you I'd return. Are you willing to trade?"

"Not until I see Iona."

MacNeil snickered. "Are you telling me you think I have her?"

"Don't you? She would've returned home if you didn't hold her against her will."

"Maybe. But the truth is I don't have her."

Rage ripped its way through Conall's body until the only thing he saw was MacNeil's death. "Show her or die."

MacNeil shared a laugh with the soldiers beside him. "It would be very difficult for me to give her back to you. I suppose I could, but I don't think you'd recognize her."

With teeth clenched tightly together Conall struggled for control. "Why's that?"

"She's been in the ground for quite some time after I slit her throat."

Conall's wrath erupted, but before he opened his mouth to answer, a commotion to his left halted him.

His heart stopped and fell to his feet when he caught sight of Glenna.

* * * * *

Glenna wanted to run and hide the instant MacNeil's evil eyes alighted on her. Instead her gaze sought Conall. He stood in the tower above the gatehouse, his black hair cascading around him. His steady gaze gave her strength.

"Come, Glenna."

She looked to the man who had killed her parents and separated her from her sisters and began to tremble. She couldn't do this. She wasn't ready to face him. Her powers couldn't be controlled and one move on his part would prove it.

And with that fear her eyes again found Conall. His willingness to give everything for the return of his family touched her deep inside. If he could face a monster, knowing he might die, then she could face the devil and vanquish her demons.

She took a deep, calming breath and folded her hands together. "You will return Ailsa. Now."

"Not until you come with me." He nudged his horse and rode closer to her.

Contempt ran rampant through her. After everything he had done to her, she wouldn't back down from him. Not now. Not ever. She wanted answers and she would get them. "Tell me, MacNeil. Why did you kill Iona?"

He placed a hand on his hip and laughed. "She got in the way. She would've filled your head with nonsense, just as these people have."

"All they've done is give me the answers I've needed for years."

"Enough talk. The past can't be changed. Now come down from there and we'll go home."

"Not until you return Ailsa to Conall."

Indignation twisted MacNeil's face. "Fine," he spat, and motioned for a soldier to get Ailsa.

"One other request," she said. She almost laughed aloud at the incredulous expression on his face.

"What?" he asked between teeth clenched tightly together.

"The MacInnes clan wants revenge. Give them Effie."

The MacNeil mulled this over for a moment. Effie began calling out to him. With a small wave of his hand another soldier grabbed Effie.

"Nay, MacNeil," Effie screamed. "You canna do this to me. I was to give you sons."

The soldier roughly hauled her facedown over his horse as MacNeil's words reached Glenna. "You might have given me sons, Effie, but with Glenna I'll have the world and sons. All you could give me would be your little black heart."

Glenna should feel pity for Effie, but no such emotion could be found. Effie had sealed her own fate when she took Ailsa. Glenna waited until Ailsa and Effie were safely inside the gates before she turned her attention back to MacNeil.

"You surprise me," she told him.

"Really? Then that means you don't really know me."

"Not true," she countered. "I know a great deal. I know you killed my parents."

"Lies. All lies. Why are you listening to these people? You're a MacNeil, lass."

Finally she would be able to do what she had wanted for a long time. She brought around the MacNeil plaid she had hid behind her back. "I was never a MacNeil," she said and set it afire.

She was glad he was too far away to see the surprise on her face that her powers had actually obeyed her. MacNeil let out a roar but stopped his soldiers when they would have attacked her. This time Glenna did laugh.

"Find something amusing, lass? You'd be dead now if I hadn't stopped my soldiers."

"I think not. After all I am a Druid, and just who do you think inhabits this forest?"

The amicable expression faded from his face. "So you think you know everything now?"

"She knows enough," Moira said, and came to stand beside her.

MacNeil narrowed his eyes. "Who are you?"

"Don't you know?" Moira asked. "I would think you'd know me upon sight since it was my cousins you killed that night."

He clenched his hand into a fist and stared at his clan's plaid burning to ash.

Moira raised her hands above her head. "The prophecy is about to come to pass. You managed to slay our parents but all three of us escaped."

* * * * *

Conall yearned to listen to all Glenna said to MacNeil, but the moment Effie rode through the gates his clan erupted in violence. They screamed for her death as he pushed through his soldiers to get to Ailsa. Not until she was safely in his arms did he allow himself to believe she was home.

"I've got you, love. You're home now," he said as he crushed her to him.

"I never doubted it, Da."

He squeezed his eyes shut and buried his face in her neck. She had so much faith in him, and it reminded him of someone else who had that much faith in him. Glenna.

"Ailsa," he said as he set her on her feet. "I need you to go to your chamber and stay there until I come for you."

"Are you going to bring Glenna back?"

"Aye, love, I am."

She leaned over and kissed his cheek. "Good luck, Da." With that she ran between people's legs and then through the castle door.

He might have lost a sister, but he had gotten his daughter returned, thanks to Glenna, and he would be damn sure to get Glenna back as well. But first he had to calm his clan before they killed Effie.

"Conall," Angus yelled above the shouts of the clan. "We have a wee problem."

* * * * *

MacNeil lifted his sword as a signal to his men. The entire army raised their bows, crossbows and swords, but Glenna wasn't worried. There was nothing they could do with the MacInnes clan safely inside the walls.

A shout from a MacInnes soldier alerted her that something wasn't right. She turned and saw buildings ablaze within the bailey.

"Now, Glenna," Moira said urgently.

Glenna concentrated all of her energy but couldn't put out the fires. "I can't," she whispered as fear overtook her.

"Don't let him win," Moira urged as she took hold of Glenna's hands. "You can do this. I believe in you."

Glenna gazed into her sister's green eyes, eyes that she somehow knew looked just as their mother's had. She nodded and searched her mind for a way to combat the fires. If she couldn't put them out herself, then she would find something that could.

She concentrated on the blaze sweeping rapidly toward the barn. "Moira, stop the wind," she called.

Please let this work.

Her eyes focused on the barn as she waited for the men to get all the animals out. When the last animal ran from the building she focused her powers, and to her amazement the barn caught fire.

"Moira, push the fire."

Chapter Twenty-Four

Conall emerged from the barn to see the fire closing in. It would soon reach the castle. His clan was no longer safe here. "Angus, get them to the caves."

But the clan had stayed focused on Effie even while the fire burned. When the flames had started, he had glanced at Gregor, thinking he had betrayed him, but Gregor had stayed by his side.

Whoever set the fire was Glenna's attacker, and the only one who could give him those answers was Effie. If the clan didn't kill her first. Before he reached Effie, a loud explosion sounded behind him. He turned to find the barn ablaze, but the original fire had yet to reach it.

"There," Angus shouted, and pointed to the cliff.

Glenna had saved them. He and his clan watched as the two fires melded and fought for control until there was nothing left to burn. He wanted to go to her, to thank her, but his clan had turned back to Effie.

He reached Effie to see her huddled in a ball as his clan threw anything at her they could get their hands on. "Enough," he bellowed to gain their attention.

They looked at him, the violence still in their eyes. "She betrayed the clan," someone yelled.

"Aye, she did. But Ailsa is returned home thanks to Glenna."

"Banish her," a woman hollered.

Conall looked down at the once-proud Effie. Her red hair and face splattered with mud and rotten food, her gown torn, shoes missing, and defeat shown in her eyes.

He knelt beside her. "You've got one chance to answer me or I'll let them finish you off."

She swallowed and nodded.

"Why do you hate Ailsa?"

"She prevented you from marrying me."

Conall jerked he was so surprised. "Explain yourself."

"I'm the one who convinced Mary not to tell you of the babe. I knew if you found out you'd marry her."

"You've already told me this." He sighed and waited for the rest.

"I thought I had everything under control until she looked at the brat and said she wanted you to know."

"So you killed her," he deduced.

Effie nodded though no tears were on her face. "It was easy to convince Mary's mother to keep Ailsa from you."

Conall sighed at her words. How an innocent child could do this to a person appalled him. "And Glenna?"

Effie raised her eyes to his and hatred burned there. "When I saw the way you looked at her I knew I had to get rid of her."

"I know you didn't try to kill her. Who did?"

She cackled. "You'd like to know, wouldn't you?"

"We know he's a Druid. Tell me his name."

"Even if I did you'd never be able to hurt him. He's too powerful."

"We'll find him. Give the clan a reason not to want your banishment. Give me his name," he tried again.

Effie's eyes burned bright with her secret. "I'll die before I betray him."

Conall knew his time was short, and he needed as many answers as he could get. "How do you know MacNeil?"

"I was but a child when I came to this clan. We lied about where we came from."

"And what clan was that? MacNeil's?"

"Nay."

"Tell me," he threatened. He had grown weary of her vague answers. He needed truth, and with his power gone, he didn't have that assurance.

"Nay," she yelled, and scrambled to her feet. "You'll never find that out, or the man who tried to kill Glenna. He'll get her yet, you know."

Conall stood and spotted the dirk in her hand. He didn't know how she had gotten it, and it didn't matter. He just wanted her to drop it so they could continue to talk.

"Put it down, Effie."

"I'm fulfilling my family obligation."

"And that is?" he asked as he took a step toward her.

"To make sure no Sinclairs ever live again."

Conall rushed toward her, but she had already buried the dirk in her stomach. She crumpled to the earth, her lifeless eyes open to the sky.

* * * * *

The Shadow ducked behind a tree. He had been curious to see how Effie handled herself. He had been more than a little surprised when she had ended her own life. He had never held much respect for her until that moment.

Things hadn't gone to plan. Whenever MacNeil was involved, things never went as planned, he thought to himself. He would have to give MacNeil more incentive to go according to plan.

How many times had he told MacNeil he should have checked those girls at the Sinclairs? Countless, in fact. But MacNeil had assured him they were the older sisters. Even then he had known MacNeil had erred. Now MacNeil would learn just how much his error had cost him. Not all the Sinclair sisters had to die.

In fact, only one needed to give up her life, and he had already decided Glenna would be that sister.

He sighed. He had thought killing her would be easy, but she had fought like a she-cat. The only saving grace is that she hadn't seen his face and given him away.

Although the fact they knew he was a Druid disturbed him. He would have to rethink staying by Moira. Maybe it would be better if he went away for a little while.

Voices brought him back to the present. He looked to find some men carting Effie's body away. He needed to get back to the circle and begin planning the next stage, and he needed to check on Moira. He wouldn't put it past MacNeil to disobey him yet again and kill Moira instead of Glenna.

MacNeil would survive this day, so he didn't waste any thought on him. Nay, his mind turned to keeping Moira for himself and making sure one of the sisters died.

Together he and Moira could rule Scotland like the *sidhe* once did before they left this earth. Once more magic would reign supreme in this land. No more hiding what they were. The power of the Fae would push aside kings and rule people's tiny minds. It would be so very easy, and since he had found a way to block himself from the Fae he could move around freely.

He would just have to stay away from Dartayous. That warrior saw through his shield and could very well ruin all his carefully laid plans.

* * * * *

Glenna rounded on MacNeil once the fire was safely out. "You of all people should know my abilities."

"Your kind all deserve to die. I kept you alive," he spat. "And look at the thanks I get in return."

"You killed my parents," she yelled, barely controlling her fury. "The prophecy will come to pass. Your days are numbered."

He laughed, the sinister sound as black as the devil's heart. "You can't fool me. You don't have the other sister. And I'd wager you don't even know where she is."

"I don't think you'd care to gamble on that," Moira said, a haunty blonde brow raised.

MacNeil's lip curled in a sneer. "Oh, I can assure you, wench, I'll find her faster than you."

"I doubt that."

MacNeil shrugged nonchalantly. "I have an ally you'll never find, an ally who's already tried to kill Glenna. He'll succeed next time. That I promise you."

Glenna had had enough. Her confidence in her powers gave her self-assurance she had never had. With just a simple thought she erupted a fire around MacNeil and his men. Moira brought a gust of wind into play and the flames danced around the horses' hooves.

The men hired by MacNeil began to yell to each other to flee. MacNeil saw the confusion and sought to gain their allegiance. "I'll give you another bag of gold each if you stay and fight."

"Ye didna say nothing of the Druids," a voice called out.

"They're nothing. We outnumber them. It's two wenches against an army," he argued.

But the soldiers would have nothing of it. Glenna extinguished the blaze, and the hired men fled for their lives. She and Moira shared a smile until the banging of the castle gates flying open reached their ears.

"Nay," Glenna said, and grabbed hold of Moira's hand when she spotted Conall running toward MacNeil.

* * * * *

Conall had seen enough. He refused to hide behind the castle walls while Glenna and Moira battled MacNeil. Battle was for men, not women, not even Druid women.

Angus sidled up next to him. "With the mercenaries gone, our men equal the MacNeil soldiers."

It was all the encouragement Conall needed. He brushed past Angus and Gregor and ran down the steps to the bailey. His soldiers lined the battlements and stood ready in the bailey.

"It's time, men. Now's our chance for revenge," he said, and was met with a chorus of cheers. He turned to Angus. "Keep the archers going."

"If you think you're leaving me behind yer daft," Angus said, and signaled to a soldier before following Conall.

Conall nodded to the guards. The gates flew open as he roared the MacInnes war cry. The MacNeil soldiers who remained were surprised at the attack since their attention had been on Glenna and Moira.

He found MacNeil and made his way toward him as MacInnes men continued to yell the war cry. MacNeil saw him and spurred his horse. Conall planted his feet and waited until the horse was almost upon him. Then he stepped to the side and slashed his sword across MacNeil's calf.

MacNeil cried out and clutched his leg while at the same time jerking on the reins. The horse reared and sent MacNeil tumbling to the ground. But Conall didn't get the chance to end MacNeil's life as soldiers swarmed around him. Conall lost track of MacNeil as he fought, the sweat stinging his eyes, until something bumped into him from behind.

He turned and found Angus at his back. "Just like old times, aye, my friend."

"Frankly, I'm getting too old for this," Angus said, and stuck his sword into a soldier's belly.

Conall finished off his last solider and watched as MacNeil advanced on Gregor from behind. Conall dove at MacNeil and landed his shoulder into MacNeil's stomach.

Gregor turned and looked at him. "He's all yours. Good luck," he said, and continued fighting.

Conall jumped to his feet and smiled when he saw the pain MacNeil was in because of the cut on his calf. "I drew first blood."

"But I'm the one who'll win the day," MacNeil taunted.

Conall swung his sword and lunged. "Don't be so sure. You have much to pay for."

MacNeil sneered. "You're not man enough to kill me. You couldn't even keep your sister or daughter safe."

With a lunge and a fierce thrust, Conall stabbed MacNeil in the shoulder. "I don't care if I have to take you piece by piece. I will have my revenge."

* * * * *

"Hold," Aimery told his people. They itched to join Conall's men and fight, but it wasn't meant to be. Their presence in the Highlands, and in fact the world, must continue to go unnoticed. Things could get out of control if people knew the Fae were still among them.

It was enough that they were able to watch this battle between the MacNeil's and MacInnes' soldiers. There would come a time when they would have to fight.

Chapter Twenty-Five

Glenna watched, horrified, as her vision played out before her eyes. She couldn't let Conall die. She refused to let her vision come to pass. They fought fiercely and violently, their blades clashing loudly over the roar of the battle.

Conall's sword moved faster than MacNeil's, and MacNeil was tiring, but still Glenna knew anything could happen. If only she could aide Conall somehow. She held her breath, hoping Conall would gain the upper hand until he stumbled over a fallen soldier. He hit the ground hard as MacNeil raised his sword above his head.

She called out to Conall, thinking to save him until she saw him kick the sword from MacNeil's hands. But then it was too late. She had distracted him.

He turned and it was then she realized she was the cause of his death. Her vision hadn't showed her everything.

* * * * *

Conall jerked around when he heard Glenna scream his name. He didn't understand until he saw the horror on her face. The sound of a sword slicing toward him reached his ears.

He rolled, but not in time as the blade cut across his back. Agony blazed a fierce trail across his back, and the burned ground he rolled on sent stinging pain lightning around the cut. But he pushed aside the throbbing and sprung to his feet. He turned and saw it was MacNeil's commander who had tried to kill him.

Out the corner of his eye he spotted MacNeil crawling away, but the commander stepped in front of Conall to stop him. Conall cast a glance at MacNeil before turning his full attention to the soldier.

With his sword clutched in one hand, he reached into his boot and pulled out his dirk. He wanted this fight over with quickly for he had other, more interesting game to catch.

The commander was no match for him. With each thrust of Conall's sword the soldier raised his arms and left his body unprotected. Conall swung his sword and sliced the soldier nearly in two.

The commander's body hadn't touched the ground when Conall saw MacNeil seize a crossbow. Before Conall could reach him, MacNeil had already shot the bow, and Conall watched the arrow find its mark. In dismay, he saw Glenna collapse.

Moira's scream rent the air as Glenna fell. And suddenly his mother's words that fateful day, when he was but seven and told the prophecy, came to mind. Every word of the prophecy screamed in his mind as he stared at Glenna's fallen form.

The impact of the prophecy, even the part that he had forgotten, pounded heavily in his chest. He had been a fool to want to forget something that affected his life so thoroughly. If only he had remembered sooner, he thought.

Anger suffused him as he turned to MacNeil. "You've done enough damage in this lifetime. It's time your life ended," he said, and held the tip of his sword to MacNeil's heart.

He heard Moira call his name, but revenge for all MacNeil had caused him rang loudly in his head. He shut out Moira's voice and focused all of his anger and hate at the monster who had created it all.

"Conall, Glenna needs you," Moira called once again.

Conall's blood sang for vengeance but his heart cried for Glenna. She had healed wounds he hadn't even known he had. And she needed him. He couldn't deny her, yet he couldn't allow MacNeil to live.

MacNeil laughed and came up on one elbow. "Seems you have a choice. Kill me or save Glenna. I wonder which one you'll choose."

"Conall," Gregor called as he ran toward the forest. "Hurry!"

Conall didn't have much of a choice, and he would be a fool to waste any more time. He looked into MacNeil's eyes and spit on his chest. "You'll live this day, but I'd watch my back if I were you," he said, and hurried after Gregor.

* * * * *

Glenna tried to block out the agony screaming through her thigh as Moira and Frang carried her into the safety of the stones.

"Did Conall survive?" she asked for the tenth time, but they wouldn't answer her. "Please, I need to know."

"He lives," Moira whispered, and wiped at her cheek. "Now worry about yourself."

Glenna felt something wet hit her face and she realized Moira wept. "No tears, sister. You're the best healer around. If I can be saved, it's you who'll do it."

Moira ducked her head, and Glenna knew her words had affected Moira. Glenna bit her lip to keep from crying out as they placed her on top of a long, flat boulder.

Her eyes drifted open to stare at the blue sky. The clouds drifted lazily above her, oblivious to the battle below them. She couldn't help but wonder if the Fae were as unaware. If only she had thought to go to them for help, maybe none of this would have happened.

Only a fool would think like that.

And she was being a fool. She hadn't learned enough to save Conall and had barely saved his clan. If Moira hadn't been beside her she might not have been able to gather the courage she needed to control her powers.

"Drink," Frang ordered as he held a cup of her lips.

The cool liquid quenched her parched mouth as it slid easily down her throat. Instantly the pain faded away until Frang grasped the arrow and pulled it from her thigh. She tried to hold the scream inside but blinding pain surpassed her effort.

* * * * *

Conall ran to the top of the cliff but Glenna was nowhere to be found. Only blood was to be found on the rocks. "By the saints, where is she?"

"To the stones, perhaps," Gregor said.

Conall inwardly groaned but ran to the stone circle anyway. He reached the circle and called out to Glenna when he saw it was cloaked.

"You must come in for her," Moira said.

"No more games. I need to see her. I need to know she's all right. Just tell me that," he urged.

"If you want her, come and get her."

Conall cursed and hit the stones. "I'm through with the tricks, Moira."

"Open your mind, Conall. I know you remember the prophecy now, but it isn't enough. If you love Glenna, then you must come for her. You must believe in her, in us, and yourself."

Conall looked at Gregor and saw him wave. "What are you doing?"

"I'm waving to Moira," he said.

Conall ran his hands down his face. This day wasn't turning out as it should have. For some reason the *fi-fiada* was only cloaking the circle from him. "You can see in?"

"Aye."

"I didn't think you believed in what the Druids could do."

Gregor crossed his arms over his chest. "I most certainly believe, as would you if you'd let yourself."

Conall turned back to the stones and told himself he believed, and he did believe. But it wasn't enough. Moira wanted him to take the Druids into his life again as his mother had reared him.

He told himself he could do it, but his heart knew it was a lie. How could he after all the Druids had allowed to happen to his family?

"You can't continue to blame the Druids for what's happened," Gregor said as he stepped closer. "They can only do so much. They don't have the power to change the world."

Conall bowed his head and placed his hands on the stone and remembered Glenna's smiling face, the sun glinting off her dark brown locks and her sweet sigh as they made love. Suddenly he knew he would open his heart to anything as long as she was by his side.

He raised his head, ready to tell Moira just that when he found himself staring inside the circle. He didn't ask how they knew, only gloried in the fact he could enter now.

Moira stood beside a long, flat boulder where Glenna lay motionless. He let his sword drop as he ran to her side. Her eyes were closed and he feared the worst.

"I'm too late," he whispered, and placed his hand on top of hers.

"Never."

He found himself looking into the most beautiful soft brown eyes ever to grace a living soul. "I thought I'd lost you," he told Glenna.

"Moira wouldn't allow me say anything."

Conall laughed. "Will you forgive me for being so stubborn?"

"Only if you kiss me."

He bent his head and claimed her sweet lips. "I love you," he said once he was able to pull his lips from hers.

"And I you."

He wiped the tear that trailed down her check. "Will you come back with me now and be my wife and mother to Ailsa and whatever children we're blessed with?"

She wrapped her arms around his neck. "Nothing could stop me."

And then he felt the truth in her words. "My power is back."

Moira smiled through her tears. "I knew it would once you fully accepted Glenna for what she was. It's a good day."

"Aye, MacNeil is gone," he said.

She shook her head. "You've remembered the prophecy and your part in it as well as holding the Druids' beliefs once again within your heart."

"It is a good day," Glenna said. "Now let Moira see to your back. I won't have you bloody at our wedding."

* * * * *

The Shadow gathered his cloak around him. He had been defeated here, but there was still another sister he could reach. He hadn't been able to learn of her location, but if he knew Frang and Moira they would send someone for her and he would merely follow. But first he needed to see MacNeil. Effie's death changed things.

A new strategy would have to be formed. If they waited for the other sister to join Moira and Glenna, then it was over for them. But he wouldn't give up without a fight, and in the end he knew he would win.

People like him were ruthless, and when one was ruthless, they could make things happen. And making Moira love him would be a simple act.

Chapter Twenty-Six

☯

Glenna surveyed the damaged done by the fire from the safety of Conall's strong arms. "We lost so much."

"It can be rebuilt. You saved all of us."

She smiled and rested her head on his shoulder. "I almost couldn't do it."

"But you did, and that's all that matters."

A shriek sounded before Ailsa charged at them. "You did it," she called out to Conall.

Glenna smiled as Ailsa wrapped her arms around Conall's legs. She looked up at Glenna, and said, "He told me he'd bring you home."

"He's a laird. Did you expect anything else?"

"Come," Conall said, and ushered them into the hall where it overflowed with the clan waiting for them.

Cheers erupted when they spotted Glenna in Conall's arms. She now had everything she had always dreamed of, a man to love her, a daughter, sisters and a clan who accepted her.

"Let me stand," she told Conall, and he grudgingly set her down.

She faced the clan who had hated her beyond sense but now welcomed her with open arms. They were good people who had been terrorized by the MacNeil. She couldn't and wouldn't judge them for their actions.

"I have news," Conall declared. "Glenna has finally agreed to become my wife."

Again the hall erupted in deafening cheers. With Conall at her back to help her stand she greeted each member of the clan, her heart swelling with each smile.

*****

"I'm so very happy for you."

Glenna turned to find Moira behind her. She had stayed within the stones to ready herself. "You knew all along, didn't you?"

Moira smiled and came to stand beside her. "There is always a chance things won't work out like they're supposed to. I was worried that Conall wouldn't accept you for a Druid. In which case, we would've had a problem."

"Truthfully, I didn't think he ever would accept me," Glenna said.

Moira smiled and raised her face to the sun. "It's time."

Glenna took a deep breath and followed Moira from the stone circle to the cliff that overlooked MacInnes Castle. Almost the entire clan and all the Druids had come for the event, some on the cliff but others watched from below.

The Druids on the cliff had formed a large outer circle that held a smaller half circle inside. To her amazement she spied some Fae as well.

All the eyes on her began to make her nervous until she spotted Conall. He stood beside Frang near the edge of the cliff. His black hair hung loose around his shoulders still damp on the ends from a recent bath.

She thought about him in the loch and her stomach gave a delighted flutter. They would most likely spend many days in the pleasant loch water.

Conall was magnificent to look upon in his blue and green plaid kilt. But it was his eyes that held and calmed her. She kept her gaze locked with his while she walked to stand across from him.

"I was worried you might change your mind," he said.

"Never. We are meant to be together."

"Then together you shall be," Frang said as he raised his hands to let everyone know the wedding ceremony was about to begin.

Frang blessed the inner and outer circle as Moira walked to his side. "Welcome."

"Welcome," everyone replied.

Frang raised his face to the sky and closed his eyes. Four of the eldest Druids walked until they stood at the four directions.

"Great Spirit," Frang's voice rang out, "we ask for your blessing for this ceremony. Let the four directions be honored that power and radiance might enter our circle for the good of all beings."

Glenna smiled at Conall as the Druid to the north said, "With the blessing of the great bear of the starry heavens and the deep and fruitful earth, we call upon the powers of the North."

"With the blessing of the stag in the heat of the chase and the inner fire of the Sun, we call upon the powers of the South," a Druid priestess who represented the South said.

The Druid to the west raised his face. "With the blessing of the salmon of wisdom who dwells within the sacred waters of the pool, we call upon the powers of the West."

Glenna eyes glanced at the woman who stood at the east. She smiled faintly at Glenna before she said, "With the blessing of the hawk at dawn soaring in the clear pure air, we call upon the powers of the East."

Frang lowered his arms. "We stand upon this earth and in the face of Heaven to witness the sacred act of marriage between Conall and Glenna. Just as we come together as family and friends we ask for the Greater Powers to be present here within our circle. May this sacred union be filled with their holy presence? By the power vested in me I invoke that love is declared."

"By the power vested in me I invoke the bright flame be present in this sacred place. In her name peace is declared," Moira said.

"In the name of ancestors whose traditions we honor," Frang said.

Moira said, "In the name of those who gave us life."

"May we all unite in love," they said together.

Moira captured Glenna's eyes. "The joining together of man and woman in the sacred rite of marriage brings together great forces from which may flow the seeds of future generations to be nurtured within the womb of time. A union based on true love finds many expressions. This union is truly holy."

Glenna's eyes fluttered as she gazed into Conall's quicksilver eyes. They held such promise she wondered how she ever thought to leave him. She pushed aside her thoughts as the time drew near for her part.

"Who walks the path of the moon to stand before Heaven to declare her sacred vows?" Frang asked.

Glenna swallowed and smiled as Conall winked at her. She stepped forward. "I do."

"Who walks the path of the sun to stand upon this holy earth and declare his sacred vow?"

Conall came to stand beside her. "I do."

Glenna's soul rose up in elation at hearing his words. His hand brushed hers and she longed to have his strong arms around her. But for now she would have to be content to hold on to his hand.

They walked together around the circle. First one way then the other until they returned to the east.

Frang smiled at them. "Conall and Glenna you have walked the circles of the moon and sun, will you now walk together the Circle of Time, traveling through the elements and time?"

She and Conall shared a smiled before they answered, "We will."

Still holding on to his hand they walked to the Druid who represented the South. "Will your love survive the harsh fires of change?"

"It will," she and Conall answered.

"Then accept the blessing of the Element of Fire in this place of Summer. May your home be filled with warmth."

Conall led Glenna to the Druid of the West. "Will your love survive the ebb and flow of feeling?" the Druid asked.

"It will," she answered.

"Accept the blessing of the Element of Water in this place of Autumn. May your life together be filled with love."

Their steps brought them to the Druid of the North. "Will your love survive the times of stillness and restriction?"

They shared a brief smile. "It will."

"Then accept the blessing of the Element of Earth in this place of Winter. May your union be strong and fruitful."

At last they came to the Druid of the East. She smiled warmly before she said, "Will your love survive the clear light of day?"

"It will."

"Then accept the blessing of the Element of Air in this place of Spring. May your marriage be blessed with the light of every new dawn."

Glenna's eyes misted as Conall squeezed her hand. Although the ceremony was nearly done, she and Conall had been joined by their souls since the day they met.

"Do you swear to keep sacred your vows?" Frang asked.

Conall took her other hand as they faced each other. "We do," they said.

Moira placed one hand on Glenna's shoulder and the other on Conall's. "Then seal your promise with a kiss."

Glenna wrapped her arms around Conall's neck as he clasped her to him. The kiss sealed their souls, hearts and bodies together. They were mates who had found each other again and would continue to do so through time.

Dimly, Glenna became aware of Frang blessing their union and their children. Gradually Conall ended the kiss but didn't release her. Glenna knew that once they returned to the castle he wouldn't allow her to leave the chamber for at least a sennight, and she welcomed that reprieve after all they had been through.

While she and Conall stared into each other's eyes the Four Directions and their Elements said their blessings. Frang and Moira finished their blessings and ended the ceremony.

"It's done," Conall said, and ran his hand down her face, the love shining brightly in his eyes.

"Aye. It's done."

* * * * *

Gregor watched Conall carry Glenna back to the castle where a large feast and celebration awaited them. It seemed that things were back to normal at the MacInnes' clan. Conall no longer cast aside his Druid blood, and the MacNeil was gone. For now.

If all Moira had said was true, MacNeil would be back. Of that he had no doubt. MacNeil wanted the sisters dead, and he would keep going after them until they were gone. Only then would MacNeil rest easy.

Gregor rubbed his medallion through his shirt and vest. Home. He hadn't seen home in over ten years. Hadn't even gone near that land. Now he yearned to see it. All because his sense of right and wrong had found its way back into his heart, emotions once again made their presence known.

He was proud of himself for doing the right thing and standing beside Conall, but he was also annoyed with himself because his mercenary life was now over. What was he to do now? Wander Scotland forever? Nay.

He was tired of wandering. He had become comfortable in Conall's home, and it made him ache for one of his own. He looked up to find himself alone on the cliff. Everyone was at the castle celebrating. It was a perfect time to leave. He knew better than to see Conall. If he did, he knew Conall would offer him a place in the clan, and Gregor wouldn't be able to pass up that boon.

If he was to leave, it needed to be now. He turned after one last look over the castle and the sounds of revelry and found Frang staring at him. The wise Druid priest gave him a nod. Gregor returned the greeting and hurried to his mare. Better get out soon, he told himself. Great powers pulsed here and he didn't need to be caught up in them anymore.

Epilogue

Glenna was thankful for the support Conall gave her as she hobbled out of the castle. The wedding feast had commenced as soon as the ceremony had ended and had lasted all day.

The sun had begun its decent when Glenna felt Moira's call. She had told Conall, but he had refused to let her out of his sight. After several hours of telling him she needed to go to Moira, he had given in, albeit grudgingly.

"Enough of this," he grumbled, and lifted her in his arms. He carried her until they reached Moira, who stood beside Gregor.

"Where will you go now?" Glenna asked Gregor when she saw his horse standing nearby. Their presence seemed to agitate Gregor, as if he couldn't get away from them fast enough. She didn't understand that after all he had done for them.

He shrugged. "Somewhere."

"I have a job for you," Moira said, stopping Gregor in his tracks.

Gregor raised a blonde brow. "I'm not sure I'm the man you want."

Moira just smiled. "How does this sound?" she asked, and threw him a small bag that rattled with coins. "Half now and half on completion."

He eyed the bag in his hand. "What do you want me to do?"

"Bring our sister Fiona to us."

Glenna watched as he mulled over Moira's offer. She hadn't known Moira would ask him to bring Fiona here, but she agreed he was the man to do it. Gregor was the type who other men avoided, and the need for Fiona to get here quickly and quietly was of utmost importance.

"Please," Glenna begged him. "You're the only man who can get her here without letting her fall into MacNeil's clutches."

"All right," he agreed. "But know I'm doing this for the coin not because I like you."

"Of course," Conall said, wearing a knowing smirk he didn't try to hide.

Glenna elbowed him in the ribs and gave Gregor a big smile. "Good luck," she called out.

Conall wrapped his arms around her as Gregor mounted his horse and rode out the gates. "He'll get her here."

"I know."

"Good. Then let's go enjoy the night," he whispered seductively in her ear before he kissed the sensitive spot on the back of her neck.

"But Moira."

He glanced up and found Moira gone. "She's left."

Glenna laid her head on his chest. "Then let us not tarry here a moment longer, my laird."

Conall looked down at amazement at the nymph who had captured his heart and soul. It still astonished him that she was now his wife.

His.

Mine.

Also by Donna Grant

eBooks:
Druid Glen 1: Highland Mist
Druid Glen 2: Highland Nights
Druid Glen 3: Highland Dawn

About Donna Grant

ಬ

Donna Grant is the award winning author of more than twenty-five novels spanning multiple genres of romance-- Scottish Medieval, historical, dark fantasy, time travel, paranormal and erotic — to both electronic and print publishers.

Donna was born and raised in Texas but loves to travel. Her adventures have taken her throughout the United States as well as Jamaica and Mexico. Growing up on the Texas/Louisiana border, Donna's Cajun side of the family taught her the "spicy" side of life while her Texas roots gave her two-steppin' and bareback riding.

Despite the deadlines and her voracious reading, Donna still manages to keep up with her two young children, three cats and one long-haired Chihuahua. She's blessed with a proud, supportive husband who's learned to cook far more than frozen chicken nuggets.

ಬ

The author welcomes comments from readers. You can find her website and email address on her author bio page at www.ellorascave.com.

Tell Us What You Think

We appreciate hearing reader opinions about our books. You can email us at Service@ellorascave.com (when contacting Customer Service, be sure to state the book title and author).

Why an electronic book?

We live in the Information Age—an exciting time in the history of human civilization, in which technology rules supreme and continues to progress in leaps and bounds every minute of every day. For a multitude of reasons, more and more avid literary fans are opting to purchase e-books instead of paper books. The question from those not yet initiated into the world of electronic reading is simply: *Why?*

1. **Price.** An electronic title at Ellora's Cave Publishing runs anywhere from 40% to 75% less than the cover price of the exact same title in paperback format. Why? Basic mathematics and cost. It is less expensive to publish an e-book (no paper and printing, no warehousing and shipping) than it is to publish a paperback, so the savings are passed along to the consumer.
2. **Space.** Running out of room in your house for your books? That is one worry you will never have with electronic books. For a low one-time cost, you can purchase a handheld device specifically designed for e-reading. Many e-readers have large, convenient screens for viewing. Better yet, hundreds of titles can be stored within your new library—on a single microchip. There are a variety of e-readers from different manufacturers. You can also read e-books on your PC or laptop computer. (Please note that Ellora's Cave does not endorse any specific brands.

You can check our website at www.elloracave.com for information we make available to new consumers.)

3. *Mobility.* Because your new e-library consists of only a microchip within a small, easily transportable e-reader, your entire cache of books can be taken with you wherever you go.

4. *Personal Viewing Preferences.* Are the words you are currently reading too small? Too large? Too... ANNOYING? Paperback books cannot be modified according to personal preferences, but e-books can.

5. *Instant Gratification.* Is it the middle of the night and all the bookstores near you are closed? Are you tired of waiting days, sometimes weeks, for bookstores to ship the novels you bought? Ellora's Cave Publishing sells instantaneous downloads twenty-four hours a day, seven days a week, every day of the year. Our webstore is never closed. Our e-book delivery system is 100% automated, meaning your order is filled as soon as you pay for it.

Those are a few of the top reasons why electronic books are replacing paperbacks for many avid readers.

As always, Ellora's Cave welcomes your questions and comments. We invite you to email us at Service@elloracave.com or write to us directly at Ellora's Cave Publishing Inc., 1056 Home Avenue, Akron, OH 44310-3502.

MAKE EACH DAY MORE *EXCITING* WITH OUR

Ellora's Cavemen Calendar

☥ www.ElloRASCAVE.com ☥

Ellora's Cave Romanticon

Annual convention for women who refuse to behave

WWW.JASMINEJADE.COM/ROMANTICON
For additional info contact: conventions@ellorascave.com

Discover for yourself why readers can't get enough of the multiple award-winning publisher Ellora's Cave. Be sure to visit EC on the web at www.ellorascave.com to find erotic reading experiences that will leave you breathless. You can also find our books at all the major e-tailers (Barnes & Noble, Amazon Kindle, Sony, Kobo, Google, Apple iBookstore, All Romance eBooks, and others).

www.ellorascave.com

Made in the USA
Lexington, KY
22 March 2013